CW01499091

Taz Towers was born in Nuneaton. He spent most of his life working in heavy industry and in the entertainment industry before deciding to write a book of fiction based partly on his own life and partly on true events.

Dedicated to my great friends, Bram, Kingy, Sola and Angie, without their help and inspiration this book would never have been written.

Taz Towers

THE SHIP CALLED
THE PHARAOH

AUSTIN MACAULEY PUBLISHERS™

LONDON • CAMBRIDGE • NEW YORK • SHARJAH

A CIP catalogue record for this title is available from the British Library.

ISBN 9781398491588 (Paperback)
ISBN 9781398491595 (ePub e-book)

www.austinmacauley.com

First Published 2023
Austin Macauley Publishers Ltd®
1 Canada Square
Canary Wharf
London
E14 5AA

Liverpool Present Day 1960

It's 10:15 PM and in the 'Harbour Lights' pub on Liverpool dockside, the bar is crowded and buzzing, a man in his '50s is eyeing up some young girls and watching them as they dance and kiss with their boyfriends. The music can be heard streets away, not that it matters, there are no houses for miles, these docks haven't been worked for decades and never will be again.

Two 'scallies' 60 yards away from the pub can hear the music, but they're not here for the dancing, they are examining the potential 'swag' in cars parked in the derelict streets that serve as a free car park for the pubs and clubs. They turn the corner and something attracts their attention, a figure is standing there apparently waiting for something or someone, but they are not concerned about that, this is their 'patch' and they won't tolerate newcomers from other gangs, they will defend their patch as they always do with violence.

'Hey, what the fuck we got here,' says one of the 'scallies' as they both confront the stranger. 'No fucker ever tell you this is our patch,' as one of the men automatically opens a flick knife and the second man menacingly raises a crowbar, resting it across his shoulders as they both walk straight toward the stranger increasing their speed with every step.

Their intention was obvious, but as they got within four metres of the stranger, the response was immediate, no time for shouts from the scallies, just two 'tup, tup' sounds were heard, one bullet to each man's heart and two of Liverpool's worse were lying on the pavement. The stranger approached the bodies and kicked each, checking for life and then a second bullet was fired into each man's head, death was quick from a silenced hand-gun, the stranger slipped quietly back into the shadows.

In the 'Harbour Lights,' a brawl began between two young men and a 52-year-old man who tried to force one of the young girls to dance with him even though he could hardly stand because he was so drunk. The 52-year-old Paddy was a well-known brawler; he is heavy set and strong, he only uses the 'Harbour

Lights' because it's just a few streets away from his terraced house in the semi-derelict area of the harbour.

The landlord has had lots of trouble with him over the years and only tolerates him because he is a big drinker, but the pub has a new clientele and now caters for a much younger and far less violent crowd, it's no longer the dock land of the 1940s, John the landlord would now really prefer Paddy and his type were gone. After John and two doormen had dragged Paddy off one of the young girl's boyfriends, he was forced to leave the pub, the swearing, aggression and violence was frightening the patrons and John called for calm. Paddy left the pub shouting 'Fuck off, all of ya bastards.'

He couldn't walk straight, he was seriously drunk and he stumbled along on his way home. He could still hear the music from the Harbour Lights as he turned a dark corner and stopped to steady himself against a wall.

Even though he was drunk and the street was very dark, through his hazy vision he thought he saw a person lying on the pavement up ahead. Instinctively, he looked around and then walked towards the body only to realise as he got closer that there were two bodies. Paddy heard a sound from across the street, he raised his head and motioned to shout at a stranger who stepped from the shadows a few yards away across the street, but he didn't even utter a sound as blood poured from his mouth and neck dripping onto his boots as he began to choke.

Paddy reached up and felt something protruding from his neck, unknown to him it was a steel cross-bow bolt that had passed straight through the side of his neck, through his throat and into the wooded shop door frame he was standing next to. As the bolt impaled him, a dark figure moved from the shadows and crossed the road deliberately standing right in front of him to be clearly seen.

Paddy was still alive but only just; he was bleeding heavily and unable to utter a single sound, his throat was squeezed and blocked by the bolt, his hands struggled to free himself as he slowly choked in silence on his own blood. His eyes opened wide in complete horror as he watched the dark shadowed figure load a second bolt and then slowly raised the crossbow to point at him.

First, it pointed at Paddy's face, but then menacingly slowly and deliberately lowered down past his chest, past his stomach until it pointed straight at his groin. All the time Paddy gripped the bolt through his neck with both hands and watched in terrified horror.

The trigger was pulled and a second steel bolt ripped through Paddy, this time through his groin passing straight through his pelvic area and into the ground behind him. Blood poured from him onto the pavement creating a huge pool, the figure stood and watched as Paddy's strong hands desperately tried to free the bolt through his neck. His face distorted in agony as he gurgled air and blood; the seconds ticked by as his body struggled until eventually his hands stopped, his arms slowly dropped to his side and he gave a final shudder.

He was then completely still, as his whole body hung from the bolt through his neck, the 'Harbour Lights' music played on as three dead men lay in the street. The dark figure stood for a few moments and then checked Paddy's limp body to be absolutely certain he was dead before turning and disappearing into the Liverpool night.

Crime Scene Present Day 1960

Paul Bramley is a DI with the Liverpool police and has been a detective for more than 25 years, he has just arrived at the scene of the crime to join his colleague Dennis Goodburn, a support team, uniformed police and forensic officers. Most of the area around the 'Harbour Lights' is cordoned off.

'What the fuck is this all about, Dennis,' asked Paul, 'No killings for weeks and then three on the same night, the press is gonna love it and why a crossbow, Dennis, when scallies can get guns like fucking sweets in Liverpool.'

Dennis Goodburn is a DS and has worked with Paul for over 7 years. 'It's nothing to do with lack of guns, Boss,' said Dennis. 'That crossbow killing is a deliberate execution to send out a message to somebody and probably gang related.' Both detectives walk away from the scene under the yellow cordon tape. 'Not that you need to worry, Boss,' says Dennis, 'You're off down south on your holidays on Sunday, aren't you?'

'Yeah, I was,' replied Paul. 'I was going for ten days, Den, I'm seeing an old DI mate of mine, but I can't let three murders wait, the Super would have my bollocks.'

As Paul got in his car he said to Dennis, 'Den, I am gonna slip off to see Colin tonight, for fuck sake keep it quiet. I'll be back in the morning so do some background on the victims, get everything back from forensics that you can and keep me posted on it while I'm away I'll give you D.I. Colin Kings home phone number and the number for the Dugdale Arms pub, under no circumstances, phone his station or talk to anyone except me or Colin King himself. I'll be back here before lunch tomorrow. I want to clear this up as quickly as possible, we don't need no fucking William Tell's on this patch.'

Jack's business 1946 Liverpool

Jack Grantham was a sergeant evacuated from Dunkirk following an injury in France in May 1940. He was a very good soldier, he was a first-class sniper and had seen a lot of horrors in France as the Germans advanced to the English Channel and he had seen lots of killings and had killed many times himself, like many front-line veterans it had made him emotionally hard, he was one of the lucky ones to get back home, many men he fought beside didn't.

Jack took ownership of his Mum's and Aunties houses after they were both killed during a German air raid in 1941, he lived in his mum's house. Jack was well known locally as a Dunkirk hero and used his contacts on the council to provide him with details of bomb-damaged properties that were repairable, he would contact the owners and buy the property for next to nothing and gradually during the war bought houses from bomb victims, it was not long before he owned lots of properties.

Many wartime landlords made money from the bombings in the same way and many of them exploited bomb victims who had very little or no money. They had no scruples about increasing rents whenever they wanted to and they did this often, as the property was very limited. Jack was exactly this type of landlord, he believed he'd done his bit for his country as a soldier, unlike the generals who just give orders and never risk their lives on the frontline and then become millionaires writing their memoirs. Well, he was going to become rich from war too, a different route perhaps but the same goal, wealth from war.

Jack had various shops trading in 'Black Market' contraband from where he conducted lots of illegal and lucrative businesses, one of which was providing returning servicemen with his working girls at various properties owned by himself. He provided accommodation for the prostitutes that worked for him at extortionate rents and Liverpool was perfect for operating an illegal black market, it was a port city and of course, he had an endless supply of returning service men as customers for every one of his brothels.

Rose (Thomas) Newton

Rose did not have a very good start in life and grew up on the edge of the city in a very rough area, she did not have loving parents and in the main was left to fend for herself. Her mum was an alcoholic who was often beaten by her dad right in front of Rose, who had also witnessed her mum having sex with various delivery men as payment; she understood why, because her dad didn't work and gave her mum no money to buy food or run the house.

He was a petty thief very well known to the police and often in prison; even when he was out of prison, he never held down a job for long. Her mum was quite pleased to see him do time, she had one less person to feed and clean up after and it at least gave her a break from the frequent beatings. Rose promised herself that she would not allow herself to live a life like her mum had done, a life of misery and beatings.

Moira was Rose's best friend and she came from a similar family background, her dad was also in and out of prison and thought nothing of using his belt on her mum and Moira. They talked often about the existences that both their mothers tolerated and thought there must be a different way to live life and perhaps even be happy like in the films. They were always together in the neighbourhood, just hanging around the streets or parks; one night, two foreign sailors on shore leave bumped into them in the park and gave both of them cigarettes and drink, they were only 14, one thing led to another and they both lost their virginities, both on the same night in that very park; the sailors gave them money and were gone.

It was their secret and they discussed every detail of their experience with each other and realised from that moment, that was their way out of poverty, earning money from sex with men, they were both very young and pretty and knew they could charge men a lot of money. As their experience grew, they began to offer a whole range of sexual services and they soon had lots of regular clients in the park or outside pubs, as well as soldiers and sailors passing through the docks.

They soon discovered, however, that prostitution is a dangerous profession, many of their clients were sailors and nearly all of them carried weapons, there was always the danger that they might not be paid or they could be beaten up, raped or even killed, most of their clients could be on a ship and in another country the next day.

The danger was not only from their clients but much closer to home. The nature of prostitution is by and large led by young and beautiful girls and the older prostitutes even though they were only in their twenties and thirties were missing out on business to younger baby-faced teenagers and they didn't like it. For several years both girls worked the streets, but neither girl wanted that life forever.

Everything changed in 1932 when Rose was 19 and tried to break away from the business when she met Bob Newton, he was a young soldier aged 21. Rose loved Bob and they lived together at Bob's parent's house, he was away most of the time training with the army but when Rose became pregnant that year, Bob's parents felt ashamed and they disowned her and when she was close to giving birth and Bob was away with the army, training, they told her when she gave birth to the baby she would have to leave and find somewhere else to live.

Rose moved out of the house a few days after giving birth, she was still only 19 and in a time when unmarried mothers were shunned, she was left to bring up her new baby Theresa on her own; when there was no benefit system, Moira helped her enormously and even helped her get a flat. Rose reverted back to the only way she knew of earning money, prostitution; she thought that Bob would find her and rescue her when he found out but he never did; she never knew that Bob's parents had told him that Rose had left him for another man and he never saw her or Theresa again.

Three years later in 1935 Rose again tried to escape her life of prostitution when she fell in love with a Royal Navy sailor and became pregnant again, but as soon as he found out she was pregnant he was gone and again, she was left alone, now she had two girls to bring up alone. To give herself a level of respectability she had always told everyone, friends and any neighbours and even Theresa that she was a widow and that her husband, Theresa's daddy had been killed as a soldier and now gave her new baby the same surname of Newton, Theresa and Bridget Newton.

Ironically some years later, Rose heard through friends that in 1939 Bob Newton really did die as a soldier; he had been sent to France with the Expeditionary Force, he was one of many soldiers that never got back to Dunkirk, his body was one of the millions never found on the battlefields of France.

Rose was one of Jack's tenants, he knew from Moira that she was a prostitute, but not regrettably working for him. Rose was a beautiful looking woman and he knew that she was struggling to afford the current rent and he wanted Rose for himself and increased the rent purposely forcing her into a corner financially. Jack offered her a deal that was too tempting for her to refuse, she could live in a property of her choice with her girls, she would not have to pay rent and Jack would even pay her an agreed amount of money every week, but she must do everything and anything he asked her to do.

War time Britain was hard for everyone, there were no properties available because of the thousands of houses destroyed by bombings, they would take years to rebuild. Everything like food and clothes was rationed and fruits like bananas and pineapples and certain other foods were a luxury only the rich could afford, even when the war ended rationing would be here into the 1950s. Homelessness and hunger, almost to the point of starvation, was everywhere; there was no work and the country had been bombed almost into oblivion.

If Rose accepted Jack's offer, she could have food, nice clothes, cosmetics and anything and everything she wanted from Jack's black-market operations; she could also live in a nice home when many people had nothing; she felt very lucky, it was a good offer. She knew Jack thought she was gorgeous and it was not that much of a problem to control him, she enjoyed sex more than him, although not necessarily with him and she could always get what she wanted for herself, Theresa and Bridget, as long as she always gave Jack whatever he wanted.

Jack made it quite clear to Rose that this arrangement meant she was sexually exclusive to him and she could not have any other men clients and although this was all part of the arrangement, it was still an easy decision for Rose to accept the offer. It only took a few weeks for Rose to slip into this more comfortable and far easier way of life.

Jack didn't know it, but Rose already had other men, in fact on average she would sell her services two or three times a week to her three regular clients. Rose was not going to give up this opportunity of earning money unknown to

Jack. Apart from this, she didn't just like sex she loved it, but sometimes Jack didn't visit or was away for weeks and she was not going to deprive herself of regular sex waiting for Jack to call.

On some occasions Jack was away for months and often came back tanned, she knew he'd got it made and if he could have a wonderful life fucking all his working girls, she was not going to miss out either, she would have her men clients and earn a lot of money. With this arrangement Rose could have as much sex as she wanted and get paid the very best price for it, she just had to be very careful.

All three of Rose's regular clients owned businesses and although none of them knew about each other, they all knew about Jack, so the sex always took place at their houses, the back of a car, they could not use hotels or boarding houses. Jack was far too well connected; over the war years he had bought numerous properties, including hotels becoming a very rich man with his brothels and black-market outlets; Jack had a lot of influential people in his pocket because he could get hold of anything for them.

Jack believed that Rose was totally dependent on him and she allowed him to believe that. In reality, she was able to earn and save money secretly for the day when she could escape this life, rationing couldn't last forever and she knew none of her clients would ever inform Jack of their liaison, they were taking more of a risk than her. Jack had a fearsome reputation for violence and would kill every one of Rose's clients and their family without a second thought if he ever found out about them.

Moira

Moira was also in one of Jack's houses, she had returned to prostitution for the same reason as Rose, in this broken, bankrupt bombed-out country homelessness and near starvation were everywhere. Rose and Moira had been friends long before Jack was on the scene, they had a history of both performing sexual acts for clients since they were 14 years old, now Moira and Rose would team up, especially for Rose's clients who could all afford to pay extortionate rates to live out their fantasies.

Rose knew that Jack had sex with Moira whenever he wanted to and Moira had never attempted to hide the fact. Rose knew that she was in the same sex trap as herself; they were both owned by Jack just like all his other girls; if Jack ever found out that any of his 'property' was having sex with someone else or doing private jobs, they would be history; this rule applied to Rose just as well as everyone else.

Rose never forgot the time when Jack accused her of fucking around and beating her up so badly, she needed hospital treatment. Jack owned private nursing homes and hospitals and had doctors and nurses on his payroll so Rose was nursed privately and her injuries escaped the public gaze. Rose knew that she had to leave as soon as she had sufficient finances.

Jack visited her whenever he chose, the visits were always just for sex, but fortunately for Rose, they were not too often, but she was well aware that if she didn't comply with Jack's demands, there was the ever-present threat of violence and eviction, he was that mercenary. Rose tolerated the situation for the sake of Theresa and Bridget because she had nothing else, the arrangement lasted right up until 1946 when Theresa was 14 years old and Bridget was 11.

Jack had amassed an absolute fortune from his black-market businesses to the point where he had now become legitimate in post-war industry. He had a lot of influence and Rose knew that eventually Jack would find out about her clients and she and the girls would pay the price and this was the very reason Rose needed a different life, a new life and soon.

One of Rose's clients was a butcher; Cyril, who was infatuated with her, he had offered to marry her on many occasions and he had meant it, he had pleaded with her to leave Jack and they'd move away to somewhere new, even abroad. But Rose knew he was just dreaming, it was almost impossible to escape from Jack and anyway she didn't love Cyril any more than Jack. With this current arrangement that Jack obviously knew nothing about she could save all the money that Jack thought she was spending on food thanks to Cyril, who gave her any meat products she wanted for free as well as paying her for sex.

Cyril was a lovely man but he had little appeal to Rose; for a start he was 72, far too old for her. Although he loved sex with Rose it was definitely not mutual, he seldom lasted longer than a few minutes. Rose would often immediately visit one of her other clients to get some sexual satisfaction; obviously, Cyril was not aware of this.

Cyril had a fetish and only ever wanted one type of sex to the exclusion of everything else; as a matter of fact, he was very naïve for such a mature man, he thought he was exclusive to Rose and the only man to perform this sexual act with her and she allowed him to think that because he paid ridiculous money just to live out his fantasy and Rose cashed in on it. Cyril loved his fantasy sex with Rose and on quite a few occasions had sex with Moira and Rose at the same time; he was living his dream to have both of them and he would pay a fortune for just a few hours with them.

Moira and Rose told Cyril that the reason they had to charge him so much more than other clients was because he was so huge, both girls had seen many naked men over the years and they both agreed Cyril had the biggest dick they'd ever seen.

Cyril didn't care about the additional charge he was rich and it boosted his ego to hear the girls tell him that he had the biggest dick either girl had ever seen. They both joked with him, that he had cut off a horse's dick and grafted it on himself, they both knew that he wouldn't last very long with two curvy young women all over his body, purposely getting him overexcited. With the money, Cyril was willing to pay they could not refuse, even if they both still felt the effect of his dick the following day.

Jack's Business 1946

Since Theresa was now 14, Rose had taken a job as a barmaid at the 'Queens Head'. Theresa was old enough to babysit Bridget. Rose needed to distance herself from just Jack, her clients and other prostitutes and pursue her own social circle, she needed a way out of this life that she was trapped in. Apart from this, Rose had noticed that since Theresa had started to develop last year at thirteen and begun to wear bras, Jack had started to spend more time with her and frequently played games that involved touching or tickling; she didn't like this unnatural interest he was showing in Theresa, she was only too aware of her own life at fourteen. Rose didn't want that life for Theresa.

Rose didn't like it when Jack visited and was in the house with the girls while she was at work in the evenings and liked even less this unnaturally close relationship that had developed between Jack and Theresa, but if she was to make the break from Jack, she needed the money from her clients and the new social circle of friends and contacts she was developing around the pub, she needed a life completely independent of Jack.

Rose recalled when Jack started to visit a pub that Theresa passed on her way home from school. One particular Wednesday in the summer Jack called Theresa across to the pub, to a bench, he was sitting at with three men; they were all talking to Jack as Theresa came across the street. The men looked frightening to her; they all had dark clothes and had beards, she recognised all the men talking to Jack were Irish, she went to a catholic school and many of her teachers were Irish, but these men had really heavy accents.

Jack said, 'Theresa, sit at the end of the bench, my little darling. I just have to have a word with these men, I won't be long.'

Jack spoke to the men in a really quiet voice, almost in whispers, she could hardly hear a word Jack said. Then Jack spoke to, Theresa, saying, 'Would you like some pop.'

Theresa replied, 'Yes please,' and Jack went into the bar to get the drinks, leaving her with the three Irish men.

The men looked at Theresa but said nothing, she innocently asked if the men were teachers, one of the men who sat closest to her turned and glared back at her, leaned into her face almost nose to nose and said in a thick Irish accent, 'Do I look like a fucking teacher;' he had a big scar running all the way down his left cheek from his eyebrow to his chin and a blue scorpion tattooed on the back of his left hand; he frightened her, but then Jack returned with his and Theresa's drinks.

Jack sat down and said to the Irish men, 'You know the arrangement,' and they nodded, drank up their beers and left. Theresa was so shocked and frightened by the men she told her mum when she got home. That was how Rose had learned of Jack's meetings with these men and Theresa at the pub and she realised that Jack's relationship with Theresa was not as it should be.

Theresa and Bridget normally went to bed at around 9:00 PM when Rose was working at the pub. When Jack came around to Rose's house it was usually around 9:30 PM. One day Rose came home and discovered Jack rolling around the floor, playing a game with Theresa, it was way past her bedtime and such a game was inappropriate for a 14-year-old girl.

This was another reason she needed to keep him sweet and well-provided with sex, to keep his interest in her and away from Theresa; he was fairly easy to keep sexually satisfied she knew exactly what he liked and what to wear to keep him interested, she knew all his preferences and his favourites but he was very loud and now the girls were of an age when she needed to be discrete.

Unknown to Rose, Theresa had heard Jack and her mum having sex and would often sneak across the landing, attracted by the noises coming from her mum's bedroom; she was at that age of sexual discovery and she would watch them having sex and her mum moaned quite loudly too.

Theresa had heard bad language at school and had also learned a lot of really bad words from the bedroom and was surprised that mainly it was her mum who said them even though she whispered them; watching her mum and Jack having sex through a partially open bedroom door was only possible because Rose had always been paranoid about bombing and even though the war was now over, she still always left her bedroom door partly open to listening for the girls.

School

Theresa talked to her friends at school and like most normal 14-year-old teenage girls they often talked secretly about sex. Most girls at school hadn't even seen a man's naked body, but she had and although it remained a secret from most of her friends that she'd already seen lots of graphic sexual activity performed by her mum and Jack, she had only told Angie; she was Theresa's best friend and they confided in each other.

Angela's mum had been killed in an air raid when Angela was 11 and she had told Theresa that her dad had said she had to do all the things her mum used to do like the housework, wash the clothes, ironing and cook the dinners, but more recently when Angie got to 12 and 13 her dad had told her she had to do all the grown-up things that her mum used to do now she was a big girl.

One day Angela saw Theresa in the park and ran up to her, Theresa kissed her and wished her happy birthday, which was today.

'Thank you,' said Angela, who took Theresa's hand and led her very quickly, much quicker than usual to a quiet place; as they both sat down Angela suddenly turned to Theresa first looking over each shoulder to make sure no one could hear, she was very excited. Angela looked at Theresa and made her swear to keep a secret and tell no one, not ever.

Theresa said, 'Of course, I'll keep a secret Angie, what is it,' she asked inquisitively.

Theresa put her arms around Angela reassuringly and promised to keep her secret, 'Tell me,' she said excitedly. 'Tell me.'

Angela told Theresa that her dad had come into her bedroom about a month ago and said now she was nearly 14 and soon leaving school, she couldn't go to work because she had to do the housework that her mum used to do and 'other things.' She went on, he told her that he had brought her some grown-up clothes now she was a big girl and produced a bag and told her to open it.

In the bag were a lady's black negligee, black silk pyjamas, lacy underwear, stockings and a pair of new high heel shoes and dad had said to her, 'Do you like those new clothes that I've bought you for your birthday my little darling.'

She did like the clothes, they made Angie feel like a proper grown up. 'Yes, I like them, dad,' she'd replied, she went on, 'Can I try them on before my birthday, dad,' and Angie told Theresa that her dad said, 'Of course you can, my little darling, I love you and I want to see you in them myself.'

Angie told Theresa that her dad had said, 'Angie, you'll be 14 in a few weeks and you'll be all grown up and you'll need to wear grown-up clothes like these and that's why I bought them for you.' He went on, 'And now because you are grown up, I'm going to love you even more, just like I loved your mum.'

'But you told me you always loved me, daddy,' Angie replied and she told Theresa what he said next, 'Of course, I always loved you, Angie and I still do, but in the past, you were a little girl and I loved you as a little girl, but now you are a grown-up young woman and I'm going to show you how I will love you as a young woman and how women love men back; would you like that, my little darling.'

'I'm not sure, daddy,' replied Angie. Ahe went on, 'I don't know how to do those grown-up things.'

'Don't worry Angie my little darling, that's what the clothes are for. I'm going to show you everything you need to know and I'm gonna show you tonight.' Then he had told her to lay out the new clothes on her bed, he kissed her and took her by the hand and said, 'Come with me, my beautiful little darling.'

Angie told Theresa how her dad took her to the bathroom with him where he took off her pyjamas, put her in the bath and bathed her.

'Yes,' I know,' said Theresa. 'You've told me this secret before.'

'Yes I know,' said Angela. 'But this time daddy stripped, he took off his shirt and vest and then unzipped his trousers and took them off and then took off his underpants and he was completely naked. And he got into the bath with me and told me to bath him.'

Angie was giggling with excitement. Theresa gasped and covered her mouth. 'Did you see his thing?' asked Theresa excitedly.

'Of course, I did,' replied Angela. 'When he stepped into the bath it was right in front of my face. Daddy talked to me and kept kissing me as he bathed me gently; he has bathed me quite a few times before, normally when it was bed time and in the last year or so dad had begun to do it with just his underpants on, although when he bent over to wash me, I could see a big bulge in his underpants, really close to my face. But this was the first time he'd stripped completely and I'd actually seen his cock this close.'

'So, that's not new,' said Theresa, 'You told me you'd seen his cock before.'

'Yes, I have, I told you, sometimes when he comes home drunk and he can't get completely undressed I would find him laid on his bed half naked, but then it's just soft.'

'What was it like this time then,' asked Theresa excitedly.

'It was hard and big but don't tell anyone please.'

'I won't,' implored Theresa. 'Honest. I won't tell anyone. What happened next?' asked Theresa?

'Dad said, 'This is what mum used to do,' as he kissed me and slowly stood up in the bath and his cock was right in front of my face and he said to me, 'Now you're grown up, you can do what your mum used to do, my little darling Angie; this is how women show they love a man, like you love me,' and he put my hands around his cock.'

'What did you do,' asked Theresa, covering her mouth with her hands in excitement, 'When you touched his cock.'

'It felt funny, but I liked to look at it and touch it,' replied Angela, laughing. 'But I saw this coming though Theresa,' said Angie, 'Cos over the last few years since mum died, dads always bathed me, but in the last year or so he's bathed me far more often and kissed me a lot and sometimes kissing my shoulders, back and legs, especially when he's drying me and I know I shouldn't say it but it feels really nice. He said not to tell anyone or they'll take me and him away.'

'So, then what happened,' asked Theresa excitedly.

'Well, when dad had dried us both he told me to put the black silk pyjama top on, just the top, not the bottoms, the stockings and shoes, just them nothing else and walk around the bedroom in front of him. I did it, Theresa and I felt really grown up and sexy and dad couldn't take his eyes off me and he kept saying, 'You're beautiful, my little darling,' and his cock started to get hard and grow. I don't mean like Andrew's at school that time he showed his cock to us in the playground, that was little, but dad's cock was really big and I mean really big and it had lots of hair around it, then dad got into bed and told me to get into bed with him.'

'Honest,' asked Theresa excitedly.

Angela had been a total virgin and felt very excited about all these new things she was experiencing but she also felt guilty about replacing her mum and even guiltier that she had enjoyed every bit of her new secret sexual life. Angela told Theresa since this started her dad had just loved her more and more and bought her anything she wanted, but she reiterated not to tell anyone, citing the case of Mr Roberts who lived on the same street; when his wife had died and he also began a relationship with his daughter Paula who was 13, Paula had been so excited she told her friends at school, who in turn told their mums and of course, their mums informed the police who took them both away, they were not seen again.

Rose and Jack

Theresa was just like any other 14-year-old and after hearing about Angela's secret had again that evening sneaked across the landing to watch but the bedclothes often obscured some of the activity, but not tonight, it was a warm night, the bedroom light was on and the bedclothes were on the floor and Theresa could see everything. She had to be careful to stay out of the light spilling through the door and stay in the shade on the landing, she thought she knew what they had done previously but could not normally see exactly, now she could see everything clearly and up close.

Theresa watched them as they whispered and moaned but was quite puzzled that mum was forever complaining about Jack to her, but here she was fucking him (one of the words she had learned whilst watching and listening to them) and apparently enjoying it as much as Jack by the sounds she was making. Theresa had to be careful not to get caught she was so close she could hear Jack whispering something about his favourite and her mum whispering back, 'Do you now, you bad boy.'

'You fucking know you love it, darling, as much as I do,' said Jack as he kissed Rose's neck and shoulders working his way all the way down her back to her bottom.

Rose knew she had to give Jack whatever he wanted for the time being for several reasons, Theresa was not old enough to understand the complexities of sex but Rose knew very well that when Jack was in the house with Theresa, he showed far too much sexual interest in her, from little bits of information that Theresa had let slip. Rose knew exactly how to use her sexuality to obtain favour and gifts from Jack, it was her only currency so tonight she would give him whatever he wanted to keep him under her control, at least until she could work out a plan for a better life for her and the girls.

Jack continued to kiss Rose's gorgeous womanly bottom, who laughed as she whispered, 'I'm not sure that what you want is even legal in this country.'

Theresa watched as Jack slowly moved up her mum's back as Rose lay on her stomach, she was nearly looking straight into Theresa's face. Theresa quickly moved backwards from the light pouring from the bedroom, her mum had not seen her but Theresa needed to be very careful. She stayed in the dark shadow of the landing and listened. 'Is this what you want,' she heard her mum say. Rose continued, 'And what will you buy me in the morning, big boy.'

Theresa knew that Jack loved it whenever mum spoke like that, it's nearly always the same; Jack gets very excited and tells mum she can have anything she wants. Theresa carefully peeped into the bedroom but her mum's face was looking straight towards the partially open door, she moved back quickly into the darkness not daring to look in case her mum saw her.

She heard her mum let out a long Ohhhhh; Theresa almost gave herself away as she peeped from her hiding place to see what Jack was doing to her mum but quickly moved back because now Jack's chin was on her mum's head as they both lay face down and both were looking directly toward the open bedroom door.

Theresa just caught a glimpse of Jack gripping her mum's shoulders and her mum's face buried into the pillow to muffle her moans. She stayed in the shadow as she heard what sounded like Jack coming with his heavy breathing and uncontrollable jerking. She listened in silence as they finished and could hear Jack kissing her mum and talking dirty, 'I fucking love your arse, baby,' Jack said as he finished and lay on her mum's back before he again continued to kiss Rose all the way down her spine back to her bottom.

Theresa edged further back into the darkness and slipped quietly back to her bedroom across the landing.

Theresa lay awake thinking about the day and how Angie had experienced sex before her and with her own dad. She also thought of how Jack is always in a good mood the next morning when he's had his 'favourite' as he calls it and always treats mum and us to something special the next day. Although Theresa was never quite sure of everything and was still a little confused about what exactly Jack's 'favourite' was and why mum seemed to enjoy sex when most of the time Jack was a brute.

Theresa had learned one of the most important lessons in life and was aware that her mum used these nights to do special things with Jack to get exactly what she wanted, by giving him his 'favourite,' she had also learned how a woman can make a man do almost anything just by letting him do things to her. Angie had told her that her dad would buy her anything she wanted now since she had started having sex with him.

One night it was about 9:00 PM the girls had gone to bed. Bridget was fast asleep but Theresa was still awake and she heard a key in the door, heavy steps come up the stairs and then some shuffling in the bathroom, a few minutes later her bedroom door slowly and quietly opened and Jack was standing there wearing a dressing gown and smelling of whiskey; he had a camera in his hand, a camera that Theresa had seen before and that she really liked, Jack knew she liked it.

The light from the open bedroom door fell over Theresa's bed and Jack saw she was awake and crept quietly to her bed, in a hushed voice he said, 'I've come to show you something, my little darling,' and put his finger to his lips saying, 'Shussssssh,' so as not to wake Bridget.

Jack sat beside Theresa on the bed, 'I know you like this camera and you would like it to keep it for your own, wouldn't you, my little angel,' he continued, as he proceeded to show Theresa how it worked. Jack stood up, bending forward allowing his dressing gown to fall wide open pretending not to notice that he was exposing his penis, he sat back down on the bed with his dressing gown still wide open and his penis in full view.

Theresa had noticed and she just stared in amazement, she had seen his penis before but never quite this close, it looked bigger and was surrounded with hair, just like Angie had said about her dad. Jack was well aware that Theresa was staring at his cock in fascination as he put his arms around Theresa's shoulders pretending to demonstrate how to point the camera and take pictures. He held her hands on the camera all the time gently pressing his penis against Theresa's bare arm.

Theresa felt it pressing against her and realised it was getting harder and looked at it in amazement and said, 'Jack what's happening.'

'Oh that, don't worry,' replied Jack as he stood up, putting his index finger over his lips to say 'Shussssssh' and allowing his dressing gown to fall completely open to reveal his now erect penis. 'It's what men have got instead of ladies, my little darling,' he said in a hushed quiet voice, 'I wanted to show it to you, my little princess, see how it gets bigger, that's because it likes you.'

Theresa was a little afraid but fascinated at the same time and kept both her hands on the camera as she stared at his erection, he didn't know that she'd seen him erect many times and had also seen her mum sucking him, but this was the

Theresa pretended to calm down as Jack reassured her that she had not hurt him but just made him very happy and put his arm around her.

After a few minutes she asked Jack, 'What's that stuff on my arm that came out of your thing.'

Jack replied, 'That's what supposed to come out of my thing, you did what all big girls do and you did it very well,' he said as he wiped the sperm from her arm with a handkerchief from his dressing gown pocket. He gave Theresa the camera saying, 'Remember what I told you; if you tell your Mum, she'll make you give the camera back and ask why I gave it to you and then you'll be in serious trouble.'

Jack kissed her on the forehead and said, 'You've been a very, very good girl but go to sleep now before your Mum comes home,' with that he left her bedroom and went to his own room. Theresa did not tell her mum and kept the camera well hidden.

Over the next few months, the bedroom visits became a regular thing every time Rose was at work. Theresa knew that she'd be in trouble if her mum found out but she was getting quite a bit of money together, she wasn't hurting anyone and she was amazed how easily she could please a man. She often thought were all men this easy to please after Jack's visits to her room. One night, Theresa was just coming out of the bathroom wrapped in her towel when she heard Jack. She was getting a bit tired of these visits and she tried to make it to her own room before Jack got to the top of the stairs but was too slow.

Jack approached her on the landing smelling of whiskey, as usual; he took Theresa's hand and said, 'You look lovely wrapped in that towel; come into your Mum's room, I've got something to show you.' Jack whispered, 'Shusssssh, be quiet so we don't wake your sister.' Jack led her to his and her mum's bedroom. 'Look how beautiful you look my little angel,' he said. 'Let's see how gorgeous you are under that towel.'

'I mustn't, Jack, I shouldn't be here in mum's bedroom,' said Theresa trying to grip the towel tighter.

'Shusssssh,' said Jack, 'Your mum won't know, will she and it's my bedroom as well you know, now let's see your beautiful body,' he said, as he slowly removed the bath towel. Theresa crossed her arms attempting to cover her breasts, Jack whispered, 'No, don't cover your gorgeous body, my darling; let me see it all, I've got some money for you.'

He took a five-pound note from his pocket, Theresa had never seen a five-pound note, Jack waved the note above his head as he gently pulled her arms away revealing her naked breasts and was amazed how developed she was, a young woman's body and a young girls face. Jack whispered, 'Kneel down, my little darling. I want to see if you can do what your Mum does; I'm sure you can, I'm sure you can do what all big girls do.'

Theresa slowly knelt in front of him as he unzipped his trousers; she leaned backwards uttering an alarmed Oooooh, he ran his fingers through her hair and moved her head closer; now Theresa was looking straight at his cock, she had never seen it this close, it was almost touching her lips.

'That's it, my little darling,' said Jack. 'Open your beautiful mouth like a big girl.' Theresa had watched her mum do this to Jack and knew exactly what he wanted her to do and how to do it. She did as she was told and Jack gently pulled Theresa's head toward him. 'Oh my God, my little darling, you are soooo good.'

Theresa, nearly choked as he gradually pushed his cock as deep as he could into her mouth. Theresa was trying to remember exactly how she'd seen mum do it. Jack was caressing Theresa's head and face with both hands as he began to lose control, pushing himself deeper and deeper. Theresa had her hands pressed on Jack's thighs trying to hold him back as she almost choked, but couldn't compete with Jack's strength as he pushed deeper into her mouth, she was starting to get frightened with Jack's urgency.

Suddenly, they both heard a key in the front door, it was Rose arriving home from work and she was earlier than usual. *Fuck it, fuck it, fuck it,* thought Jack to himself as he quickly pulled himself out of Theresa's mouth, wrapped the towel around her and quickly bundled her from the bedroom back across the landing to her own room with the money in her hand.

Rose heard the rushed movement upstairs and heard Jack walking quickly across the landing; she knew it was Jack, the girls are light and hardly made a sound. She went up the stairs, Jack was back outside their own bedroom. Rose walked towards him noticing his trouser belt was undone and his zip was open, he was breathing heavily and slightly out of breath. Rose also noticed the girl's bedroom door was wide open.

She said, 'Is everything OK, Jack?'

'Yeah,' he replied. 'Just checking on the girls.'

Rose immediately kissed him and ran her hand gently down his body sliding inside his trousers, she needed to confirm her suspicions and felt he was semi hard. Rose thought she knew exactly what he'd been doing, she had suspected for a while that Jack had far too much interest in Theresa and assumed he'd been masturbating outside the girl's room, she would have cut his dick off if she'd known what had really just been happening.

She was horrified at the implications, of what she thought, she wanted to kill him there and then but as a mother she could only protect the girls from him and keep Jack as far away by using her feminine wiles and not let him know that she was aware of what a sexual predator he really was.

Rose couldn't keep up this pretence forever and the day was coming when something had to give but for now, she needed to keep the girls safe. She kissed him as she wrapped her fingers around his penis and whispered, 'Let's take care of this big boy, Jack;' she pushed her tongue deep into his mouth and whispered, 'You must have been thinking of me to be this big when I got home, I need that cock inside me, baby,' gently tugging him into their bedroom.

Theresa had heard her mum come up the stairs and was relieved that her mum had not stormed into her room, she had stuffed the money under her pillow and was pretending to be asleep. Theresa slowly calmed down as she heard her mum softly talking to jack on the landing, this time she nearly got caught, she heard her mum and Jack go to their room and she went to close her bedroom door but she could hear noises from her Mum and Jack's room.

Their bedroom door as usual was half open and she crept across the landing and peered through the door to see her Mum naked and kneeling in front of Jack, just as she had been a few moments earlier, he pushed his penis all the way into her Mums mouth, then Jack threw Rose onto the bed. Theresa watched as Jack had sex with her mum as she whispered, 'Oooooh Jack, give me that big fat cock, fuck me, baby, fuck me,' she knew Jack loved dirty talk and he wouldn't last very long.

Suddenly, Jack moaned loudly, like that night in Theresa's room some weeks earlier, Jack held her mum's legs in the air gripping her by the ankles as he tensed and started to shudder, he pulled out shooting all over Rose's stomach. Rose watched as Jack pumped his sperm over her before he slowly relaxed in ecstasy, she knew Jack loved to do that to her and after a short while he collapsed next to her on the bed as her hands softly caressed his cock and balls until he fell asleep.

Theresa crept back to her room. Rose lay next to Jack for a while as he slept, she didn't love Jack but she did love sex and Jack did like to give her a lot of sex when he was there and most times she could turn it towards her own pleasure too; sexually he was OK and after all, he did pay most of the bills. She could do a lot worse many women were struggling with rationed food and nowhere to live and many had turned to prostitution but Rose knew her only route out of this way of life was a sexual one.

Queens Head

Rose hardly slept these days only too aware of Jack's increasing interest in Theresa, she knew she had to leave him soon, the war rationing can't last forever things have to improve she hated 'the arrangement' and always had, but she did love the sex. One night a well-dressed man came into the 'Queens Head' where Rose worked, he stood out from the crowd because the 'Queens' catered mainly for older business man types, he was also very tall and good looking, she liked what she saw.

He approached the bar and spoke to Rose, 'Excuse me, do you know a Mr Wardle.'

Rose quickly looked at the clock and replied, 'Yes, I do; you're a little early for him, he won't be in for another 15 or 20 minutes; if you're going to wait, can I get you something to drink.'

'Yes please,' the man said. 'Can I have a brandy please and would you like a drink yourself,' he asked.

'Thank you,' replied Rose. 'Is that a double or a single brandy, Sir.'

'Just a single please,' he replied.

As Rose poured the brandy, the man sat at the bar looking around the pub and she took the opportunity to adjust her dress to show as much of her ample cleavage as possible and it worked, when she placed the brandy on the bar in front of him, she wiped the bar purposely leaning forward to give him the best possible view, she knew exactly how to work men.

'Would you like anything else, sir,' Rose asked, he smiled, trying to look at her face and not her gorgeous boobs, she said, 'I'll take that as a no,' as she took the money and gave him the change.

'I'm sorry I didn't mean to stare, but you are a very attractive lady,' he said.

'Well, thank you,' replied Rose walking from behind the bar to wipe the tables, but really to lean as far forward over them without making it obvious to show him as much of her gorgeous legs as she possibly could.

Rose saw through the pub wall mirrors, he never took his eyes off her, she went back behind the bar and the man said, 'Can I have another brandy please.'

'Of course sir, see you should have had the double,' Rose replied.

'Don't call me sir, my name is Jess,' he replied

She passed him his double brandy and said, 'And my name is Rose.'

Just then Mr Wardle arrived with some friends and Mr Wardle invited his two friends to sit at a table because Mr Wardle joined Jess at the bar and ordered the drinks for all three of them.

'Hello, Jess,' said Mr Wardle, 'Can I get you a drink.'

'No thank you, John,' replied Jess. 'I've only come here tonight to deliver your merchandise as arranged,' and handed him a package.

'I expect you've noticed the beautiful Rose behind the bar,' said John deliberately loud enough for Rose to hear. Rose looked at both men and smiled in a very coy way, as John scooped up his package and tried to pick up the drinks too.

Rose said, 'I'll take the package for you, Mr Wardle,' and she took the parcel to the table as John picked up the drinks and said, 'Got to get back to my two business colleagues, I'll see you again soon, Jess' and with that Mr Wardle joined his friends at the table.

'Thanks for taking the parcel over to them, Rose,' said Jess.

'That's alright, but if the police come in, I didn't touch it OK,' she replied.

'No, Rose,' said Jess, 'It's not black-market stuff; it's just a suit, I'm a tailor, it's all very legal and above board.'

'Oh, a tailor,' said Rose as she smiled. 'That explains why you look like a male model then.'

'That makes two models in here then,' said Jess as they both laughed.

'I hardly look like a model working behind a bar in a very normal dress, do I,' said Rose questioningly.

'You look lovely in that dress, Rose,' said Jess. 'But if you want, I can make you a dress, how about that.'

Rose replied, 'Jess, I don't know Mr Wardle except as a customer, but I do know he wears very expensive suits, so how am I going to afford a dress made-to-measure on barmaid's wages,' she said with a questioning look on her face.

'I wouldn't charge you, Rose. I'd make it for you for free,' replied Jess.

'Oh, that's how you make money, is it by making clothes for people free of charge, Jess. I'm not 16, Jess; there's always a price to pay, now would you like another drink.'

'Yes please, I'll have another brandy,' he replied.

It was no surprise to Rose that the very next night Jess showed up at the 'Queens,' she knew he had taken a shine to her.

'Well, hello again, Jess, would you like a brandy.'

'Yes,' Jess replied.

'Are you delivering another suit,' she asked as she poured the brandy.

Jess began, 'Last night I didn't mean to imply anything, Rose, when I said I would make you a dress free of charge, I was just thinking ahead.'

Rose placed his drink in front of him on the bar, as he continued, Jess looked straight at Rose and spoke quietly, 'The war is over and rationing will end soon; every day thousands of soldiers, sailors and airmen are being demobbed and I want to be in the position of making wedding dresses and bridesmaid dresses and for that I need a woman to bring in the trade. I've been looking for that woman for some time and then by pure chance I popped in here yesterday to deliver a suit and there is the exact person I've been looking for behind that bar.'

'Are you making me a job offer, Jess,' she asked.

Jess looked around quickly to make sure no one could hear him and quietly said, 'Yes, I'm making you a job offer.'

A man came to the bar followed by a second man.

As Rose served the two customers, she couldn't help but think this could be her way out and she knew she could have this very handsome man, he was putty in the hands of an expert like Rose. After she'd served them she returned to the conversation with Jess, 'But why me, Jess.'

Jess immediately replied, 'I've already told you, you're attractive, you're used to serving the public and very well I might add and you hinted that your wages were not ideal, I need to change my tailor's window to have appeal to women, so why don't we give it a try; you work for me a few days a week, see if you like it and if you do you might have a career change.'

'OK,' said Rose. 'If I choose to accept your offer, where do we go from here.'

Jess gave Rose the address of the tailor's shop and she was pleased to hear that it was about fifteen miles away, which is good because it's out of the immediate area but bad for commuting. Rose said, 'Jess, well that job sounds great but that's a long way to travel by public transport.'

Jess realised that getting to the shop presented problems for her and offered to pick her up each day she worked. Rose looked at Jess and then at the paper with the address written on it. Jess said, 'Please, Rose, it could be a new start for you and you might love the work.'

Rose looked at Jess as she served another customer, she gave the man his change and returned to Jess and said with a beautiful smile, 'OK, Jess, when would you like me to start the trial at your shop.'

Jess replied, 'As soon as possible please, Rose.'

Rose went on, 'Next Monday sounds good for me, Jess, pick me up outside the 'Queens,' but please say nothing to jeopardise this bar job.'

'That's not a problem, Rose,' said Jess. 'I'll pick you up at 9:00 on Monday morning and now I will have a double brandy to celebrate and please have a drink with me.'

The Tailor's Shop

On Rose's first day at the tailor's shop, she began to change the window dressing to have more appeal to women working closely with Jess, they stopped for a coffee and walked to the kitchen, as they got to the door the trousers on one of the mannequins slipped to the floor and they both laughed. Jess saw this as a perfect opening to kiss Rose and leaned forwards to do exactly that, but Rose pulled away from his advance, there was an awkward moment and an awkward afternoon.

As arranged at the end of the day, Jess drove Rose back to drop her off a couple of streets away from her house. On the drive Jess said, 'Rose, I am so sorry for what happened today. I don't know what got into me.'

Rose replied, 'It doesn't matter, Jess, honestly; it's been a long time since a man tried to kiss me and I was just a little shocked. I'm sorry too.'

'You will come back on Thursday, won't you?' asked Jess.

'Stop the car now,' Rose commanded.

Jess pulled over and stopped, Rose grabbed his head in both her hands and pulled his face towards hers, she pressed her lips onto his in a long sensual kiss, she broke away saying, 'Yes, I'll be back on Thursday and yes, I wanted to kiss you but it's just been a long time since I've been intimate with a man,' and she kissed him again, Jess drove her home but just couldn't wait for Thursday to arrive.

Jess

Jess was not known to many people in the area, especially not Jack, he was not seen out that often, a tailor's profession is not really like many others because there is minimal face to face contact and liaison with clients, a tailor mainly works alone and in one place and there is limited contact with end clients. Jess had quite a number of well-heeled regular clients who knew him by his reputation, they would simply make first contact placing their order, he would measure them, if necessary, there would be a fitting and then he would make the garment and deliver it.

Jess was tall, single, good looking and financially well off and he had offered the job to Rose in good faith, it was Rose who had a hidden agenda, it was her who would pursue Jess. It had been a long time since Rose had been with a man because she wanted to be with him and not just for his money, she saw Jess as a potential way out and she intended to draw him into her feminine honey trap.

On Thursday the mood was far more relaxed and when Jess picked up Rose she said, 'Good morning,' and kissed him. She actually kissed him on the lips saying, 'I'm sorry for the other day, Jess and feel I have to make it up to you,' as they drove off, she looked at him and smiled as she put her hand on his thigh. When they got to his shop Rose said, 'I really am so sorry for the other day, what can I do to make it up to you, Jess.'

He said, 'Can I kiss you, Rose,' she put her arms around his waist and pushed her face to his. He kissed her, but Rose really kissed him back, she felt his urgency as he put his arms around her and returned the kisses, in the middle of a long kiss he felt her hand slowly slide around his muscular arse, she pulled him in close and squeezed her large breasts into him, the kiss continued as her warm hands slid down his leg and gently around his hardening cock.

'Jess, Oooooh, you feel so nice. I don't think we're going to get any work done today, are we,' Rose said, as she pushed her tongue into his mouth and moved her hand up and down the length of his cock.

'Ohhh, I hope not,' said Jess as he smiled back at her, took off his coat and proceeded to slowly take off her clothes. Rose did not resist and they both discarded clothes as they walked toward the stairs and had sex for most of that day in Jess's apartment above the tailor's shop.

Jess knew nothing of Theresa, Bridget or Jack and Rose wanted to keep it that way, she spent many nights thinking about how her life had gone wrong, the girls and her own welfare and future, Jack's unnatural interest in Theresa; she had saved a lot of money from her clients unknown to Jack and now her new found attraction for a good man Jess, she was in a very good position to execute her plan; she may never get another chance and the longer she waited the greater the chance of Jack finding out.

She just wanted her life back; she was not an old woman, she knew Australia was crying out for immigrants and they weren't too fussy how they got them and so she toiled with the idea of secretly releasing the girls for immigration completely unknown to Jack.

Because Jess had a car which was quite unusual, they could visit pubs miles away from the local area and keep their relationship secret, which cannot be done on public transport. This could be a chance for all three of them to escape from Jack, the girls could have a new and better start in life half a world away from a bombed out and bankrupt country and she could be with a man who she really loved being with, they could all be beginning a new life and future.

The Holiday Present Day 1960

Birmingham was not an ideal holiday destination for most people but Paul liked it, this is where his police career began 30 years earlier. He walked into his old local pub the 'Dugdale Arms' to a chorus of 'Fuck me, look who's back on the patch,' followed by raucous laughter. Paul went straight to the bar and embraced Colin. Colin King was also a DI and had joined the police with Paul as a young man.

'How are you, you old bastard, you don't get no fucking cuter, do ya,' said Paul.

'Ain't you got no fucking mirrors in Liverpool,' replied Colin laughing,

'What you havin' mate?' said Colin.

The two friends carried on drinking with the other off duty cops and then went back to Colin's house.

Nancy, Colin's wife was still up, she stood up and kissed and embraced Paul, 'Lovely to see you, Paul and it's been too long,' said Nancy.

'It's just work, Nancy,' Paul replied. 'It just never seems to end.'

'Paul, we can all make that excuse,' said Nancy. 'And I'm going to make that very excuse now, you'll have to give me all the details in the morning, I've got work early and have to go to bed, I just wanted to be up when you arrived, I've put you in Lisa's room,' and with that Nancy kissed both men and went to bed.

'Fancy a whiskey, mate,' said Colin.

Paul said, 'Yeah, I'll have one with you mate.'

They both continued drinking and chatting into the small hours and then just went upstairs to their rooms and crashed out in their beds.

Next morning in the kitchen eating breakfast after Nancy had left for work Colin was filling the kettle as Paul came down the stairs and sat at the breakfast table. 'Morning, mate, did you sleep OK?' enquired Colin.

'Like a log,' replied Paul, 'mind you I'm not surprised with what we put away last night.'

'It's the nature of the careers we chose, mate,' said Colin. 'It was never 9 to 5.'

'Precisely, mate,' replied Paul. 'As a matter of fact that's exactly what I need to talk to you about.'

'What's that then,' asked Colin.

'I got a multiple murder on my patch yesterday mate and if my superintendent knew I was here at this moment I'd be back on the beat, so I gotta get back today, I'm sorry Col.'

'A multiple murder,' asked Colin, 'You ain't had one of them for a bit, what happened.'

'Not sure yet but it looks like two local's dead from gun shots and one ex-merchant marine killed with a crossbow. I've asked my DS to keep me up to speed on it, even while I'm here.'

'Oh, fucking hell, Paul,' said Colin. ' 'Your Super' will have your balls if you're partying down here with a multiple murder to sort, mind you so will Nancy, she's organised a bit of a party, the food and a night out so she'll go barmy when she gets home to find you've gone back north.'

'I could have done with the break myself, mate,' replied Paul, 'but you just said it yourself, it was never 9 to 5.' Paul continued, 'And I could have done with the holiday and a couple of nights with Vicky, do you remember her.'

'Everybody remembers Vicky,' Colin replied. 'She had the most beautiful perfect tits. Nancy remembers them very well, she used to ask every day, are you working with that slag Vicky.' Both men laughed.

Then Paul began, 'What ever happened with that beautiful black sergeant, you had the hots for, mate.'

'Don't fucking mention Sonia in this house, Paul,' replied Colin. 'She went back to the Caribbean and had a party at the 'Brandon Hotel,' Nancy was at her sisters in Coventry for a few days, Sonia came round here to invite me, she went to the toilet and came back in the room just wearing a tiny yellow tanga against her beautiful black skin; she knew she was gorgeous, I couldn't resist her and I ended up shagging her all afternoon and she was supposed to be on duty and in uniform; why her beautiful black arse was sat on my face, her police car was parked outside for three hours and the neighbours noticed.' They both laughed.

'I went to the party and shagged her all night and half the next morning, she was fucking gorgeous,' said Colin. 'But Nancy got a sniff of it from the neighbours and it caused some shit.'

'Did someone tell her,' asked Paul.

'No,' Colin replied. 'But when a fucking police car is parked outside all afternoon, neighbours talk. And when you wear a figure hugging bright yellow mini dress at a hotel party and you're as black and gorgeous as Sonia you get noticed, mate and some of Nancy's mates work at the 'Brandon'.'

'So, what happened,' asked Paul.

'Well Jenny, Nancy's best mate saw a black girl in a yellow dress sat on a blokes face along the corridor of the 4th floor of the hotel in the early hours and the bloke was wearing a dark green suit.'

'Did this Jenny recognise you or see your face,' asked Paul.

'No, she just saw a dark green suit,' replied Colin. 'She couldn't see my face, it was buried in gorgeous black arse and pussy.'

They both laughed. 'So what happened,' asked Paul.

'I fixed myself an alibi,' said Colin. 'I bought one of the single uniform recruits a dark green suit, give him a few quid and got some photos of him with Sonia, then I took Nancy for some posh expensive dinners but it was a close call mate, could have ended in divorce.' Both men laughed again.

Jack's Business 1946

Jack Grantham bought the houses of deceased house owners with no living relatives. He had friends everywhere and paid contacts in the civil service to supply him with lists of armed forces deaths who were either only sons or women who were now widowed. He paid another friend on the local council to supply similar lists of the elderly deceased and dead bomb victims whose property was still repairable.

Jack's businesses were all illegal. He provided black-market goods and special 'services' to military personnel who were on leave and also accommodation for returning service personnel with 'additional comforts' always available, Jack's 'Girls' were predominantly war widows orphaned teenagers or any young woman struggling financially, they received accommodation, moderate pay and black-market food for their 'work.'

Jack was in the pub 'The Black Boy' with a couple of his associates looking at the women and barmaid between scanning the death list in the newspaper. The papers headlines told of Russian soldiers still occupying Berlin.

'Ain't gotta enough houses to let,' said Jack. 'They're coming back in droves.'

'Yeah, you ain't got your pick of all the girls now though have you, Jack,' said Harry laughing as he pointed to Linda the barmaid looking up her skirt as she wiped the tables and collected glasses.

Jack was looking for his next house purchase and replied, 'With all these soldiers and matlows coming back, mate, I've got it sorted for 'em, I supply everything they need; this time next year I'll have all the money and crumpet any bloke could handle.'

The Journey 1946

Rose had purposely arranged to remove the girls one day directly after school when she knew Jack would be out doing business with his associates or buying houses, he could be gone anything from three days to a week. In the past, he had disappeared for weeks on end or even months but she knew better than to ask him where he was going or where he had been, but she knew approximately how long he'd be away with the clothes he took with him, one of these times when he just disappeared, she would seize the opportunity to just disappear and begin a new life.

Rose had worked at the Tailors shop for about a month, she had to make her move soon or Jack would find out that she now only worked two days at the pub, she loved the way her life was heading and fortunately Jack was away for months at the moment thank God, she didn't even know or really care what he was doing, her time was coming.

Rose knew Jess was falling in love with her, he told her every day and she had now decided he was her way out, he begged her to move in with him but she couldn't tell him why that wasn't possible yet, but the day was arranged it was in just two days. Rose needed to keep Jess right on the boil till the time was right, now it was important to purposely dress in the most sexual way she could every day. She wore dresses that were too short and would show just a hint of her stocking tops or no panties, she knew all the tricks.

Rose was arranging the window mannequins and deliberately kneeling in a way to show off her assets to Jess and of course, it worked. Today she was going to accept his invitation to move in. Jess walked towards her and said, 'Rose, you are so fucking gorgeous. I can't think straight, you are driving me crazy, please just move in with me, please.'

'You've been looking up my dress again, haven't you, naughty boy,' she said, knowing full well that she'd no panties on.

Jess just fell on her burying his face into intimate parts of her body. 'Whoaa tiger, we're in the shop window, baby boy,' said Rose laughing as she fell flat on the floor under his weight. 'Let's move somewhere a little more private,' said Rose, she went on. 'Stand there and just wait,' as she moved into the shop, closing the window curtains behind them and locking the shop door.

Rose allowed her dress to slip to the floor as she walked back to Jess saying, 'Where were we, baby boy,' she knelt down in front of him and unzipped his trousers. 'Why I call you baby boy with a fucking cock this size, I'll never know, baby,' she slipped him into her mouth and Jess nearly passed out as his hands pulled her mouth onto him. 'Fucking hell, baby, it's like a horses cock, I've never seen one this fucking big,' said Rose, 'And it tastes delicious baby.'

Jess was just not used to such wonderfully erotic sex and couldn't take the action and dirty talk, it was all too much for him as he exploded into Rose's mouth, all Jess could hear was 'Mmmmm, Baby,' as Rose sucked every last drop from him, swallowing as she stared right back up into his eyes. Jess just pumped and pumped as Rose had her hands behind his thighs pulling him further into her throat, eventually Jess felt the last surge and fell to his knees hugging and kissing Rose.

'Please move in with me, baby. I love you so much. I couldn't bear to lose you.'

Rose kissed him pushing her tongue into his mouth, as she lay on the floor beside him, saying, 'Can you taste your gorgeous cream in my mouth, baby.' Rose's fingers caressed his cock as she said it and she felt his cock surge in response, she said, 'Baby, you're not going to lose me. I love you too, you're so handsome and kind to me and look at this fucking huge horse's cock, where will I ever find another man like you,' as she moved down his body and sucked him, saying, 'And you taste gorgeous baby boy.'

'I tell you what, baby, I love you and your gorgeous body so much, if you get this huge cock hard again and fuck me, I'll move in next week.'

Jess couldn't believe his ears and rolled Rose onto her back as he kissed her, she could feel him getting hard again, she wrapped her legs around his back as he entered her saying, 'Ohhhh, baby, fucking hell, you are soooo big.'

The Journey 1946

Some weeks later Theresa and Bridget returned home from school and there was a black car outside their house, cars were rare and it was very unusual to see one parked outside their home. They went into the house to find their Mum (Rose) had two men in the house, both of the men wore suits and bowler hats. Theresa noticed two bags and a suitcase in the hall, the two bags were Theresa's and Bridget's bags.

Rose called the two girls into the kitchen where the men were, kissed both girls on the cheek and said, 'I need you both to go with these men, it's for the best.'

Rose then hurriedly came from living room walked to the kitchen and closed the door, she put on her coat picked up her suitcase and left the house by the backdoor, she walked quickly down the back entry's, careful not to be seen by neighbours and disappeared into the back streets.

Bridget started to scream and cry and shout for her mum as Theresa hugged her to try to comfort her as the men picked up the two bags from the hall and tightly clutched the hands of both girls as they took them from the house, where they were quickly bundled into the back of the car.

The two men were each side of the girls and the driver was instructed to drive off, the car sped away. The car seemed to travel very fast and drive for a long time, Theresa was too frightened to ask the men what was happening as she hugged Bridget who cried all the way, one man lit a cigarette and finally spoke and all he said was, 'Do as you're told and you will not be in any trouble.'

The car finally stopped outside a big house in a dark street, one of the men got out and knocked on the door, a large women and tall woman came from the house and walked back to the car with the man, the girls and their bags were quickly taken into the house, the man gave the woman some envelopes and then went back to the car, the car and all three men drove off; the tall woman spoke to the girls, 'Don't be frightened you're going on a holiday tomorrow so you need to have something to eat and go to bed, you'll be staying here tonight, behave yourselves and everything will be alright.'

She took the girls who were both frightened and still mystified into a big room and gave them some bread and stew. The large woman stood by the door and waited until they'd finished then told them to pick up their bags and follow her.

She took them upstairs to a room with lots of beds and just one big table down the middle between the bottom of the beds and said, 'Choose a bed before the other girls get here; if you need the toilet, there is a potty under your bed, put your pyjamas on and get into bed,'

The woman locked the door as she left. All through the evening and night Theresa and Bridget heard cars pulling up outside, the sound of voices and the bedroom door kept unlocking and locking as other girls arrived, all of them given the same instructions, where the potty was and to change into their pyjamas and get into bed. Sometimes just one girl arrived, other times three or four, some were a bit older or a bit younger, some were crying, some were quiet and all of them were as mystified as Theresa and Bridget.

When the room was full the door was finally locked for the night and the lights were turned out. Theresa could hear some girls crying, some quietly whispering; she hugged Bridget who had managed to go to sleep and looked at the girl in the next bed, she was about Theresa's age and asked her name, the girl looked back in the half light and said, 'I'm Susan, where are we and where are they taking us.'

Jack's Business 1946

It was 10:00 and the 'Black Boy' was fairly busy, Jack talked to his contacts, he had secured more houses from bomb victims and the war just kept him so busy and rich he couldn't believe his luck. He finished his drink, nodded good bye to his friends and left, it was dark outside but only a short walk home. As Jack walked to the end of the street two young women approached him.

One of the girls spoke in Jack's ear in whispers, after a brief pause Jack looked at the other girl and then gave the one who had whispered to him some money, 'Meet me tomorrow at 10-00 in the 'Kings Head,' both of ya and don't be late.'

Jack got home and shouted, 'Rose,' there was no answer. Jack looked around the house then went upstairs to the bedroom. Rose's clothes were all gone, he ran to the girl's room, the girl's and their clothes were gone too. Jack went back downstairs and looked in every room for a note or letter, there was nothing.

He phoned around and got some of his men on the streets and down the local pubs to try and find Rose and the girls, they all drew a blank, it was if all three of them had just disappeared into thin air, reluctantly Jack returned to the house and went to the kitchen and grabbed a bottle, he then sat in his chair and cursed to himself as he poured himself a whiskey.

The Journey 1946

Theresa had woken early and immediately wondered where she was, but as she looked around the room it all came flooding back. Susan was awake and they began to whisper to each other to avoid waking the other girls.

'Do you think Mum will come and get us back,' Susan asked.

'I don't know,' said Theresa. 'I don't know where we are or where we're going, did some men come for you?'

Before Susan could reply they both heard the door unlock and it sprang open as the lights came on and two women entered the room, they were not the same women as last night. One of the women rang a school bell to ensure all the girls were awake and she had their attention, the other woman put two big bowls of water, several bars of carbolic soap and a pile of towels on the table.

'Listen very carefully, you girls,' she spoke loudly. 'Get washed and dressed, put your pyjamas in your bags and be ready to leave this room in 20 minutes. I do not want to find any clothes left or there will be trouble, is that clear.'

The room was silent.

'Is that clear,' she bellowed.

All the girls replied, 'Yes, Miss.'

She stared at the girls and said, 'When I come to collect you in 20 minutes, bring your bags with you and we'll be going downstairs for some breakfast;' both women left and locked the door.

When the women returned the girls were led down the stairs carrying their bags, they went into a big room and were hurriedly seated for their breakfast, there were a lot more girls than there were in the big bedroom and lots of women in the room by each table, some of them had keys on chains on their belts. All of them had dark uniforms like policemen wear. Theresa thought, *where have all these other girl's come from and where are we all going.*

Bridget sat as close to Theresa as she could as they ate breakfast of toast and porridge. 'Is Mum coming back, Theresa,' Bridget asked.

'I think so, I bet we'll see her soon,' said Theresa reassuringly.

Susan whispered across the table to Theresa, 'Do you think they are going to put us in prison, Theresa.'

'They're not going to put us in prison, are they' asked Bridget starting to cry.

'Shooooosh,' said Theresa. 'No they're not going to put us in prison, I don't know where we're going yet but it's not prison.'

'Quiet over there,' a voice bellowed. 'All of you girls hurry up and eat your breakfast, we're leaving in ten minutes.'

Then women came round the tables with labels, two for each girl and wrote our names on both. One of the labels was pinned to our collars and one tied on our bags. All the girls were led out of the house to a big yard where there were lots of buses waiting, there were queues of girls on this side of the yard and boys on the other side.

There were women with keys on chains on their belts loading the girls onto the buses and men with keys on chains on their belts loading the boys. The buses were quickly boarded and one women or man in uniform got onto each bus with the children. The buses moved off quickly in a long convoy, none of the children knew their destination.

The Holiday Present Day 1960

The phone rang and Colin answered it, a voice spoke, 'Can I speak to detective inspector Paul Bramley please?'

'And who is this?' asked Colin.

'It's detective sergeant Dennis Goodburn,' came the reply.

'It's your DS for you, mate,' said Colin handing the phone to Paul.

'Yes, Dennis, what ya got.'

'Hope you're enjoying your holiday, chief,' said Dennis, who continued, 'The two scallies were regular clients of ours chief with long records, originally from Toxteth; however, the Paddy was known around town to the lad's cos he was a bit handy and apparently a bit of a loner.'

'Any History,' asked Paul.

'Well he was in the merchant navy for 20 odd years, that's where he learned to box and he served on ships taking immigrant kids to Aussie some years ago, he was on the 'Nicola Star,' 'Kingdom Five' and 'The Pharaoh'.'

'Thanks, Dennis,' said Paul, 'Anything back from forensics yet.'

'Nothing back yet,' replied Dennis.

'OK,' said Paul, 'stay on it mate, I'll be back around lunchtime,' and ended the call.

Colin poured another cup of tea and asked Paul, 'Did I hear you say, 'The Pharaoh?'

'Yes, why?' asked Paul.

'Because I think you'll have the perfect excuse for your 'super' to be down here, mate.'

'Sorry Col, you've lost me.'

'Listen,' said Colin, 'Last night you had two scallies shot, but from what you told me, you know as well as me that was because they just showed up by accident on the wrong night, the real target was the guy executed with the crossbow, who was a merchant seaman on The Pharaoh, right.'

'Yes,' said Paul.

Colin went on, 'Well, last week we had a hit and run and we're still looking for the driver; the victim was an ex-merchant seaman, guess what fucking ship he served on.' Colin continued, 'What are the chances of two ex-sailors, who served on the same ship some years ago, both dying in mysterious circumstances within a week of each other, it looks like we've got a serial killer on both our patches mate.'

The New Life 1946

Rose awoke she could hardly believe she'd done it, she had escaped that dreadful existence and turned to see her gorgeous man next to her in bed, he was still asleep and she gently kissed him. She remembered their first time together, Jess had asked her to come up to his flat for a drink after work, his flat was above the shop. Straight after she finished work Rose quickly washed herself in the shop toilet, put on clean underwear and applied some perfume. She hung her coat in the hall at the bottom of the stairs, unbuttoned two top buttons on her blouse and confidently went up the stairs.

Jess had expected Rose to go home first and went for a shower, he was just coming from his bathroom bare chested with a towel around his waist, he had a good body, when he saw Rose on the landing.

'You're early, Rose,' he said.

'And your gorgeous,' she replied, as she walked to him and wrapped her arms around him and kissed him with a long deep erotic kiss.

'Gosh, Rose,' said Jess in shocked pleased surprise, she had taken his breath away with her forwardness. Rose could see he was pleased and began to kiss him all over his face and neck, he felt a warm hand on his back as the other slid slowly down inside the towel and down his leg and the towel fell to the floor as her fingers slowly curled around him.

His breathing increased in speed and Rose felt his body re-acting, she looked straight into Jess's eyes, 'Wow,' she said between the kisses and whispered 'You're not big baby, you're just fucking enormous, can I kiss and suck you please, Jess,' she whispered and with that Rose slid down his body kissing his chest and stomach as she slowly went down onto her knees still looking straight up into his eyes.

As Rose knelt, she diverted her gaze from his eyes to a rock hard and very large erection. 'Oh, Jess,' she said, 'It's huge and beautiful.'

Jess was in awe of her sexuality and loved the way she touched him and the way she talked her sexy talk.

Rose's warm hands gently caressed him. 'Can I taste you,' Rose whispered in a soft sexy voice, whilst looking up at Jess, he was in the world of heaven as Rose's tongue and lips traced their way along him, she could hardly get her fingers all the way around him, he was so thick. She said, 'Wow Jess, you're really honestly hung like a fucking horse, this is the biggest cock I've ever seen.'

Rose's tongue was taking Jess to the very edge, then she opened her mouth and her beautiful soft red lips closed tightly over his bursting penis. Jess already knew Rose was a beautiful woman but couldn't believe how lucky he was to find someone this sexually experienced, he was not going to let her slip away. It was like a night in Heaven's dreamland as her head rocked backwards and forwards gently and slowly sucking him.

Jack's Business 1946

Jack awoke from his drunken state, still in the armchair with the dregs of the whiskey bottle in his damp lap. 'Fuck it' he cursed as he realised, he was still in the chair from the night before, with wet trousers. Suddenly, he remembered Rose and the girls were gone and still didn't know where, he quickly washed his face in the sink and changed his trousers and looked round the house for any clues as to where they had gone.

He could hardly inform the police, they were the last people Jack needed in any of his properties, he phoned Billy and said, 'Meet me in the 'Kings Head' at 9 o'clock and bring a couple of lads and leave them at the door.'

Jack was at the bar in the 'Kings Head' when Billy arrived with two men who he left at the pub door as instructed, he walked straight up to Jack and said, 'Good morning, boss; what we got on.'

'Billy, what you havin',' Jack said.

'I'll have a scotch, boss,' replied Billy.

'Now listen, Billy,' said Jack. 'How many men have you brought?'

'Two, boss,' replied Billy.

Jack went on, 'Rose and the girls have disappeared.'

'What do ya mean disappeared, boss,' asked Billy.

'I got home yesterday and Rose and the girls were gone and all their clothes were gone too, so I know they ain't been kidnapped by some of them fucking Manchester bastards trying to muscle in so it's not a turf war, but I'm busy for the next two weeks and I want them found,' replied Jack.

'But I thought she had no money, boss,' quizzed Billy.

'I didn't think she did have, Bill, but she's gone all the same,' said Jack.

'So she's fucking got money from somewhere. OK Boss, what clues we got about where she might be,' asked Billy.

'Well, start with the 'Queens Head' and then all the local taxi's and then some of her mates like Moira. I want her found and brought back, OK,' said Jack.

'OK, Boss. I'm straight on it,' said Billy and he left the pub.

Jack walked quickly through the bar of the 'Kings Head' and into the snug at the rear of the pub and the two girls from last night were sat there it was exactly 10 o'clock, he joined them with no introduction and looked across the table at the two girls Jill and Sheila, then he said, 'Look, there are hundreds of girls in your situation, Sheila,' as he looked at the young blonde woman. 'Has Jill told you how we operate.'

Jill replied, 'She knows the deal, Jack; she won't let you down.'

'OK,' said Jack. 'Just don't fuck me about.'

The barmaid brought the drinks and they waited for the barmaid to leave the table and be out of earshot and then, Sheila spoke, 'I won't fuck you about, Jack, honest.'

Jack said, 'Be at my house tonight about 10:00 and wear something sexy and I've got a special job for you tomorrow just round the corner, is that a problem?'

Sheila replied, 'No, it's not a problem, Jack, honest.'

Jack put his hand in his pocket and took out a piece of paper, he slid his hand under the table and up Sheila's dress and tucked it into her stocking top and then slid his hand slowly between her legs pulling her pants to one side and pushing first one and then two fingers into her, Sheila just allowed her legs to open and smiled back at Jack as he moved his fingers inside her as he spoke, 'I've got you a place you can move in today, if you're the right sort of girl who does as she's told, Jill will tell you what I mean,' then he stopped touching her, stood up finished his drink and left.

Jill turned to Sheila and said, 'Told you, you'd be OK; he just wants to fuck you tonight to prove he's in charge, he likes to think he owns all of his girls, but after that he won't bother with you much honest and tonight he'll be half pissed anyway, he'll be done in five minutes.'

They both laughed, then Sheila looked at the paper Jack had given her and asked, 'Do you know where Albion Street is and what he meant by wear something sexy?'

'Look, Albion Street ain't all that bad honest and you've got somewhere to live darlin, I'll lend you my lacy draws that's what he likes believe me, I know, he likes to show he's boss by fucking all his girls, the only one that Jack doesn't get his dick in is Rose.' They both laughed and finished their drinks.

The Holiday Present Day 1960

Paul phoned Dennis and said, 'I want you down here, mate, with me ASAP and I want everything you've got on the two scallies and especially the ex-sailor.'

'The super will go mad, sir, I can't leave in the middle of a murder enquiry and with respect sir, you can't either,' replied Dennis.

'Listen, Dennis,' said Paul. 'I have some new evidence and I'll be in-touch with the super with regard to releasing you in the next few minutes, in the mean time I need you to do a total history search on the sailor, just sit tight until I've spoken to the super about releasing you.' Paul hung up the phone.

Paul said to Colin, 'Let me have everything you've got on this hit and run victim, mate and I can let my super know that's the reason I'm down here.'

'Well, all we've got at the moment mate is a brief description of the car and a possible colour match,' said Colin.

'Yeah, but now, I can tell the super that this is not just a hit and run but almost certainly a serial killer and ask him to release Dennis and more resources,' said Paul.

'With three murders in Liverpool mate and a hit and run in Birmingham, the superintendents gotta listen to the possibility of a serial killer.'

'No he ain't, mate,' said Colin. 'I bet your super will need more than a thin connection of two blokes who both served on the same ship.'

Just then Colin's phone rang, ''Scuse me, Paul; let me just take this, mate.' Colin took the call while Paul got himself a coffee, Col spoke down the phone saying, 'Are you absolutely certain, Mac.' Colin put down the phone and said to Paul, 'Phone your super, mate and do it now.'

'Why what ya got, Col,' said Paul as he sat down with his coffee.

'That was one of my detectives who was the detective on the hit and run, he's got a couple of days off to go to Manchester for his wife's uncle's funeral, apparently he fell off scaffolding on a building site four days ago. Mac tells me he's ex merchant navy, guess which fucking ship he served on.'

'I knew it,' shouted Paul, 'Great news, Col, great news, now it's not a thin connection.'

The Journey 1946

The buses carrying the children finally stopped and the woman guard stood up and shouted, 'All of you girls listen carefully, when I point at you pick up your bags, get off the bus and stand in line in front of that nun waiting at the door, is that clear.'

All the girls replied, 'Yes Miss.'

The girls got off the bus and formed a line, the boys did the same on the other buses. As the lines formed the children realised, they were standing next to an enormous ship bigger than anything they'd ever seen in their lives even bigger than the ones in picture books.

A man was talking to all the nuns, he looked like the ship's captain and he had about 20 sailors with him, he spoke to the sailors and pointed at the gangplanks, then all the sailors ran up the four gangplanks and stood at the top. The nuns herded the girls together still in their lines and began to take them to the bottom of the gangplanks. The nuns at the bottom of the gang planks sent each girl to a sailor at the top, when the sailor had his quota of girls, he would take them on-board the ship and another sailor would replace him and he would get his quota.

As all the children were boarded and each line embarked the nuns in charge of that line went back to the buses, when all the children were boarded, the buses left with only the nuns on board, there were no good byes or kisses or waving. Some of the children were excited, but most were frightened and cried but in a state of shock just wondering where they were, where they were going and why and will they ever be going home again, everything happened so quickly, all the buses and nuns were gone and now the sailors were in charge.

Jack's Business 1946

Sheila went with Jill to Albion Street, it was terraced houses. Curtains across the street were moving as the women entered the property. The house was filthy and stunk, there was no furniture except for a bed with a filthy stained mattress but at least it was a house and Sheila had the key. Both the women cleaned the house and then with a little help moved in some basic furniture and a clean bed. Sheila borrowed the underwear from Jill and went to Jack's house for 10 o'clock. Jack opened the door with a glass of whiskey in his hand and staggered along the hall, she could see he was really drunk.

'Come in, darling,' he said.

He directed Sheila into the lounge and said, 'Sit down and make yourself comfortable, do as you're told and ask no questions and we'll get along just fine.'

She sat down and Jack pushed a drink into her hand, she saw a bottle of whiskey and jar of Vaseline by the chair, she knew exactly what he wanted. Jack knelt by her chair and gently pushed her legs apart, he said, 'You're gonna love this or at least I fucking will,' as he ran his hands up her thighs pushing up her skirt to reveal stocking tops, she was wearing the panties she'd borrowed from Jill.

Jack's tongue licked up the smooth bare legs of her thighs, Sheila braced herself as he pushed her legs as wide apart as possible and pushing her panties to one side, she felt his tongue on her pussy.

'Take off your skirt and kneel over that chair,' said Jack, she did as she was told and she felt his body lean on top of her; he made her suck his thumb as he kissed her neck and then pressed his thumb into the Vaseline and slowly pushed his thumb into her arse, she knew what was coming.

Jack stopped kissing her neck but his head stayed there for some time but she felt nothing, then Sheila noticed Jack's whiskey glass was tipped over on the floor and she felt him go completely limp on her back and heard him begin to snore. Sheila eased his body gently off her trying to avoid waking him up and laid him onto the floor, he was completely out of it, she straightened her clothes and went quietly upstairs, found his bedroom and got into bed.

The Journey 1946

Each sailor took six of the girls at a time and their bags to their allocated cabins. The sailor who took Theresa and Bridget and four other girls to their cabin was nice looking and very big, when they got to the cabin it was tiny and there were six bunks inside.

'Stow ya gear,' he said, the girls just stood there not understanding what he meant. 'Put ya cases down,' he shouted. 'Put em under the bottom bunk and sort out which bunk you're having. Listen to me, learn and remember your cabin number and what deck you're on, you'll be punished if you get lost, you are not allowed to walk round the ship, got it.'

The sailor went on, 'My name is Ben, remember it; if you get lost the member of crew who finds you will ask, who is your sailor, but all you girls will call me sir until I tell you any different. Listen carefully, you're in cabin number 217 on deck 4, all repeat it back to me;' all the girls repeated the cabin number and deck. 'Louder,' he shouted.

'Cabin 217 on deck 4,' all the girls replied as loud as they could.

'There are six of you in this cabin and all of you can't forget, so make sure you all remember; stay here, I'll be back in a bit,' he said and with that he left. The girls could hear other girls walking past to their cabins and getting their instructions, this went on for what seemed like hours.

The big sailor returned and immediately asked all of them his name, their cabin number and deck, they all replied, 'Ben, number 217 on deck 4.'

He said, 'Good, now follow me.'

He took them down to a big room with lots of other girls and boys for something to eat, they were all sat at long tables and before the food was served a man stood up at the very top table and banged his fist on the table, the room went silent.

'Quiet everyone,' he shouted, 'My name is Captain Peterson, I am the captain of this ship, The Pharaoh, listen to me and listen to me good, you have all been told to remember your cabin number and deck because this ship is very big, do not forget your deck and cabin number, because if you do, you will be punished, you will be on this ship for about 6 weeks and I cannot afford the time for my sailors to look for you if you get lost, they are far too busy with other duties.

We are on our way to a place called Australia and you'll all be happy there. I will talk to all of you tomorrow, so now eat your food and go back to your cabins and have a good night's sleep, there will be a hooter in the morning and that means come down for breakfast, here in this same room and that means everyone, even if you are not hungry you will come to breakfast for a roll call, that's like when they call the register at school, don't be late.'

The captain left and the food was served. All the sailors ate with the children, even though they all sat together at a different table. It was easy to see Ben, he was one of the biggest sailors on the ship, he was very broad and tall. When the children had finished eating a whistle was blown and they were all told to stand and wait for their sailor to collect them to take them back to their cabin. All the sailors took their charges, including Ben and the dining room was empty once more.

During the second world war, all transportation to Australia stopped, it had become far too dangerous, there were just too many German war ships and submarines. When the war ended, the Royal Navy no longer needed such huge numbers of men on active service; they needed far fewer active war ships and submarines and many sailors returned home to civilian life as industry was desperately short of a skilled male workforce.

On the other hand, Australia was very keen to resume the transportation ships, they still wanted to increase their population and England was even more anxious to resume the ships, thousands of homes and even whole cities had been destroyed in the bombings and it had misplaced and homeless people after a devastating and destructive war.

The Merchant Navy needed thousands of men to crew these transportation ships and was only too pleased to accept ex Royal Navy men. They were already skilled and experienced sailors; Ben was one of these men; he was 25, he'd joined the Royal Navy during the second world war and after the war ended had transferred to the Merchant Navy, he knew these waters very well as he'd been stationed in the far-east during the war; he was not only respected for his wartime service by other non-combatant crew members, but he was also a very good boxer. He was a good-looking young man and many of the young girl teenage transportee's on many previous voyages found him very attractive.

The New Life 1946

Rose came back from the shower and sat on the edge of the bed and began to dress, she rolled her tan stockings up her curvy legs and thighs and fastened her suspenders to the top. She half turned toward Jess, her bare breasts brushing his bare chest, she ran her hand slowly up his neck and leaned over to kiss him on the lips.

'I better make you some breakfast, darling,' she said. Her hand slowly trailed down his bare torso and she kissed him again and said with a sexy smile, 'Do I need to pull you to your breakfast with this very, very big handle.'

With that Rose stood up to take a pair of pants from the dresser purposely and deliberately bending forwards. She knew her gorgeous backside was irresistible to most men and it had earned her a lot of money from rich men in the past who adored it and would pay a king's ransom for it.

She slipped a finger slowly into Jess's mouth as she looked over her shoulder at him and then took her finger from his mouth, trailed it down her back and slid it between her cheeks and very slowly into herself before very erotically pushing her finger back into her own mouth, all the time looking at Jess, 'See anything you like baby,' she said. Jess was getting aroused by the second as he watched this sexy woman.

Rose stopped her teasing and slipped on her dress, then she applied some bright red lipstick and whispered to Jess, 'Do you think such a huge donkey would fit in such a tight little hole baby, do you;' she then kissed him on the mouth pushing her tongue inside his, only stopping to whisper in his ear, 'but I love you so much you make me feel like such a bad girl, I want to feel you deep inside that tight little hole where no man has ever been.'

That statement was definitely not true but Rose knew that all men like to feel they are the first to fuck a woman in their arse, it makes them feel special. Rose then gently kissed his dick leaving a red lipstick mark around it and went downstairs to make breakfast.

Jack's Business 1946

Sheila woke at about 6am she crept down stairs to find Jack still in a deep sleep, she suddenly had an idea, she raced back upstairs and made the bed as if it hadn't been slept in then came back down and gently rolled Jack on his side, careful not to wake him, she unzipped his trousers gently tugging them down to his thighs, then his underpants exposing his dick.

She scooped some Vaseline and rubbed it over his dick and on his fingers, he drank with his right hand so he must be right-handed. She slipped off her top dropping it on the floor next to Jack and then took off her bra and put it in his hand and lay down beside him naked and as close to him as she dared get without waking him. She lifted his other arm, the hand still holding the whiskey glass and folded it around her shoulder over her breast.

Some time passed and the room was lightened by daylight she felt Jack begin to wake up and so she pretended to be asleep. Jack did wake and felt Sheila next to him, he run his hand over her breast and down her back between her ample buttocks and slipped his fingers into her arse, before kneeling up looking at her beautiful naked body. He stood up realising he had her bra in his hand and pushed it to his nose, having a smile to himself.

He tapped Sheila with his foot saying, 'Come on, get up; told you you'd love it; you all love cock, especially in the arse,' he gave her another tap and Sheila pretended to wake and stood up naked covering herself with her hands. 'Take your hands away and let me have another look at those tits,' he said. 'Too late to cover up now you've been fucked, get dressed you fucking whore.' He zipped himself up and straightened his clothes.

The Journey 1946

Next morning the girls woke up early to find one of the girls had wet the bed and another had been sick, the whole cabin was rocking from side to side, suddenly there was a deafening horn and they could hear men's voices. 'Breakfast time, breakfast time,' the voices shouted. The cabin doors were thrown open by the sailors and sea spray splashed through the door, all the girls were told to get down for breakfast and hold onto the handrails on the way down.

The breakfast was porridge, some of the girls had never tasted it and didn't like it, others felt too sick to eat. After breakfast the captain stood up and spoke, 'As you can all see today the sea is a bit rough; when the days are like this, you will be told to stay in your cabins between breakfast, dinner and evening meal.' The captain went on, 'Every one of you were shown to your cabin by a sailor; learn that sailors name, he will be responsible for you and you will do everything he tells you to do or you will be punished.'

A boy was talking at the breakfast table and the captain glared at him and 'his' sailor slapped him hard around the face, the room fell into complete silence. The boy was quietly sobbing.

'That is what you'll get if you don't do as you're told; now when you've finished your breakfast, all of you go back to your cabins and be quick about it,' with that the captain left.

That night after lights out, the door opened. Theresa was not only the eldest girl in the cabin she was the only one awake. Ben quietly opened the cabin door and beckoned Theresa to come to him with his finger over his lips as a gesture to be quiet. Theresa did as she was told and Ben took her hand and then quietly closed the cabin door. He took his big jacket off and wrapped it around her shoulders.

'Where are we going,' asked Theresa.

Ben whispered, 'Be quiet,' and with that took her up some steps and along decks to another cabin. He opened the door and said, 'This is my cabin.'

Ben's cabin was very warm and nearly as big as cabin 147 which had six beds in it. Ben removed the coat from Theresa and said to her, 'You are going to be my favourite girl on this long voyage, so most nights you will be in this special cabin with me.'

Theresa was not stupid, but she was frightened, but she remembered the captain had said the girls had to do as they were told by 'their' sailor or be punished; slowly she calmed down, at least Ben was not hurting her. Ben then got two glasses and poured drinks for them both.

'Other girls might get punished but you won't ,Theresa, 'cos you're my favourite, we'll have a nice trip to Australia and I'll look after you,' he said.

'What about Bridget, my little sister,' asked Theresa?

'Don't you worry, my little angel,' said Ben. 'You do everything I tell you and I'll make sure no one hurts you or your little sister and we'll have a great journey.'

Jack's Business 1946

The phone rang and Billy answered, 'What's happening, Billy,' said Jack.

'Well, boss, Rose reduced her hours at the pub in the last few weeks and then in the last few days left that job completely and got a job in some shop out of town apparently.'

'Where's the shop, Billy?' asked Jack.

'Dunno yet, Boss, but a couple of the lads say they saw Andrea and Rose talking together just before she fucked off; so, I think Andrea knew something and never mentioned it, so I'm gonna lean on her a bit, Boss.'

'No,' replied Jack. 'I'll be back in a couple of days then we'll find out together, Billy Boy.' Jack hung up.

The Journey 1946

'Drink up,' said Ben and Theresa sipped the big glass of wine.

'Am I staying here, sir.'

'No need to call me sir, you're my special girl so you can call me Ben,' he said. 'Yes, you'll be staying here in that big bunk and I'll keep you warm and safe, little angel.'

With that Ben began to undress, he had big muscles and arms, he stripped down to his trousers and then leaned over to Theresa and kissed her on the face, Theresa was getting frightened because Ben was so big. She carried on slowly sipping her wine as her mind drifted to her mum with Jack and Angie with her dad, she knew what was going to happen, but she couldn't get away, she hardly knew her way around the ship and had nowhere to go anyway.

Ben took off his trousers and said, 'Don't be frightened, little angel; you just get into bed and get nice and warm. I'm not going to hurt you,' with that Ben unzipped his trousers and let them slip to the floor, he was standing completely naked as he refilled their glasses.

Theresa tried not to stare, but she couldn't help herself, as he was a good-looking young man, very muscular and his cock was much bigger than Jack's. Ben turned and saw her looking before she quickly turned away. 'Don't be frightened, angel. I don't suppose you've seen a man with no clothes on before, have you,' he asked.

'Yes, I have,' replied Theresa.

Ben was very surprised and asked 'And where was that my little angel,' as he sat on the bed putting his arm around her and taking a drink of wine. 'I saw Jack with no clothes on.'

'Who's Jack?' asked Ben.

Theresa had another sip of wine before continuing, 'Jack lived in the same house with me, my Mum and Bridget.'

'And how did you see him with no clothes on then,' enquired Ben.

'Jack used to do things to my mum in their bedroom,' Theresa replied.

'How did you see them if they were in the bedroom,' asked Ben.

'I used to hear them making a noise and I would sneak across the landing to see what they were doing. Mum always left her bedroom door open a little bit in case Bridget was crying.'

'You said this Jack used to do things to your Mum, what things did he do,' Ben asked.

'I don't know exactly cos they were in bed under the covers most of the time but sometimes he would stand up and mum would kneel in front of him and it looked like she was kissing his thing.'

'Well, was Jack hurting your Mum, little angel; was your mum crying,' Ben went on.

'Well, no, she wasn't crying,' replied Theresa.

'And where did your Mum go after Jack had done these things to her in the bedroom, my little angel,' asked Ben.

'Well, nowhere, she just went to sleep in bed with Jack.'

'Well, there you are then,' said Ben. 'Jack wasn't hurting your Mum, he was loving her,' said Ben as he pulled Theresa closer to him. 'You don't think your mum would do bad things, do you.'

'No, I don't suppose so,' replied Theresa.

'And don't you worry, we're not going to do bad things either, my little angel; we'll do nice things all the way to Australia, 'cos you're my special girl; drink up,' said Ben, they both had a sip of their wine. 'Did Jack ever kiss or touch you, my little angel.'

'A little bit sometimes, when mum was working at the pub, but I didn't like it,' she answered.

'But you like the wine, don't you,' said Ben, laughing. 'Just sit there and enjoy it.'

He knew exactly what he was doing as he smiled, saying, 'Only my favourite girl can come to this cabin, get extra food and drink wine and who's my favourite girl,' asked Ben.

'Is it me?' asked Theresa.

'Of course, it's you, little angel,' he replied and started to kiss her. Theresa was not frightened but she knew exactly what Ben was going to do to her, 'You're going to be a big girl soon and Jack will be doing nice things to your Mum and you'll be doing things to me, like your Mum does to Jack, 'cos your Mum wouldn't do bad things, would she now,' and sure enough his hands began to touch her.

Theresa remembered that time back home in the shops with mum and Bridget and mum had whispered to Mrs Marshall, thinking that Theresa couldn't hear, she said, 'You know, Pat; sometimes we have all the control over men that we ever need and its right between our legs, we're sat on it.'

Theresa was beginning to understand what exactly mum meant, she had started to understand a little with the way Jack gave her whatever she wanted as long as she let him do things, she remembered how her mum called his thing a 'dick' and how Jack got excited and liked it when mum said those words and now Ben wanted her to do these things to her.

'What do you want me to do?' asked Theresa.

Jack's Business 1946

Jack arrived at one of his busiest brothels and got Billy and his men to collect all twelve girls who worked there and bring them to one room, when they were all in the room, Jack began, 'I don't fucking like the way some of you girls are cheating me and you're stupid enough to think I don't know, so tonight in the next 30 seconds I want to demonstrate how important you all are to me and how worthless you are to me; you all mean something to me 'cos you make me money, but you all mean fuck all to me 'cos I can replace all of you today,' he screamed in their faces. 'First ,I've got a bit of business with Andrea who's lied to me.'

'I haven't, Jack, honest; I haven't lied, I wouldn't lie to you,' pleaded Andrea.

'You were seen talking to Rose and you never fucking told me, you lying bitch,' said Jack.

'Honest, Jack, I was going to the—' before Andrea could finish Jack shot her once in each leg and she fell to the floor screaming; all the girls put their arms around each other in terror and huddled together hysterically as Andrea screamed in agony on the floor. 'She didn't tell me where she was going, honest, Jack,' screamed Andrea, 'Else I would have told you.'

'But you fucking didn't, did you,' said Jack and then he shot her in the stomach, he then nodded to Billy who gouged out her left eye with his knife as she let out an ear-piercing scream grasping her face with both hands. Billy threw the eye to the girls laughing, the girls were petrified and shook in fear, shock and horror.

Andrea screamed in agony and wriggled about on the floor in a river of blood.

'Now, watch what happens to girls who fucking lie to me or try and cheat me;' again he nodded to Billy who without a second thought stabbed Andrea in the vagina and ripped his knife upwards through her stomach, completely opening her body up in front of all the girls who screamed absolutely petrified as they watched the horror of Andrea's intestines spill out across the floor.

The Journey 1946

Ben slowly kissed her on the lips, stood up and walked across the cabin to get the bottle of wine, he walked back to the bed and continued, 'Look, I've got no clothes on, so let's take off your nightdress and get nice and warm in bed.'

Theresa shyly and slowly took off her nightdress and put her hands across her breasts to cover herself.

'Now, now, don't do that,' whispered Ben, as he gently took her arms away. 'I'm not covering up, am I; so, don't cover up your beautiful body, my little angel, you're gonna be in this cabin for weeks and it makes me very happy to see you with no clothes on.'

With that he put his arms around her, kissing her and pulling her close to him. Theresa finally understood why her Mum did the things she did, to try and give her and Bridget a safe, reasonable and comfortable life in a war-torn country, using the only currency she had, her own body. Now Theresa in order to protect herself and her sister, was forced into the very same situation, she couldn't run away and there was no place to hide, she knew what was going to happen.

Australia 1946

Denny Harris was sat in the bar of the Victoria Hotel in Freemantle, on the west coast of Australia, Denny owned a sheep farm on the Canning River in Maddington a small town about 30 miles north of Freemantle. Denny had made a lot of money from sheep farming but still lived a life like the old wild-west when America was practically lawless. Law and order were still sparse in Australia, police were stretched to the limit and many farmers in the outback lived by their own rules.

Denny was known in the area and had made his money long before Coppin had become successful and he wasn't in Freemantle by accident, he was there for business and knew that the man he wanted to see; Andrew Coppin would be staying at the 'Victoria'.

At that very moment Andrew Coppin walked into the bar with Jonesy and some business friends, he did not notice Denny at first and carried on drinking, laughing and joking with his friends. Denny bided his time and sure enough after a couple of hours the Coppin party were down to just three as the others drifted off to bed. It had been some years since Coppin had borrowed a lot of money from Denny to pursue a business career in Freemantle, now Coppin was an important person, a VIP and dignitary and all because of the loan from Denny.

Denny took the opportunity to approach Coppin and went to the bar right next to him and said, 'I hear you got a ship coming in, mate.'

Coppin turned to see who was speaking to him, he was shocked to see Denny and said, 'Denny, what are you doing here in Freemantle,' immediately turning to his friend John and saying, 'John, this is an old friend of mine, would you mind if we had a private word.'

With that John said, 'I'm ready for bed anyway, Andy,' and he drunk up and left for bed, saying, 'I'll see you in the morning,' and left Coppin, Jonesy and Denny at the bar.

When John had gone Coppin turned to Denny and said, 'What the fuck do you really want, Denny.'

'Do you want to talk in front of him,' said Denny nodding at Jonesy.

'Just tell me what you fucking want, Denny,' replied Coppin.

'Well, unless you've got the 5,000 Australian dollars that you owe me, I'll be looking for a bit of your cargo,' replied Denny.

'I don't know what you're fucking talking about,' said Coppin.

'You're doing OK in this town, mate,' said Denny, 'You're well respected, live on the right side of town, you got it all Andy, so don't fuck about with me. I met a guy in Darwin, he'd had a few beers, he worked on a ship called 'The Pharaoh' about three years ago and he told me all about it mate and guess what, he mentioned your name and for a few Aussie dollars and a couple of beers we had a long chat and he told me all about the game you're in.'

Denny continued, 'I did a bit of asking about in various bars, you've got a ship coming in on Tuesday and of course, it's The Pharaoh and there'll be at least 50 more on board than there will be on the ships manifest and you're here to receive the 'cargo,' as well as the white slaves.'

Denny took a drink, then said, 'Look mate, all I want is one of your young females, a nice young fresh faced one, get my drift mate, a pretty one and unregistered and then I'll just fuck off back to Maddington and we can both keep your white slaves a secret, nobody needs to know about a few prison break outs, the fucking IRA and the illegal guns, fuck me,' Denny continued. 'This country was built on criminals mate, but try and fuck me about, Coppin and constable Phillips and everybody in this town will know all about your IRA mates, the prison break outs, the gun running and your very nice little white slave racket.'

Denny took another drink, 'Ironic really, mate; a country built on importing criminals is now making big money importing the bastards again, what a piece of shit you are, Coppin.'

Coppin thought for a moment, secretly thinking, *Shit, shit, shit;* he knew if Denny got what he wanted this time he'd be back again for the next ship and the next, he looked at Denny and said, 'We can do business, mate, but I need to know how we can work it. It's gotta be final, I can give you a girl but I want you out of my life forever.'

'I'll tell you how it's gonna work, mate,' said Denny. 'Tomorrow when they're coming down the gang plank as they step onto Aussie, you'll see me over on the 'Victoria' veranda.'

Coppin butted in, 'Tomorrow, I've got business as the ship docks, Jonesy will sort the girl for you.'

'I don't give a fuck if it's you Coppin or him,' said Denny. 'But when I take my Akubra off on the 'Victoria' veranda and wipe my forehead, the one who's at the bottom of the gang plank at that moment is the one I want and you'll put your hand on her shoulder to confirm she's the one I chose and if you've put your hand on the right one, I'll put my Akubra back on, got it; then you can break her out and take her to the back of the arrivals office and deliver her to my assistant, he'll make himself known to you mate, then we'll both fuck off, out of each other's lives.'

Coppin finished his drink and said, 'You can have your girl, Denny, Jonesy will sort you out but this is the last time I ever wanna see you, mate and before you finish your drink, I need the name of the sailor you bumped into in Darwin.'

'It was your best mate, Coppin, remember Dixie Bacon,' said Denny with a loud laugh. With that Denny drank up and left the bar. Coppin said to Jonesy, sort him a girl out off the ship Jonesy just to humour him, he'll be disappearing soon after and we'll get the girl back.

After a very early breakfast next morning Coppin made a phone call to one of his henchmen Ridgeway a notorious and violent individual. 'Ridge, I got a job for you, mate, a big payday but I need you today in Freemantle, but be discrete.'

'No worries, mate,' replied Ridgeway. 'I can be there in a couple of hours.'

'Meet me in the 'Ship' down parry street near the prison, do you know where I mean?' asked Coppin.

'Yeah, I know exactly where you mean, mate,' replied Ridgeway.

'See you at twelve,' replied Coppin and continued, 'And keep nice and quiet mate, it'll be worth your while.'

The New Life 1946

In the morning Jess gradually woke as he felt soft lips tracing down his neck and her warm hands undo his pyjama bottoms and continue to slowly slide down his stomach and her fingers slowly wrapping around their goal. He moaned softly turning around and kissing her deeply on the lips, then her full breasts, then gently opening her nightdress Rose slowly opened her warm thighs, grasped his erect penis as she pushed her tongue deep into his mouth. Breaking the kiss to whisper, 'Ohhhh baby, you feel sooo good and soooo big.'

Rose gripped his dick in her hand and moved his cock up and down her moist pussy, positioned him and then slid her hands around onto his tight muscular arse and pulled him all the way into her letting out a deep long moan, 'Ohhhhhh baby, I thought I'd only dreamt you were like a donkey, but it's true.' Rose kissed him deeply and whispered, 'Ohhhhhh, I want to feel your big fat donkey cock all the way inside me, baby; oh yes, fuck me.'

Jess had never experienced such a sexy woman, what a lover, they made love for what seemed like hours kissing her as he went as deep inside her as he could to the sounds of her, 'Ohhhh baby, give it to me, I want it all the way inside me,' she kissed him and pushed her tongue deep into his mouth, breaking the kiss just to say, 'Give me your cream, baby, give me all that spunk inside me and in my mouth. I want to taste you, baby; give it to me, give it me now.'

She overwhelmed Jess with her sexuality, he could not hold back a second longer his hips rammed into her as he gripped her tightly and let out a bear like growl, Rose gripped his muscled tight arse as her legs gripped tightly around his back, pulling him into her as she said, 'Yes baby, yes, I want it all inside me;' she pressed her lips onto his in a deep kiss as he gradually and slowly stopped surging.

Jess rolled over onto his back in ecstasy saying, 'Rose, that was beautiful.'

Rose rolled half on top of him, kissing him on the lips as her hand slid down his stomach and her fingers wrapped around him he was still half hard, she squeezed the last drops of semen from him and then brought her hand to her lips, licking her fingers and saying, 'Baby, you taste gorgeous.' She kissed him saying, 'Next time, baby, I want you all in my mouth, will you please,' she said as she kissed him softly.

Jess returned her kisses, he could not believe he not only had a beautiful woman but probably the sexiest woman in the world in his bed and in his life. They both slept for a while with their arms wrapped around each other, then Rose slipped quietly from the bed and went for a bath.

The Journey 1946

Ben said to Theresa, 'Now, you love your little sister, don't you.'

'Yes,' replied Theresa.

'Well, I'm going to make sure that you and your little sister are alright, my little angel; all you have to do is everything I tell you to do,' said Ben, as his hands began to caress her.

Theresa knew that sometimes mum had done things for Jack just to keep the peace and she had witnessed with her own eyes how other sailors slapped children and shouted at them and she knew they were miles from home in the middle of an ocean and there was no one to help or protect her and Bridget except Ben. Some sailors were cruel in the extreme to their charges and purposely chose very young girls or boys who were only 9 or 10, Ben was at least a bit better than those sailors, he liked older girls who were approaching adulthood and he hadn't been brutal to Theresa or Bridget. Theresa thought what would mum do in this situation.

Theresa again remembered Mrs Marshall saying to her mum, 'You have all the control over men that you ever need and its right between our legs.' Theresa had been forced by circumstance to learn the art of being a woman and she was old enough and bright enough to know that she and Bridget needed Ben, she thought if Angie can do it, then she can too. With all these things in her head Theresa simply tried to imitate what she'd seen her mum do, when she had crept across the landing to watch mum and Jack, she had watched her mum do this many time, but this was her very first time, her heart was pounding.

Ben on the other hand had done this many time before, it was normal practice on such a voyage for some of the sailors to choose one, two or even more of their charges on every trip. It was so easy, choose a young beauty and do exactly what you want to do to them, there are no restrictions, live out your fantasy, these kids were never coming back, they were on a once in a lifetime one way trip, there would be no consequences to face regardless of the horrors committed.

The captain turned a blind eye to such practices because of his own business interests, it was easier to ignore the sailors and recruit at lower wages with such sexual benefits on offer. Obviously, no shipping company would ever openly offer these benefits, but everyone in the business knew exactly what went on and what was available.

Ben said, 'All we have to do is look after each other, my little angel. I'll look after you and Bridget and you look after me; you heard the captain tell everyone that they must do as they're told and some sailors hit the children, but I'm not going to hit you, Theresa; we're going to do nice things, my little angel.'

As Ben continued Theresa's mind drifted to the secret whispers, she had heard at meal times about a young 13-year-old some years earlier who had been brutalised and she had threatened the offending sailor how she would tell when she got to Australia. She never arrived in Australia, she was not even recorded on the ships manifest so she didn't even exist, she was invisible, she was taken from her bed one stormy night and put over the side into a cruel, cold and unforgiving sea. Theresa resigned herself to what was about to happen.

Jack's Business 1946

Andrea still squirmed on the floor in agony, the girls were unable to help her as Jack just spoke as if a woman wasn't dying in agony at his feet. 'I believe in a fucking democracy,' Jack bellowed at the girls, 'And I want you remaining girls to pick another one of you sluts who will be dead in the next 30 seconds or if you want me to pick, I'll pick three. I have to choose who's gonna live or die every fucking day you bitches,' screamed Jack.

He then pointed the gun at the girls, swaying from right to left causing mass hysteria and screaming and then randomly pointed the gun at Sharon and blew her face away, all of the girls screamed and gripped each other in shock and panic as they were covered in her blood spatter as they watched screaming as Sharon fell to the floor dead right next to Andrea.

Andrea still squirmed on the floor slowly dying. Jack looked at Andrea and said, 'Fuck me, is that bitch still alive, Billy,' as she continued to move in a pool of her own blood and entrails, she was choking as she tried to grasp a breath in her final moments.

'Now you see this can happen to any one of you if you try and cheat me and all you fucking bitches are responsible for these two girls not me, you all knew they were working on the side, like some of you have done and are still doing, it stops now right,' Jack bellowed in a screaming voice. 'Am I fair with you girls,' no one answered, Jack screamed in the faces of the girls, 'Am I fucking fair with you,' as he placed his foot on Andrea's throat.

Andrea grabbed his foot attempting to push him away but she was too weak in her dying seconds and he was too heavy for her as her throat gurgled and finally choked her last breath.

Jack went on, 'When will you girls realise, you're only safe with me and if you hear even a fucking whisper about Rose and my girls, I need to know; now clean up this fucking mess and if I find one more fucker cheating me, you're all fucking dead, got it.'

As they left the building Billy said, 'What do you want me to do with the bodies, boss.'

'Leave Pete and three of the lads behind to make sure the girls clean that fucking place up,' replied Jack, he went on, 'Then let Pete and Bob take the bodies to Pete's, cut 'em up and feed 'em to their dogs.'

Billy went back inside the building to give the instructions and Jack drove off.

The Journey 1946

When a young girl has spent a few days on board a ship like The Pharaoh and has witnessed the way many of the crew treat other young children, they soon become petrified of the consequence of non-compliance. For many of these children, this is the first time they have been totally alone and with no protection from family, friends, teachers or even the police. When a young child is this vulnerable and frightened for their life and they have nowhere to turn and they suddenly see a sailor who becomes their savour or guardian, getting them in your bed is not difficult.

Ben was very aware that Theresa was a virgin and that the wine had played its part in the seduction, it nearly always did, it's always a great starter, Ben should know he did this on every voyage. The idea of a young virgin with very few inhibitions thanks to alcohol, full of oestrogen and with little or no sexual experience and with no authorities, police or parents to deal with, it's like a sailor's fantasy dream come true.

Theresa had accepted that there was no escape and she must do whatever was needed to get herself and Bridget to Australia safely. She had a good idea what Ben was going to do to her, she was frightened and felt that it really shouldn't be happening, but she also knew it was better than being beaten or put over the side of the ship.

Theresa thought of her mum and Jack, she realised at that moment, why her mum had fucked Jack, from this point on she was in unknown territory, she was crying with happiness not because of this new world of sex she was forced into, but because she had realised what a powerful weapon she possessed just like her mum, she could make a man like Ben do exactly as she wanted and wondered what would have happened to her and Bridget if she had been a boy.

She was suddenly brought back into real time as she realised what he'd just done to her. 'We'll do this a lot on this journey, my little angel,' said Ben as he rolled over and put a cigarette in his mouth.

Theresa lit his cigarette for him, saying, 'You mustn't tell anyone what we've done, especially my mum.'

Ben liked her to light his cigarettes, 'Don't worry, little angel; no one will ever know, I won't tell anyone, this is our little secret,' he said reassuringly as he smoked his cigarette.

Theresa turned on her side. When he had finished his cigarette, Ben got in bed and lay down beside her and put his arms around her; again, her mind drifted, she thought back to home, is this what mum felt like with Jack, is this what all grown up girls do, she felt guilty, but it wasn't of her making. But she did feel enormously powerful as she closed her eyes and went to sleep.

The Holiday

After a long phone conversation between Paul and the superintendent it was obvious that three deaths, of ex-merchant seamen, who had all served on the same vessel and all died in the last few days in suspicious circumstances was more than just coincidence. The superintendent had already got a killing on his own patch and what looked like a third murder just down the road. It stretched police resources but an operations team was set up to begin immediately.

The investigation was to headed by Paul who was assigned three detectives, one of whom was Dennis Goodburn and uniform back up. The 'super' told Paul the Police Federation's National Conference was in six weeks, this looked like a multiple murder and if he didn't have some results before then it would look very embarrassing, the pressure was on.

In the ops room the team were assembled. Paul, Colin and Dennis stood at the front of the room and Paul started with introductions, 'Good morning, everyone. I am detective inspector Paul Bramley, this is DI Colin King whom I'm sure most of you already know and this is my colleague from Liverpool detective sergeant Dennis Goodburn; we have put together the team you see in this room and together we're looking for and intend to find what at this moment looks like a serial killer who I believe will kill again soon if not found; let me hand you over to DS Goodburn who'll bring you up to where we are at present.'

Dennis addressed the team, 'I apologise for the speed at which this team was put together and after this initial brief we'll all have coffee and get more acquainted, that'll be in about twenty minutes, but first some detail.'

Dennis continued, 'Three men have so far been murdered in a variety of ways, all three were members of the same ship's crew; at the moment we have no suspect or suspects and no motive.' He went on, 'We need to catch this person or persons as quickly as possible and at the moment, we have little to go on.'

The Journey 1946

As soon as Theresa woke up, she worried about Bridget but felt that now, they would both be safe with Ben, she had never slept with a man, let alone woken up beside one especially such a big man with big arms around her and it felt strange but she felt very protected and safe. Suddenly she remembered last night and she knew it was true and it wasn't a dream.

Theresa wished she was back in the park with Angie so she could tell her all about last night, she couldn't help but think about her mum and Jack and just like Mrs Marshall had said, men can be controlled and now she knew how. It could be a lot worse, Ben wasn't being brutal to her or Bridget, Ben began to wake and got up out of bed and dressed.

He would miss Theresa 'cos she was such a beauty, but she was just one more girl on a one-way trip to Australia. He put a cigarette in his mouth and Theresa jumped out of bed and dutifully reached up on tip toes and lit it for him placing his lighter back in her pocket. Theresa started to feel the power of sexual control that she had first felt over Jack now she could feel it over this big man.

Ben said, 'Think we ought a go down a deck to my ship mates' cabin and get you some perfume for you, my little Angel, for being such a good girl last night; what do you reckon.'

'Thank you, Ben,' said Theresa as she kissed him and got dressed. 'But I need to check Bridget's OK first,' she continued.

'Don't you worry, my angel, nobody will even go near Bridget; you can check her after we get your perfume,' Ben replied.

'But I thought we were not allowed out of the cabin except for exercise and meal times Ben, will we get into trouble.'

'Listen my little Angel, you aren't allowed out, but I am and I know when the captain is busy with his meetings, so come on,' Ben said as he chuckled. He led her by the hand out of his cabin and down towards his ship mates' cabin, before going down to where Bridget and the rest of the girls were.

A sailor welding the guard rail saw them hand in hand, a giant sailor a foot taller than the 14-year-old girl he held hands with, looking at Ben the welder smiled and said, 'Her first cock, mate.'

Ben let go of Theresa's hand grabbing the sailor by the throat and snatching the welding torch from his hand. Ben held the torch close to the sailor's face and said, 'You ever fucking disrespect her again with talk like that, matey and I'll put you over the fucking side one dark night and I'll do it nice and quiet, you understand me.'

The sailor was petrified as he was lifted completely off his feet and, could only answer a muffled, 'Sorry mate,' he gasped through the strangling grip around his throat, 'I'm sorry, mate; honest, I didn't understand,' he pleaded as Ben gripped his throat. Ben lowered him onto his feet as he struggled to breath, pushing the still blazing welding torch back into his hand.

As they walked away Theresa said, 'I was frightened I thought you were going to throw him overboard or burn him with that thing he was holding, what was it Ben.' She'd never seen a welding torch before.

Ben said, 'It's a welding torch for mending steel, you'll never need to touch them, my little Angel; it's a very dangerous tool and it can seriously burn you, that flame will melt steel.'

Over the weeks Ben took Theresa to lots of places on the ship but he hadn't realised how well she'd memorised the lay out and decks and she had got to know her way around the ship like a member of the crew.

Whenever she could, Theresa would sneak down to see Bridget but it required stealth as their cabins were on different decks and quite a long way apart but Theresa knew all the places to hide to avoid being discovered. She would kiss and cuddle Bridget, tell her how much she loved her and talk about home and share whatever gifts she could with Bridget, such as chocolate and soda drinks that Ben had given her, but wouldn't see in Bridget's cabin. All the children only saw each other during mealtimes which like exercise times were compulsory to attend for roll call.

One night she was returning from Bridget's cabin, she heard thick Irish accents coming from a cabin she was passing, she could not make out everything they were saying because they spoke in hushed voices, but she did hear talk of guns and of other men to join them on the next voyage. The children saw all the sailors and most of the crew at meal times but Theresa had never ever seen or heard Irishmen anywhere on the ship, it was if they were ghosts.

All of a sudden, the cabin door flew open and the men walked straight towards her, she was petrified and thought she'd been seen as she closed her eyes and pressed herself as flat as possible under the dark stairs against the ships cabin, all the men were temporarily blinded as they emerged from a light cabin into the night darkness of the deck and did not see her.

About eight or nine men approached, as she hid, she could not see them in the darkness but she recognised Captain Peterson's voice and also that most of the other men had thick Irish accents, she knew the accent very well, from her teachers at Catholic school, many were Irish. All the men passed so close to her that she could smell the tobacco and whiskey on their breath, they had not seen her as their eyes had not yet adjusted to the dark. Captain Peterson led the men to a big steel door four or five cabins down the deck and they swung open the huge door throwing light along the deck but not as far as Theresa.

She waited and listened but heard nothing, after a minute or so she crept along the deck and peered through the hinge in the door, she couldn't see everything, but she could see it was a cold room store, where the ships meat was kept and the men looked as if they were bringing out sides of beef and laying them on a massive steel table and chopping them up. Why would they do this at night Theresa thought and why these Irishmen.

She quickly and silently climbed through the door to get a better look and hid under a table that was three or four tables away from them. She could hear them talking and Captain Peterson was giving instructions as they slammed down the sides of beef. Suddenly they were using the very next table to her as another side of beef slammed down over her head, but this time an arm fell down, she covered her mouth to avoid screaming as she nearly passed out, suddenly realising they weren't sides of beef, they were frozen human bodies.

Jack's Business 1946

Sheila's door burst open as Sheila and Lucy were counting money on the bed. Billy held the door open casting a shadow across the room, at six foot eight inches and 24 stone he was enormous and Jack walked in.

'Well, well, well, what have we got here, Sheila and Lucy girls; how do you like Albion Street, Sheila. I see you've settled in and a little bird tells me it's very good for business and you've been working on the side and doing very well by the look of it, eh Billy. Oh by the way, do you girls know Billy, he does special work for me; don't you, Billy,' said Jack, the girls said nothing as Jack picked up the pile of money. Billy just stared at the girls in silence with a cold icy stare. 'Now this must be a present for me girls,' said Jack putting the money into his coat pocket.

'Thanks for the money, girls. I know you wouldn't cheat me, eh. We weren't going to cheat you, Jack; we were just gonna bring it to you, honest,' said Sheila, the girls were frozen with fear.

'Did you both hear about them poor girls Andrea and Sharon. I hear they've gone to the dogs so to speak, eh Billy,' said Jack.

Billy looked at Jack and replied, 'Yeah, Boss, dogs to dogs,' they both laughed.

'We've actually brought you a present girls, haven't we, Billy.'

Billy opened the door and two men bundled a girl into the room and threw her on the floor, her own stockings had been taken off and used to tie her hands behind her back and to gag her mouth. 'Do you know who this is girls,' asked Jack.

'Yes, it's Debbie,' both girls answered simultaneously. She had been badly beaten up, her face was bruised and there was blood on her dress from her nose.

'Show 'em the present, Billy,' said Jack.

Billy took out his knife, it flicked open menacingly and perilously close to Lucy's face. Both girls took in a gasp of air, they were petrified. Billy slowly sliced along the bed head cutting a strip of wood as if it were paper, demonstrating how razor sharp the knife was.

'Show 'em the other present, Billy; go on; you'll love this one, girls.'

Billy took a bottle from his pocket, unscrewed the cap and allowed a tiny drop to fall onto the carpet, a plume of smoke rose up from the carpet as it immediately burned from the sulphuric acid, the girls were crying with fear.

'Now, you know the rules about working on the side. I remember you telling me, Sheila, how grateful you were for the nice house I got for you and how you'd never cheat me,' then Jack got nose to nose with Sheila and shouted, 'You fucking lying bitch.' Sheila was frozen in fear, then he walked away from her and said in a calm voice, 'So who wants to be first, eh.'

'Jack please,' screamed Sheila. 'I was gonna bring you the money, honestly.'

In terror Lucy tried to run for the door but Billy grabbed her by her long hair slapped her face, picked her up with one hand and threw her onto the bed.

Sheila went on, 'You can have all the money, Jack, please.'

Jack replied, 'But you'll just do it again, won't you,' he said to the two terrified girls.

'We won't, Jack, honestly, we won't,' screamed Sheila.

'Well, 'course you won't,' said Jack, ''cos Billy's gonna make sure neither of you will ever work again.'

Billy unscrewed the top off the acid bottle and held it above Lucy's face as she screamed her pleas to Jack, 'No Jack please, please, for God's sake.'

'For me girls, it's just which one we scar first, you've got nothing to offer me. I can have another two girls taking your place in an hour,' said Jack. 'I tell you what, Sheila, if you pour the acid on Lucy's pretty little face, I'll let you off; now I can't be any fairer than that, can I.'

'No, please wait, Jack,' screamed Sheila in desperation.

Billy just stood in silence staring at both girls menacingly as Jack spoke, 'Billy boy, let's demonstrate to the girls on Debbie.'

Billy picked up Debbie and cut away her dress and bra with his flick knife, they fell to the floor, Debbie was naked except for her panties and only just conscious from the beating she'd had. 'See with only one half of ya face and one tit you're out of fucking work in this game girls,' said Jack. 'Show 'em, Billy.'

Sheila lay face down across Debbie to protect her, holding up her hand and screaming, 'Please Jack, don't cut her, please.'

'But you've got nothing to offer me, have ya,' said Jack. 'I've got all the money that you three fucking sluts should have paid me anyway, so now what you fucking got.'

'Please, please, Jack, I have got something,' screamed Sheila.

'And what the fuck is that then,' said Jack.

'I know where Rose is,' said Sheila.

There was silence for a very long moment and then Jack waved Billy away with a hand gesture, Jack nodded at Billy and he released Debbie who dragged herself across the floor back to the bed hugging Sheila crying deliriously, as she screamed, 'Thank you, thank you,' both girls were shaking with cold fear.

'Oh and how long have you had this information,' said Jack.

'I only found out today, honest, Jack, on my way here, honest.'

There was another moment of silence that felt like an hour, 'Where is she then,' said Jack.

Sheila gave Jack all the information about the tailor's shop and of Rose's whereabouts. Jack said, 'In my world there are no second chances, if this information is not correct, Billy will be coming back to use the acid on all three of you, from now on every fucking penny you earn I want my fucking cut, understand.'

'Yes,' screamed both girls as they hugged Debbie, crying with relief.

As they left Jack turned and said, 'You two mean as much to me as Andrea and Sharon and don't forget she,' pointing to Debbie, ''As got a pretty little seven-year-old, if any of you three, ever fucking tries to cheat me again, Billy will pour acid on all you three tarts and the fucking kid; she won't be so pretty, no more then will she, is that clear.'

'Yes,' they both said, hugging Debbie, the door slammed closed and Jack and the men left.

The Journey 1946

It took all of Theresa's control to remain quiet, as she saw frozen humans, she had never seen men chop up any bodies before, let alone human bodies, it was like the Hell she read about at religious instruction at school. She heard Captain Peterson say, 'Remember remove all fingers, heads and tattoo's and crush the jaw bones and teeth on all the bodies, we don't want any prints, faces or marks, they have to be totally untraceable and over the side for the sharks before dawn, I'll leave you with it.'

Theresa heard the men laughing and making jokes as they chopped off the heads and fingers and she nearly fainted when two fingers fell on the floor very close to her, the Irishman who bent down to pick them up was only a foot or so away from her but he was too busy talking and laughing and didn't see her. She knew it wouldn't take them long to complete their grisly work so she needed to sneak away very soon. When she was out of the cold room she needed to get back to Ben's cabin before he returned, it was already getting light and she was still in a state of shock after seeing dead bodies.

Theresa continued to make her very dangerous visits to see Bridget as the voyage progressed but never saw any of the Irishmen again, Ben went about his sailors' function and Theresa slept with him in his cabin at night mainly but sometimes he would also take her to his cabin in the daytime. Theresa spent the whole voyage as a privileged passenger by comparison to some children.

Ben brought her gifts like make up, lingerie, lipstick and of course wine. He had got her some nylon stockings and he loved it when she wore them for him and she knew it and when she wore them, she thought of Angie and how she felt like a grown-up woman, like her mum. In the eight-week voyage Theresa was learning a lot about sex, drink, men and life generally, now those times watching her mum and Jack may well have saved hers and Bridget's lives.

She was smart enough to realise that if she kept Ben happy, they might just have a chance of survival and like her mum, Theresa would do whatever it took.

One night halfway through the voyage, Theresa and Ben were in bed, she asked how much longer it would be before they reached Australia.

Ben said, 'Don't you worry, my angel; you'll be there in a few more weeks.'

Theresa had accepted the trapped life with Ben, there was very little option, between the small talk she accidentally mentioned the Irishmen she'd seen to Ben and was totally unprepared for his reaction.

Ben flew into a rage, then dragged her from the bed and picked her up shaking her like a doll and said, 'When did you see these fucking men, when have you left this fucking cabin and not told me,' he was angrier than she'd ever seen him, she was petrified as he shook her like a doll. 'If you've told anybody else about this, I can't protect you; they will put you and your fucking sister and me over the side of the ship, we'll all be dead, do you understand.'

Theresa shook with fear and quickly replied, 'Ben honestly, I've told no one, I swear to you.'

'Did you tell Bridget,' asked Ben in a hushed voice pressed against her face.

'No, Ben, I said nothing to anyone especially Bridget, I swear, honestly.' She could see he was really angry with her and she begged his forgiveness, she said, 'I'm sorry, Ben, honestly but I've told no one, please forgive me,' she pleaded.

Ben screamed, 'No, it's time for you to go back in the same fucking cabin as the girls, no more special treatment, wine, presents or lip stick. I can't protect you or your sister from those fucking killer Irish bastards, no one can; they will kill all three of us without a second thought.'

'Please, please, Ben, forgive me I've told no one else, don't send me back I'll do anything, please.'

Ben slowly put her down and said, 'Listen, we are only halfway through this voyage, girl; you mention these men to any person ever, even in Australia and they will definitely kill us all; it's too risky, you'll have to take your chances back with your sister in her cabin.'

Now Theresa was really frightened and started to cry, she was terrified of Ben leaving her and Bridget and she remembered the story of how the 13-year-old girl just disappeared, she'd seen how other children had been treated in the past few weeks by other sailors, she also knew that other sailors liked her and if Ben disowned her as his special girl, she and Bridget would be anyone's property. She had to convince Ben to keep her, or her and Bridget might not even get to this new land of Australia.

She begged him again and said, 'I promise I'll never mention those men ever. I promise, please let me stay. I'll do anything for you.' She threw her arms around Ben and hugged him, he kept pushing her away, she knew she had to do something or her and Bridget were as good as dead.

She stopped crying and put her arms around Ben, he pushed her away again, but she persisted with kissing his face, then his lips and eventually Ben began to calm down and lay back on the bed putting his arms around her and gradually started to hug her again. She knew she had to make him happy for her and Bridget's sake, suddenly she was back in the moment as Ben said, 'I will only forgive you this one time, you can never talk of people you see or hear, you must be deaf and blind to everything on this ship or you will not survive, do I make myself clear and for the rest of this trip you will you do as you're told and that includes never leaving this cabin without me.'

Theresa squeezed him hard and kissed him all over his face saying, 'Thank you, thank you, Ben; yes I'll do as I'm told in future.'

Theresa realised that she had very nearly lost her protection on this long and dangerous voyage, which had become infinitely more dangerous with the Irish connection, she dared not risk this happening again and thought back to her mum and how she would use her feminine wiles on Jack. She realised now was her time to prove she was a grown-up woman and become so important to Ben that he would never make her leave.

Theresa looked at Ben as he sat in his chair and drank his whiskey. She put on that soft, cute feminine voice that women use so well and said, 'Ben, I'm so sorry and to prove it I'm going to do something very special for you, close your eyes,' she said, as she walked to his chair. Theresa was only too aware that her breasts were touching him as she gently placed her hands on his face softly closed his eyes. 'No peeping,' she said. Ben sat in anticipation with his eyes closed, Theresa took off her night dress and put on the suspender belt, black stockings and high heeled shoes that Ben loved so much to see her in, this was all she wore.

'You can open your eyes now,' said Theresa.

Ben's mouth dropped open. Ben could not believe what was before him, he touched her and his hands got more intimate, she didn't know exactly what Ben was going to do or what was going to happen next but had a very good idea. 'Good girl, good, good girl,' said Ben as he took off his clothes and got into bed with her.

Theresa knew that now was the time she had to do whatever it needed, whatever he was going to do to her was nothing compared to being given to the other sailors as spoilt goods, she must be strong.

Australia 1946

When Ridgeway arrived at the 'Ship,' he walked in and went straight to the bar, he had brought Weeronga with him, 'Weeronga' was an aboriginal tracker and his name means quiet in aborigine. Ridgeway ordered two beers and looked along the bar, Coppin was there and looked back, then Coppin picked up his beer and walked to one of the booths, Ridgeway followed with Weeronga.

'Gooday,' said Ridgeway as he sat down in the booth, 'What ya got in mind mate,' he asked Coppin.

Coppin replied, 'The Pharaoh is arriving today, mate and a bloke will be there to take a girl from the ship; he'll probably have a mate or two with him. I want him to get clear of Fremantle and then I want him and his mates to disappear permanently and the girl returned to me, get my drift, mate.'

'What payday we looking at, mate,' asked Ridgeway.'

'100 Australian for each bloke and the same for the safe return of the girl,' said Coppin.

'Well, now mate,' started Ridgeway. 'It's been a while since I took care of a couple of blokes for you and it was a 100 Australian back then, can't do it for less than a 200 Australian a piece, mate and half up front,' replied Ridgeway.

'You always do a good job for me, Ridge, make 'em disappear but I need the girl back tonight in the next ten hours, she's got an appointment, if you can do that Ridge it's a deal,' said Coppin.

Coppin, explained to Ridgeway how he'd recognise Denny when the 'The Pharaoh' docked and exactly where Denny would be standing on the 'Victoria's' veranda as arranged, he also told him the likely destination for the girl was Denny's farm in Maddington then very discretely Coppin passed three hundred Australian dollars under the table in the booth saying, 'Remember I need the girl back tonight, mate and in the same condition she was in when she left; don't let me down, Ridge.'

Coppin then left the 'Ship,' he knew he was onto a winner, for around six hundred Australian he was financing losing Denny and Dixie Bacon forever, getting the girl back and losing a 5,000 Australian debt to Denny.

'The Pharaoh' arrived in Fremantle on time at 14-00 and as it was tying up a huge crowd gathered as the gangplanks were slid onto The Pharaoh. In the crowd with other officials was Jonesy. He looked across to the Victoria hotel and could clearly see Denny on the first-floor veranda with a beer in his hand. Denny could see Jonesy and looked straight at him as he raised his glass and grinned. Suddenly porters were going up the gangplanks, whistles were blowing and sailors were coming down, the quay was a hive of activity. Denny didn't know that in the crowd watching him was Ridgeway.

After some time, children appeared, hundreds of 'em, making their way down the gangplanks to the quayside. Theresa clutched Bridget's hand as all the children were marched from their cabins along the ship's decks. Theresa was desperately looking everywhere for Ben somehow thinking that he could or would help her and her sister. She had this idea that somehow, she would be with Ben and happily return home with Bridget, these were just the dreams of a 14-year-old suddenly thrust into a very ugly and adult real world, a world that has little romance and even less true love.

Ben knew very well that Theresa was only 14 years old and she had served her purpose, he had just enjoyed yet another voyage of sexual fantasy and he had done as he had promised and kept both girls safe from other crew members. They had both been a convenience to each other on the voyage, but now he had no further interest in her or use for her.

Theresa didn't know it yet but she would never see Ben again, she started to realise that sex worked both ways, she had been able to afford some protection for herself and Bridget by allowing Ben to do as he wished with her, but now he was gone, her power over him was also gone, if it had ever existed, all of her sexual collateral had been used up in the heat of Fremantle.

There were nuns all around on the quayside and the children were marched off the ship carrying only their one suitcase and told to form rows and stand in line. There were buses, cars and open backed trucks all around. As the children came down the gangplanks and stood on the quayside, Denny saw Theresa and as she got to the bottom of the gangplank, he looked at Jonesy and removed his 'Akubra' and wiping his forehead Jonesy acknowledged and put his hand on Theresa's shoulder as if to guide her, but really identifying her as the girl that

Denny wanted. At the same time, he looked back across at Denny, who nodded and replaced his 'Akubra'. Theresa was the chosen girl.

A nun rang a bell and screamed an order for everyone to be quiet, then she spoke to all of the children to be quiet and listen carefully, she presented a much older nun and said, 'this is mother superior, she is the head of the convent that we'll all be going to very soon, I want you all to listen to Mother Superior very carefully,' she said and then the senior nun began to speak.

'I am mother superior and all of you children are very lucky to be here away from England, it is a bad country and will take years to rebuild after the war, you are now in Fremantle a big town in this new country, you will have a chance of a much better life here and a completely new beginning.' She went on, 'you will not see bomb sites here, it doesn't rain all the time, there is always sunshine, you won't be eating rationed food, you can eat as much as you like, you will all be happy here. All the kind people that you see around you have come to take you to their own towns and homes to begin a new life in your new country.'

She went on, 'I'm sorry to have to tell all of you that there has been a terrible accident in England; all of you children are extremely lucky to have been on this ship and missed this terrible accident; the children were shocked and frightened, some began to scream and cry; at that moment nearly all the children were screaming hysterically, asking if their family was still alive, some ran off only to be caught and returned, others just collapsed on the floor crying, others panicked and almost all became delirious, the nuns had to restrain them.

All of the nuns had canes and many of the nuns used them as Mother Superior went on, 'Because of this tragedy none of you can ever return to England; this new country is your new home forever; it's called Australia; now all of you follow the nuns to the convent, it's a short walk,' then Mother Superior walked away.

In the general confusion and all the shouting, activity and noise, no-one noticed Jonesy lead Theresa and Bridget to the back of the crowd where three nuns led them away, the girls did not know where they were being led. Everything was strange in this new country, the dust and heat, the strange accent, neither of the girls had ever seen an aborigine before, so they both noticed this black man carrying a spear, he was half naked with white paint on his face and body, he looked frightening to them.

The rest of the crowd were a mix of Australians, sheep farmers, horse breeders, sailors, nuns, drinkers and prostitutes. There was such a mix of people and lots of horses and traffic and with ships arriving in Fremantle no one noticed Ridgeway and Weeronga in the crowd, but they followed Denny's every move.

Ridgeway also noticed the men who silently walked down the other gangplank, at the end of The Pharaoh, this part of the ship was roped off from the general public, he knew they were not crew and he also knew from their clothes and lack of tan they were not Aussie's either. Ridgeway knew exactly who they were and what was going on.

Convent

All the children were walked up the street by the nuns, away from the quayside to Fremantle's convent school where they all received drinks and food from the nuns, who tried to calm them all down from the shocking news they'd all just heard. All the nuns at the convent were experts in tropical medicine and all had sufficient medical training to examine the children to ensure they were in good health before they were allocated their new homes.

The children arrived and walked into a huge entrance hall where there were lots of nuns, all the children were taken to showers and ordered to strip and shower. Each child was then taken in turn to one of the fifty bedrooms for a medical examination by a nun, each nun had approximately seven children to examine and all of the examinations were expected to be competed in two hours in time for Mother Superior's meeting with Coppin, the examinations were thorough but rudimental. This allocating of children was conducted very quickly, the usual target time was four hours.

In that time the children would arrive in Fremantle, be examined, allocated a new home and then be dispersed to all parts of Australia, to speed up this process the convent had a copy of the ships manifest some weeks before the new arrivals set foot on Australian soil, they had all the detail of each child arriving and could choose an appropriate new home. As far as the convent was concerned the further the new arrivals were from Fremantle the better.

This business was performed by the convent on a regular basis and they made it look inhumanely efficient. This business made the convent thousands of Australian dollars, an appropriate donation to the convent from the new family was agreed some weeks before any ship arrived and Coppin paid 100 Australian dollars to the convent for every placement.

The Australian and British governments paid for the Ships to help populate Australia and to rid the British of war orphaned children and troublesome teenagers, everyone was a winner apart from the children. After their examination all the children were given a vaccination and a report was made listing any irregularities and immediately sent to Mother Superior in time for her scheduled meeting with Coppin.

Coppin

Mother Superior and three senior nuns arrived at Coppin's office in Fremantle as usual to discuss the new arrivals and any 'Overspill.' The nuns were invited by Jonesy to sit at the desk and offered refreshments, Mother Superior's most senior nun Sister Mary quietly read the medical report from the convent as Mother Superior began in her soft Irish accent, 'Well, hello Mr Coppin, it's nice to see you again, but tell me do you feel threatened at all by my good self or my nuns.'

'Of course not,' said Coppin laughingly, 'What made you ask reverend mother.'

'Well, I thought perhaps you were expecting a visit from someone else because when I look around this office, I can see a lot of guns.'

Coppin turned around and said to Jonesy, 'Shift that shotgun off the table and tell 'em all to put their fucking jackets on and cover them shoulder holsters.' He immediately turned back to mother superior saying, 'Reverend Mother, please forgive my language, now how can I help you today.'

'I think we both know your business is not the boy scouts,' said Mother Superior, 'But today I counted 250 placements that are being dealt with ready for allocation as we speak; now when I was at school, which I have to admit was a very long time ago,' she said with a chuckle, '250 x 100 was 25,000 and I don't think that's changed much since my school days.' Pointing to one of her nuns, Mother Superior went on, 'Sister Mary here tells me only 23,000 was delivered to Sister Bridget at the convent yesterday.'

'No it was definitely 25,000 reverend mother,' said Jonesy.

'Well I hate to,' began the reverend mother, but she was immediately interrupted by Coppin, 'Jonesy, if the reverend mother says it was 23,000, it was 23,000, go and get 2000 out of the safe. I do apologise, reverend mother, I'm sure it was simply an oversight and I'll find out who was responsible for the error, now what other business do we need to deal with,' continued Coppin.

'Well, firstly, I do hope you are not too harsh with the person who made the error, Mr Coppin.'

'Don't you worry, reverend mother, I don't need to tell you how to run your convent and you don't need to tell me how to run my business, I will take appropriate action, now what other business have we got.'

Sister Mary leaned over and whispered into Mother Superior's ear as she pushed the medical report along the table to her.

The Reverend Mother began, 'I have the medical report in front of me, Mr Coppin and I notice the 'Overspill' is 50 this time.'

'Is this an accommodation issue, reverend mother,' asked Coppin.

'Accommodation has never been an issue, Mr Coppin,' replied Mother Superior who went on, 'The 'Overspill' increases with every ship and many of them are in what you might call, your higher price range.'

'I know from my sources that tomorrow morning within a few hours you will have dispersed this 'Overspill,' which for you is extremely efficient and also very convenient; however, it's the length of time that I have 'Overspill' on the convent premises, for sometimes as long as 16 hours and more recently the numbers have increased, so therefore my share of risk is much greater, there's always the possibility of government inspectors paying us a visit.'

Coppin replied, 'You know as well as me, reverend mother, that the Australian authorities have very few government inspectors and you also know why, Australia needs a population and they're not going to upset the apple cart, the inspectors they've got are for show, just to be seen doing things correctly.'

Coppin went on, 'Look if an inspector came to the convent, one girl looks the same as another, they'll go with the ships manifest and if it says 300, they'll accept your figures, they won't be doing a head count, but to keep you happy I'll look at reducing the times you have 'Overspill' at the convent by later sailings or picking them up earlier on the auction day.'

Coppin went on, 'For each 'Overspill', we currently pay you 100 Australian, can I suggest we increase that to 150 on the next shipment and for the current The Pharaoh arrivals we'll increase it to 125, would that help to ease some of your religious and moral conscience issues, your reverend mother,' asked Coppin.

'No need to be facetious, Mr Coppin,' said Mother Superior. 'The increased financial support is most agreeable and acceptable, thank you.'

'Now anything else reverend mother,' asked Coppin.

'I see from my report that one of the 'Overspills' has a facial birthmark but much worse, two of the girls have syphilis.'

'WHAT,' bellowed Coppin, 'Fucking hell, how old are the two girls.'

'Well, from my report both the girls are fourteen.'

'Fucking hell,' screamed Coppin, 'My best stock, are they placements or Overspill.'

'They're all three Overspill,' replied Mother Superior.

'Oh no they're fucking not,' said Coppin. 'I can't lose as much as 2,000 Australian on each girl, you'll need to find me three of your placements all about 13, 14 or 15 to replace the two girls with syphilis and the other girl with the birthmark and I want the prettiest.'

'If you wish me to continue with my report, Mr Coppin, I would appreciate less bad language,' said Mother Superior, she went on, 'There are fifteen girls in the higher age range who are no longer virgins, it's difficult to say how long ago they lost their virginity.'

'Fucking hell,' screamed Coppin. 'I need those fifteen non virgins replaced as well Reverend Mother, my prime customers pay for virgins and my reputation relies on me supplying exactly that.'

'You can't just keep taking my girls, Mr Coppin; all of my girls are already allocated to families, it was organised months ago,' said Mother Superior.

'Well, get it unorganised,' replied Coppin, 'tell the eighteen families affected that they now have a replacement girl or can have first pick from the next ship, now what else Reverend Mother, we need to get your placements gone within the next three hours, some of the families are already here.'

Mother Superior spoke as the nuns all rose to leave, she said, 'Mr Coppin, if we keep replacing girls you will create suspicion with the government authorities; they will begin to wonder how we could supply replacement girls and work out that you have 'overspill'. I'll expect a visit tomorrow at the convent, Mr Coppin, with the increased funds, let's not have any more financial oversights, good day.'

Convent

Sister Mary arrived back at the convent and instructed the nuns to proceed, there were a dozen desks already set out each one had a great big number above it and had a nun sat at it with an empty chair next to the nun and two chairs on the opposite side of each desk, the desks were all spaced about ten feet apart. One nun at the door was holding a list and directing one or two people to each desk to join the nun already sat there.

A senior nun rang a bell and commanded. 'Now listen for your name to be called out and then go to the desk with that number above it as you're instructed by the nuns.'

The children did as they were told and as they went to their respective desk, they were introduced to their new family and quickly whisked away before any of the children had any time to get upset.

When all the vehicles had left the convent, there were children left of various ages, referred to as 'Overspill,' but about twenty of them were girls between eleven and fourteen, they asked the nuns what was happening to them and the nuns told them that because Australia was such a big country, the remaining people would be arriving tomorrow and that all the children would stay in the convent tonight.

The remaining children were given something to eat and told that after their meal they would all go to bed because the next day they may have a long journey, it had been a tiring and stressful day. The children were totally unaware of the morphine in their food.

Coppin

When the nuns had left Coppin turned to Jonesy and said, 'Jonesy, these sailors have gotta keep their fucking hands off the overspill, non-virgins have no value to my fucking customers; the sailors can fuck as many of the placements as they want; go and find that Peterson bring him back to the office in the next fucking hour before 8 o'clock and tell him to bring the ships log and manifest.'

Jonesy left the office. Coppin phoned Marcus and Marcus answered, 'Marcus, I've got a job for you tomorrow morning at six, you'll need two good men, come to the office now, I'll give you the details.'

Marcus arrived at the office, Coppin told him to get a couple of beers for each of them, 'Sit down, Marcus, I've got a job for you early tomorrow morning before you open the farm gates.'

'OK, boss, what is it,' replied Marcus.

'I want two reliable men, good men, who you got,' said Coppin.

'Well, tomorrow morning Johnny and Dave are on the gate at the farm,' said Marcus. 'What's the job, boss.'

Coppin replied, 'Two 'overspills,' you need to collect them from the convent at 6 o'clock in the morning. Sister Brenda will be your contact, she'll have 'em ready, you need to lose 'em permanently in Croc Lake, got it.'

'Got it, boss,' Marcus replied. 'Johnny and Dave can do that job on their way to the farm,' just then Jonesy returned with Peterson, holding a pile of documents and the ship's manifest.

'Jonesy, get us some more beers, Marcus is just leaving,' Coppin said. Marcus knew when he was being invited to leave and he left the office.

Coppin turned to Captain Peterson, 'Sit down, Peterson; have a beer with me and Jonesy.'

'What's this about, boss,' asked Peterson.

'Well, I've just gotta tell you one of your crew has probably cost me 4,000 Australian in stock and another 400 Australian in disposal; he's one of your fucking crew, do you want to pay me the 4,800 Australian that he owes me,' shouted Coppin.

'Well, I don't know who it is or what he's done,' replied Peterson.

'But are you gonna fucking pay me 4,800 Australian,' bellowed Coppin.

'I haven't got that sort of money, boss,' replied Peterson, at that point Jonesy stood up and pulled his Jacket back and reached for his gun.

'Whoaa, whoaa,' said Coppin. 'Sit, Jonesy. I'm not after you, Peterson, if I was, you'd already be dead. I want to know which fucking cabin the two syphilis girls were in, cos the sailor in charge of that cabin give it to 'em, now open your fucking manifest and log book, the girls names are Sarah Jane Sudds and Amanda Scott, find them in your log and tell me in the next five fucking minutes which cabin they were in and the name of the fucking sailor who they were allocated to and you'll have no worries; me and Jonesy will just sit here enjoying our beers, won't we, Jonesy.'

Convent

At the convent the children were woken in the morning at 7 AM by a loud bell and told to be ready for breakfast in 15 minutes, they were all told they would be vaccinated after breakfast before leaving. Any missing children were explained away as being collected in the night. As the children ate their meal, Sister Brenda and Sister Ann prepared the vaccinations, they looked at each other to ensure all of the children were busy eating as they loaded the syringes with a second dose of morphine.

The Kidnap 1946

Bridget was only kept with Theresa to avoid both girls screaming, making a scene and alarming all the other kids, but as soon as the two girls were at the back of the Fremantle shipping offices out of site of the crowd and the other children, they were separated. Bridget started to scream and cry as she tried to grasp Theresa. She was held tightly and forcefully by three nuns and was told if she was quiet, she could see Theresa a little later and was taken to another room. Bridget was told by the nuns that older girls like Theresa had to go for an examination and after that she would be able to see her again.

On hearing this Bridget calmed down and was returned to the other children outside, the huge crowd hardly noticed as Bridget returned. Theresa began screaming 'Please don't take my little sister, please I'll do anything you want,' she was ignored, her hands were quickly tied by the nuns and she was gagged, two men quickly came into the office and in spite of her struggling and kicking out she was picked up and carried outside to the back of the offices and thrown into the back of a pick-up truck, her suitcase thrown in behind her; because of the noise of the crowds at the front of the offices, no one heard or even saw the truck quickly drive off down the back streets.

In the back of the open truck, it was almost unbearable because of the noise, heat and rough bumpy hard dusty roads. Theresa was frightened out of her brain and upset, she knew the nuns had lied, she wasn't going to be examined and she was being taken away from Bridget, a long way away to God knows where.

The tools and materials rattled against the steel sides of the vehicle as they bounced around in the back of the truck on the rough dirt road hardened by the sun, Theresa rolled around from side to side, she was not aware of the destination, Maddington, it was only 35 miles from Fremantle but it seemed like a thousand-mile journey to her.

Bingo was driving and Denny sat in the passenger seat with his sawn-off shot gun on his lap, she was being thrown about in the back of the truck but she knew that she had to try and escape soon or Bridget would be gone forever, never to be found again.

With this thought in mind, she wriggled and wriggled her tied hands on a sharp piece of the trucks damaged floor which was bare metal and clearly sharp. The two men were oblivious to what she was doing as they laughed and drank beer in the front of the truck. She could hear them through the missing rear cab window, most Aussie's removed them for ventilation.

She heard them say, 'She's a cute little 'Sheila' with a nice pair o' tits, we'll toss a fucking coin mate when we get back to see who gets first go,' both men laughed.

Coppin

Peterson scrambled through his books, conscious that Coppin and Jonesy watched him turn every page, he was sweating profusely, suddenly he blurted out, 'Found 'em, those girls were allocated to cabin 506; its Lawrence's cabin, they call him Lol and he likes the females and brothels,' said Peterson.

'Well, what do you know, Peterson; that wasn't that difficult was it, now I'm assuming you'd prefer it if I dealt with you, am I right,' said Coppin, 'You don't want Jonesy dealing with you do you.'

'No,' said Peterson.

'Now, you can't afford to pay the 4,800 Australian that your fucking Lol has lost me, can you, Peterson,' asked Coppin.

'No,' replied Peterson.

'Well, this is what you can fucking do then,' said Coppin. 'Tonight, you'll go with Jonesy around the bars and brothels and find Lol before he fucks and pisses all his wages away. I want him robbed of any money he's got left and both his legs broken, then you'll take him back on board the Pharaoh tonight and fill him with morphine.'

Coppin turned to Peterson, 'And you, Peterson, will keep him sedated on morphine in the sick bay until you sail; his name will not appear on your returning crews log, he'll just be one of those men that jumped ship and when you're a day out of Fremantle, you'll put him over the fucking side. Peterson.'

'But that's murder, boss,' replied Peterson.

'Yes,' said Coppin. 'But you can either do it my way in a couple of days' time, out in the middle of the huge Indian Ocean or I'll leave this office right now and let Jonesy deal with it his fucking way, what's it to be, Peterson.'

Peterson looked at Coppin and watched as Jonesy stared back into his eyes and rubbing his hands together nervously with his head bowed he replied, 'I'll do it your way, boss.'

Coppin went on, 'Any outstanding wages you're holding for him and the entire contents of his cabin come back to this fucking office before you leave Fremantle, got it,' said Coppin.

'Yes, I understand,' replied Peterson.

Ridgeway

Ridgeway was in no hurry to be seen by Denny, he was not in the habit of giving targets any hint of his presence and he also knew that Denny was armed and dangerous. He knew where Denny lived and where he was heading, he had all the information that he needed from Coppin, there was only one road to Maddington.

Ridgeway knew he could get to Maddington and back in about six hours so there was no rush. Ridgeway and Weeronga watched Denny and Bingo leave with the girl, but they had time on their side and they went to the bar in the 'Ship' and ordered some beers.

'No worries, mate,' he said to Weeronga. 'Another beer then we'll go and earn some easy money.'

The Canning River 1946

The truck slowed down for a junction and Theresa saw the road sign Fremantle 18 miles, she continued to twist and pull her wrists in desperation against the sharp metal floor as the truck drove along the dirt track every minute, she knew she was getting further away from Bridget, already they were 18 miles away.

Her wrists and hands were cut and bleeding as she struggled to get free, she kept accidentally rubbing her skin on the sharp metal floor instead of the rope. She could feel the warm blood running down her fingers, then suddenly one hand slipped free, the blood had acted as a lubricant at last both hands were free.

Theresa looked to see if the two men had seen her, they had not, she stayed low but carefully looked around the back of the truck for anything she may be able to use to help her escape. There was an oxy acetylene set in the back of the truck, just like the one that the sailor had used on the ship that morning when Ben nearly threw him over the side. Could she remember how to work it, come on Theresa think, she remembered you just turn the key at the top and light the gas, she desperately felt in her pockets and thank God, she'd still got Ben's lighter.

She could hear the two men talking and laughing in the front of the truck as they slowly got drunk, they had to shout to each other because of the road noise. They didn't hear the hiss of acetylene as Theresa gripped the handle of the oxy acetylene cylinders, opened the valve, lit the flame with Ben's lighter and quickly thrust the flaming gun nozzle through the rear window. Denny heard the movement and turned just in time to receive the full oxy acetylene flame directly into his face.

'Ahhhhhhh,' Denny screamed as the flame engulfed his eyes, set his Akubra, hair and face completely on fire. 'I'm blind,' he screamed and in his panic his fingers accidentally squeezed both triggers blowing away half of Bingo's head and neck.

Bingo was dead instantly and fell onto the steering wheel, the truck was now completely out of control. Denny was blind so he could do nothing as the truck veered straight into the Canning River, tipping over onto its left-hand side and sliding into the water. Theresa was thrown into the water as the truck entered the river, she was just yards from the bank.

Denny Harris in the passenger side was being crushed under Bingo's dead body which was still burning and pushing Denny under the water. Eventually, the flames were doused by the river but Denny's face was horrifically burned and he was blind, screaming in pain and drowning under Bingo's weight. Theresa screamed in panic and scrambled to the bank digging her fingers into the mud and scampering backwards up the river bank as the horror scene unfolded before her. The blood-stained water swelled around the truck which had almost stopped bobbing around in the river.

The scene would have been idyllic except for the events of the last few minutes, Theresa was in a state of extreme shock she could not believe what had happened how two men had just died by her hand. After a minute or two she tried to think straight. She had not meant to kill two men, what would happen now and how could she get back to Fremantle, would anyone find her in such a desolate quiet and remote place and how could she find Bridget. The horror was over, but at least she was free, she put her head into her hands and began to cry, apart from the gentle flow of the river it was silent.

Suddenly an earth-shattering scream broke the deathly silence, with no warning Denny burst through the driver's door gasping for breath as he broke the surface. His face was burned black and his eyes were just empty sockets of blood and he began to wade through the water towards the river bank and Theresa. He was still grasping the shot gun as he screamed, 'You're gonna get so fucked, little bitch,' he got closer screaming at Theresa, 'When I get hold of you, bitch, you'll wish you were fucking dead. I'm gonna fuck you, then drown you and then carve you alive into bits, bitch.'

He was only feet from the bank, he couldn't see Theresa, he couldn't see anything but he could hear her desperate breathing. Theresa scrambled as far up the bank as she could, trying to remain as quiet as possible and control her breathing, she was frozen to the spot. She was petrified as Denny got closer every step and cocking his head to one side to hear her panicked breathing, he continued to scream his threats.

He pointed his shot gun towards the sound of her breathing and blasted, he missed, but only just, Denny stood still and again listened intently for Theresa's breathing or any sign of movement. 'You've gotta move or breath some time, bitch,' Denny screamed, 'And then I'm gonna cut your eyes out, cut off your hands and drag you back in the river for the crocs.'

Theresa was so petrified by the threats she screamed in terror giving away her position, Denny aimed toward the sound and let off another round, he missed again but he was very close, so close in fact, that Theresa had shot-gun pellet scratches to her shoulder and face. Again, he stopped moving in the water and listened for any sign as he reloaded his shot gun. He realised he was very close, placing one foot on the river bank Theresa tried desperately not to breath, Denny was now just a couple of metres away.

Denny couldn't see anything and was in a lot of pain, but now he was stepping onto the riverbank and the shotgun was perilously close to Theresa, he knew she was just feet away as she held her breath, not daring to breath or move. He was just one step away from her and if she tried to move, he would know exactly where she was, if she didn't move, one more step and he would trip over her or walk into her she struggled to hold her breath, in desperation she threw a small rock into the water to her left and Denny pointed the shotgun and let off both barrels in that direction.

Theresa breathed in panic giving away her exact position as she ran up the bank, but she had bought a few seconds of time before Denny could reload. Denny heard her and turned to look straight at her, he broke the shotgun to reload, this time he knew exactly where she was. Denny raised the barrels and pointed them straight at Theresa, this time he would not miss, 'Ready for the crocs, bitch,' he shouted, she knew this was the end.

Suddenly, the river erupted behind Denny as an enormous dark shadow lunged from the water, he stood no chance as the enormous crocodile, attracted by the blood in the water, dropped onto him crushing him into the river bank as it's jaws almost tore off his head. Denny hit the riverbank with a sickening thud, as he tried in vain to escape his fingers gripped the trigger as he fired the shotgun in desperation, it just blew away his own face and chin.

He screamed and gripped the bank but the giant beast had its prey in a deadly grip and just disappeared backwards dragging Denny into the blood red water of the Canning River, with Denny locked in its huge jaws, the only evidence that he'd even been there a few seconds earlier was the shotgun, field glasses that he'd dropped on the bank and his finger tracks in a trail of blood all the way down the bank and into the water.

Theresa trembled on the bank in shock for what seemed like hours, then she gradually moved backwards up the bank further away from the water's edge for fear of the crocodiles return. The truck slowly stopped bobbing in the river and the red water began to run clear, it was only six metres into the river, but her suitcase that had been thrown from the truck was jammed in the reeds about three metres away from her, but although she was relieved to be alive, she was still too petrified to attempt retrieving it from the water and moved further up the bank until she felt as safe as she could.

She had only meant to escape and get back to Bridget but now two men had died in the most horrific fashion and she was very frightened and cold. It was getting late and she felt very alone.

She sat on the bank for some time pondering with the thought of retrieving her suitcase and a plastic water container from the reeds in the river, she struggled with her most basic fears but realising that time was passing and the possibility of saving Bridget was getting further away with every minute. With a sudden rush of courage, she charged into the river screaming her lungs out as she did it, grabbed her suitcase and a water bottle and raced back to the bank, running as far up the bank as possible before dropping to the floor still screaming and crying with relief as her heart pounded.

The Kidnap

Theresa was soaking wet, cold and trembling she struggled to put together the events of the day. Reality kicked in and she realised that Bridget was getting further away by the minute and she didn't even know what bus or truck was taking her or in which direction they'd be heading, she knew she was about 20 miles from the nearest civilisation and she was at the scene of a killing.

After a while, she stood up and looked both ways up and down the dirt road, there was no sign of life and she was frightened and very hungry. She looked around for any shelter from the sun and some large trees on the opposite side of the road to the river surrounded by some quite high bushes. She approached the riverbank for the last time to retrieve the field glasses and shotgun. Theresa didn't know anything about guns, she also didn't know if there were any snakes or wild animals like Lions or Tigers that might eat her but she might be able to protect herself with a gun.

She had no idea that Lions and Tigers do not live in Australia, she dragged her suitcase over to the bush and knew she had to keep hold of her case it was all she had and the case was twice as heavy at the moment because of the wet clothes inside, so she emptied them out and laid them out on the bushes under the tree in the hot sunshine to dry.

After making sure she was completely alone she stripped naked to dry the clothes she was wearing? She tried to make herself as comfortable as possible as she took stock. Would anyone use this road, would anyone help her, she had some drinking water but how long could she survive without food, how far away was the nearest town, could she walk there, how much daylight was left before night time approached and most pressing what was happening to Bridget and where was she.

Theresa just cried, she had never felt this lost, frightened and isolated, she had never been a stupid little girlie, her hard-working class life had dictated that she would never be allowed to be a child for long. The past few weeks she had grown as much as ten years because she had no choice, she stood up, pulled herself together, stopped crying and tried to think of what she could do, she thought what her mum would do, well, she wouldn't cry that was for sure.

Just then Theresa thought she heard a car and tilted her head to listen more intensely. It was a car, she could now see dust, it was coming straight towards her. She used the field glasses, they were quite far away but she could see two men in a truck, she suddenly froze in fear as she recognised the passenger, it was the black man she had seen at the quayside, the man with the painted face and body.

She quickly gathered her clothes throwing them into the case, pushed the case and belongings under the bushes and hid behind the tree. The car was now very close, it stopped at the place where the truck lay on its side in the river, the two men got out, they had their guns ready and carefully looked around, the men were so close and the place so desolate and quiet that Theresa could clearly hear their voices.

'If they'd survived this mate, we'd have passed 'em walking back to Fremantle or they'd have walked on or got a lift, what do ya reckon mate,' she heard Ridgeway ask Weeronga.

'If you were trying to find help, would you walk back towards a city or into the outback mate,' replied Weeronga. 'Only one person left this river mate,' replied Weeronga, 'And it was the girl, look at the tracks.'

Weeronga knelt on one knee gently touching the tracks with his fingers. 'No deep boot prints here, mate,' he said. 'Just a girls footprint, look at the size and she's dragging something, it's not a body, it's a box or bag and the tracks are heading that way.'

Both men turned and looked in the direction that Weeronga pointed. Theresa pulled herself closer to the tree frozen in fear, hoping she hadn't been seen, holding her breath and trying not to make a sound as both men looked in her direction. She watched in horror through the undergrowth as both men began to walk straight towards her and cocked their guns.

'Careful mate,' said Weeronga. 'Denny was walking around with a sawn off and Bingo had a rifle, this little beauty could be armed with both the bastards' guns.'

Theresa kept low and scrambled as far as she could into the undergrowth as the men crossed the road, she could go no further without running into open outback with no cover and she'd be easily seen but she could hear the men's voices they were so close, they were very close.

'You were right, mate; she's here somewhere and she ain't gone far.'

The men searched the small area and it didn't take more than a few minutes before they found the petrified girl at the edge of the growth area still completely naked.

'Well, look what we got here, mate,' said Ridgeway with a broad grin. 'She's got herself ready for me, mate,' he said laughing. 'Stand up, Sheila,' said Ridgeway, he went on, 'what did ya do to the two men in the truck, you've earned me and Weeronga 3,000 Australian, ya little beaut.'

Theresa answered, 'They got eaten by crocodiles,' and both men laughed out loud.

'Oh and the fucking croc didn't fancy a bit of younger meat, eh,' replied Ridgeway. Then he turned to Weeronga and said, 'Go and check the truck mate, she might be telling the truth, why you're doing that I'll get acquainted with missy here.'

Weeronga walked back across the road and waded into the river toward the truck.

Ridgeway moved closer to Theresa and ran his hands down her naked back and onto her buttocks. 'Have you got a name to go with this beautiful young tight arse girl,' Ridgeway asked. Theresa was so frightened she could hardly speak. 'Come on, girl; spit it out,' continued Ridgeway as his hands squeezed her so tight, she could hardly breath.

'My name is Theresa Newton,' said Theresa.

She looked petrified as Ridgeway loosened his belt and his shorts slipped to the floor revealing himself, he ran his big hands over Theresa's buttocks and pressed himself against her warm young naked body saying, 'You're gonna have some of that, girl, but first we're gonna go and find out what Weeronga's found then me and you are gonna have an afternoon of fun.'

With that he pulled his shorts back up, grabbed Theresa by the hand and walked out of the bush and back across the road to the Canning River, calling out, 'Weeronga mate, where are you.'

Ridgeway began to call again, 'Weeronga, Weeronga,' as they neared the crashed truck there was no answer from Weeronga but suddenly Ridgeway's hand almost crushed Theresa's as his grip tightened, she looked at his face just in time to see him fall to his knees spluttering and choking, releasing her hand

and clutching at his throat as he continued to fall flat on the floor blood gushing from his neck.

Theresa screamed in panic, covering her mouth with both hands. The pool of blood just got bigger until finally Ridgeway stopped moving, there was a crossbow bolt sticking out of the back of his neck.

Theresa was still screaming as she looked at yet another dead body, she didn't see or hear where the shot was fired from, but she did see Weeronga was lying some yards away, he had suffered the same fate. Theresa still naked, looked in horror at the pools of blood around the two men; she dropped to the floor desperately looking for cover and to see who had killed these men, was she next; she was mortified as she lay as low as she could breathing heavily in fear. Four people had already died this day at this killing scene, would she be next.

Skinner 1946

Theresa kept as low as possible as she crawled past the two dead men, she was trying to get back to the trees or grass or any cover at all. She was still naked looking along the river bank through the short grass, she saw a man, he was dressed in khaki shorts and shirt, wearing an Akubra and holding a crossbow. He walked towards Theresa, she clutched at the grass in vain hoping that he wouldn't see her.

He walked straight up to her pointing the crossbow at her and spoke, 'Get up and put your hands on your head.'

She did as she was told. 'Don't kill me, please don't kill me,' she pleaded.

The man said, 'Shut up and tell me where the others are.'

'What others,' replied Theresa.

'The ones from the truck crashed in the river,' he said. 'Unless you're gonna tell me you drove the truck here by yourself.'

'No, I can't drive, they brought me here and now they're both dead,' said Theresa. 'But it wasn't my fault, one got shot and the crocodile got the other one,' she said.

The man said, 'so there was just two of 'em and now they're both dead, is that what you're telling me,' he asked.

'Yes,' replied Theresa.

'Well, who were they,' the man asked.

'I don't know,' Theresa replied, 'But they called each other Denny and Bingo.'

He lowered the crossbow and said, 'Put your hands down.'

She screamed in terror as he grabbed her hand pulling her into the river with him, wading out to the truck to check her story, Bingo's body lay in the truck under water, lifeless and blackened by fire. Theresa was terrified that the croc would return as they waded back out of the river and the man asked, 'Where are your clothes.'

She replied, 'In the bushes over the road.'

He took her immediately over to where she said her clothes were, he first checked for any weapons and then said, 'Put something on quickly and follow me.'

Theresa grabbed the first thing she could, khaki shorts and top as the man walked quickly to Ridgeway's car, Theresa following closely behind. He jumped into Ridgeway's truck and said, 'Get in,' to Theresa. They reversed up to the bodies and stopped, 'Help me,' he said as he loaded both the bodies into the car, when they'd done that, he said, 'Wait there,' and Theresa did as she was told, then he drove the car with the bodies inside, into the Canning River ramming the truck a few times that was already on its side in the river until it turned completely onto its roof. Then he rammed it behind the reeds and kept ramming till both vehicles were out of site behind the reeds in the river.

The man jumped out of the car and waded to the bank where Theresa had waited. He said, 'Follow me,' and both of them walked towards another part of the river and there under thick undergrowth was his car hidden. 'Get in,' he said and she did, he drove back to where her clothes were laid out and said, 'Collect your case and clothes and be quick, leave nothing.'

Theresa did as she was told, in the meantime he tied a branch to each side of the rear of his truck and then picked up an item of her clothing and soaked it in petrol from a jerry can in the back of his truck. He waded out to Ridgeway's truck in the river and undid the fuel cap, stuffed the rag into the opening and lit it and went back to his truck and watched as both vehicles in the river above the water line burst into flames.

As they drove away the branches dragged on the dirt road hiding his tyre tracks, then they heard an explosion from the crash site. 'Who are you,' asked the man, 'and what were you doing with those men.'

'I'm Theresa Newton,' she replied. 'Those men tied me up and took me from the ship and I'm trying to save my sister, are you going to kill me,' blurted out Theresa.

'No, why would I want to kill you,' he said.

'Because you killed those men,' said Theresa

'I didn't kill those men to save you girl, I've been tracking them bastards for months, I saw their car and knew they'd be close by. Answer my question what were you doing with those men,' he asked again.

'Those two men took me and my little sister from the ship,' she shouted out.

'Which ship and where's your sister,' he asked.

'It's a ship called The Pharaoh and those men took me and left my little sister Bridget with the nuns in a place called Fremantle, I just told you and if I don't go and get her, she'll be lost forever.'

The man repeated his question, 'But who gave you to those men.'

Theresa told the man how they had arrived on 'The Pharaoh' and were taken by Denny and Bingo, she went on to say how she had escaped and then the other two men came after her. 'Now can we try to find Bridget please, please help me. I know I shouldn't ask a complete stranger but there is no-one else and I don't even know your name.'

'Whoaa, calm down,' he said. 'At this moment in time there are four dead men in the same place and before long someone will be missing them and they'll go looking for them and they'll find them and we need to be a long way away from here before that happens, now climb into the back of this jeep, lie on the back seat so I can see your face and then cover your face with that blanket.'

'Why have I got to cover my face and what about Bridget,' pleaded Theresa.

''Cos I don't want you to know the route I take; now cover your face, we'll talk about your sister soon, just do as you're told and cover up and shut up, you can call me Skinner.'

Next thing that Theresa knew, the man was pulling the blanket back off her face, she had fallen asleep and it was dark, she had no idea where they were. He picked up her bag and said, 'Come on quick.'

She followed him up the wooden steps and into a wooden cabin where he started the generator and put on the lights. He lit a fire in the brick fireplace and grilled some lamb and potatoes, they both looked at each other as they ate. After they finished eating, he said, 'Take those clothes off.'

Theresa did as she was told, she had already seen this man kill two men without a second thought. 'What are you going to do to me,' she asked.

'Nothing,' he replied as Theresa stood there completely naked. 'I want you to go and have a shower, I want you to scrub away any traces of blood or river mud and then I want to inspect you after the shower.' He led her to the bathroom and said, 'Now shower.'

Theresa came back sometime later still naked and the man inspected her body hair and nails, he then gave her a shirt and said put this on and get some sleep and pointed to a bedroom with no door. It was early morning and Theresa was being woken by Skinner he had some clothes in his hands and said, 'Put these on,' and handed her some fresh khaki shorts and a shirt.

'Then come and get some breakfast and be quick,' said Skinner; they ate breakfast quickly and then Skinner said, 'Follow me and be quick.' He unlocked a door, they went in and Theresa let out a shocked gasp. She was faced with about five crocodiles and she stopped in her tracks. 'They're dead, they're not gonna hurt ya,' he said. 'Now take hold of these,' and handed her a shotgun and cartridges, he then picked up a sighted rifle another shotgun and another box of bullets.

'Come on let's go,' he said as he locked the door and walked quickly to the truck followed by Theresa. 'Now shut up and listen,' he said as they sped away,

'Yes, sir,' replied Theresa.

'I told you to call me Skinner,' he said. 'First of all, do not ask any questions do as you are told; secondly, there is a bottle of stain in my bag, get it out and stain your face, legs and arms, you need to look Australian, we're going to a place near Fremantle where you arrived yesterday and if anyone recognises you, we are both dead and thirdly, we are going to try to find Bridget.'

Theresa started to cry and jumped on him threw her arms around him and kissed him as she said, 'Thank you.'

'Calm down,' he said, 'what we're about to do is highly dangerous you need to do exactly as you're told, clear.'

'Yes,' said Theresa, 'I'll do anything you ask, thank you.'

They had travelled about 30 miles and daylight had broken, he stopped the truck, they were in the middle of the outback, he told Theresa to get out and bring the shotgun.

'We've got about four hours for you to learn how to drive a truck, read a compass and fire a shotgun so pay attention, my life, your life and your sister's life could depend on how quickly you learn today.'

The Holiday

Dennis stood at the front of the room and finished his brief on the three killings and said, 'Finally, we can get our coffee and then DI Bramley will continue the brief.'

'Thank you,' said Paul to Dennis, who then continued, 'We are looking for what we believe to be a serial killer, already three members of crew from a ship called 'The Pharaoh' are dead and we believe that this killer will target other members of that ship's crew. We have a killing in Liverpool, Manchester and Birmingham, we are already working closely with the Liverpool and Manchester police and now we need all of the witness statements from the area of the hit and run in Birmingham and we need them quickly, then we need the plate and owner of the car, if it's hired, who from, if it's stolen, who from and why not reported. I need this information ASAP before the trail goes cold.'

D.I. King spoke, 'Mac is already on that, Paul.'

'Thanks, Col,' replied Paul, who went on, 'Work with me, let's get on it.'

Paul went on, 'The Pharaoh operated the Liverpool to Fremantle route for some years, transporting immigrants to Australia with varying crew numbers. I need a complete list of all crew members and passengers from The Pharaoh on every Australian voyage.'

A voice from the back said, 'You're joking, Gov, we're talking thousands.'

Paul looked at the detective and said, 'If you can't work with me, I don't need you on this team.'

In reply the detective said, 'No, I didn't say I can't work with you, Gov. I'm just saying that's a big list and it will take some time.'

Just then the office phone rang, Colin took the call as Paul spoke on, Colin interrupted and said, 'Paul, we've got the autopsy on John Fisher, the guy who died on the building site, he died from rat poison.'

Paul looked puzzled and asked, 'Well, how does that tie in, mate.'

'Well, apparently from the marks on the body it was administered in a large dose in his spine between his shoulder blades, it looks like a needle dart was fired at him.'

Skinner 1946

Theresa was surprisingly quick to learn how to drive, Skinner told her, 'You don't need any highway code in the outback and you didn't need any mirror skills, you might not see another truck for four days, you just need to know how to steer, change gear, brake, accelerate and fire a shotgun on the move and that's what I'm gonna teach you.'

Skinner showed her how to break open a shotgun, load it and fire it, he explained that this was a sawn-off shotgun, its purpose was for maximum damage, noise and spread at close range. She was shocked at just how loud and frightening it was as she pulled the triggers and there was a huge recoil that frightened her.

'I don't think I can do it, Skinner,' she said.

'Then we'll go back to my cabin and we'll forget about Bridget, I can't do this alone,' he replied.

When she heard Skinner say this, she knew she had to try harder, she had to do it or Bridget was lost, the instruction continued. Three hours later they were on the road again and now Theresa was learning how to fire a sawn-off shotgun from a moving truck. They stopped by a stream for a well-earned rest, Skinner made them a coffee.

'I knew about the ship 'The Pharaoh' even before you told me, Theresa. I just didn't know any of the immigrants aboard.' Skinner went on, 'Those two men I killed are just a small part of a huge white slave trade, they would have killed you as soon as look at you. I have been tracking slave traders as long as you've been alive Theresa and today will be a very dangerous day, slave traders move very quickly and most deals are done within 2 or 3 days.'

Skinner continued, 'The girls and boys normally come into Fremantle mainly from England and are sold and shipped out on the west coast, all done before the authorities can trace them, the young girls fetch big money from Arabs. You'll have to be braver today, Theresa, braver than you've ever been in your whole life if you want to save Bridget.'

Theresa sipped her coffee and said, 'Do you think we can save her.'

'Yes, I believe we can, but my biggest problem is how I recognise her from all the other kids.'

'That's easy,' replied Theresa. 'She's 11 and got a big beauty spot on her right cheek just under her eye and she always plats her hair both sides.'

'I hope that'll be enough,' said Skinner, 'I don't know how many kids will be there today. We don't have much time, so remember when I ask or signal you to fire your shotgun, you must, you don't have to be accurate or hit anything,' said Skinner. 'You just have to make a frightening and shocking noise, but you have to do it exactly when I signal and not hesitate, do you understand.'

'Yes, I understand,' said Theresa.

Heinz Bergen

Too many hours had passed with no word from Ridgeway, Coppin thought, he should have found Deny by now and reported back. All the states of Australia are huge and all have limited police resources for tracing, following and catching hardened criminals such as bank robbers, rapists, paedophiles and murderers. For decades all states have unofficially used experienced man hunters and mercenaries to catch and often 'deal' with serious criminals. Everyone's a winner, the threat and suspect disappear and the state has clean hands and achieves all this at an all-in-one price if they can find the right man.

Heinz Bergen was that man, no one knows how many men Heinz has hunted and killed and nobody cares, it is the lawless outback and all the states are willing to look the other way and simply pay the price, dead or alive. Coppin walked into a downtown pub and sat discretely in the corner, as he knew Heinz Bergen was a regular in this place, he really did not want to send more men after one girl but he could not let things get out of hand, if the girl was dead or had somehow escaped and the police or authorities found her, his business would be worthless; not to mention the possibility of a very long prison sentence, if it was necessary he would employ Heinz Bergen.

Coppin had another beer and waited patiently, he was just about to leave when in walked Heinz, Coppin watched as he got a beer and spoke to some guys at the bar. Coppin waited for about ten minutes and then walked over to Heinz and said, 'Fancy a beer, mate.'

'I will have a beer, Coppin,' said Heinz, who went on, 'I saw you sat in the corner, Coppin and thought this is not your regular watering hole, so something tells me this is not a social call.'

'Are you still in the game, mate,' asked Coppin.

'And what game is that,' enquired Heinz.

Coppin went on, 'The hunting game.'

Heinz took a mouthful of beer and said, 'I know what game you're in, Coppin and my good sense tells me your half arsed fucking soldiers have lost something of yours and fucked up and you're here to ask a professional to get you out the deep shit.'

Coppin looked down at the bar and in whispers said, 'I'm missing two men and a girl, the men were on about a four-hour job, six at most and they weren't back for an important event.'

'Let me guess,' said Heinz, 'Some of your 'stock' has escaped and missed an auction, not the first time, is it, Coppin; that's the problem mate with employing amateurs, who were the men,' asked Heinz.

'You don't need to know,' replied Coppin.

'Well, if you're gonna play secret squirrel games, mate, I'll just drink this beer and fuck off,' said Heinz.

Coppin hesitated for a few seconds and then said, 'No wait,' after another pause, he said, 'It was Ridgeway and Weeronga.'

'Well, no wonder you can't get the fucking job done, mate, Ridgeway is not a man hunter he's a part time crocodile hunter and the other fucker is an abo tracker,' replied Heinz, who went on, 'As far as I remember crocs don't carry guns and don't fucking shoot back and who was the girl,' asked Heinz. Coppin told Heinz.

Men like Heinz can be trusted to take a job or forget every detail they've heard, their reputation is built on this unlawful trust. Heinz said, 'So Coppin, are you telling me that you sent Ridgeway, a fucking crocodile hunter and Weeronga after a fourteen year old girl who escaped from an immigrant ship, who had no money, no fucking vehicle and she was in a strange country that she knows fuck all about and she managed to escape all on her own, you'll have to do a fucking sight better than that load of bollocks, Coppin; so either tell me why you've come to find me to do a job for you, that your own men can't do or just fuck off.'

Coppin reluctantly told Heinz the truth.

'So, Denny, Bingo and the girl are missing and the two blokes you sent to find 'em are also missing, right; well, this is what's happened, mate, if those incompetent bastards have not come back, there's options, Denny and Bingo could have fucked off with the girl, but they won't have, even them pair of stupid bastards know you've got a long reach and memory; they wouldn't cross you, but they've already been gone too long, so something has happened, so if you want me to find these bastards and the girl alive or dead, it's gonna cost.'

'How much,' asked Coppin.

Heinz replied, 'To clean up the tracks and all the fucking mess and make it all disappear will cost you 300 Australian for each of the five and you better look sharp mate, 'cos if they're dead, how long will it take for some farmer, passers-by, fucking do-gooder, back-packer or even a cop to stumble across 'em and if it becomes national news, I'll be out of it and you'll be hunted by every cop in Aussie. The track's getting colder by the minute, Coppin; make your mind up here and now, if you don't want it, we have never had this chat and I know fuck all about any of the five, take it or leave it, when I've drunk my beer, I'll be gone.'

Just then Jonesy walked in and straight up to Coppin, he pulled him to one side so Heinz couldn't hear and said, 'No word from Ridgeway yet, boss.'

'Fuck,' said Coppin, who thought for a few seconds and then turned to Heinz and said, 'OK, you're on it, but I need that girl back ASAP but only if she's still alive, if she's dead get rid of her as wel., I need her back tonight if possible, so you need to start straight away.'

Coppin did not want to pay 1,500 Australian but if this mess escalated out of control and into the news channels his whole multi-million-dollar business empire could simply collapse, he reluctantly agreed.

Heinz said, 'If I'm taking the job, you'll give me 700 Australian now.'

Coppin replied, 'I don't carry that sort of cash, mate.'

Heinz said, 'You came here today, Coppin, looking for me and you didn't come alone or fucking skint. I know what back up you've got outside and I know exactly where they are, you fucking know I'm not here alone. So don't fuck me about, Coppin.' Heinz went on, 'We'll go out to your car, you'll give me the cash you brought with you today, then I'll fuck off and contact you only when the job is done, when you'll pay me the 800 balance. You will not contact me again over this matter and you will pay me the balance whether all five are dead or not.'

Coppin had told Heinz that Denny had a farm in Maddington and he was certain that was where he was heading and that he had sent Ridgeway on the canning river road to Maddington. Heinz left that same day on the same route that he assumed the men had taken, there is only one road to Maddington from Fremantle and that is along the canning river road.

Heinz took Tom with him, they went back years both leaving the military and working unofficially for all the Australian states as bounty hunters, Heinz drove and Tom was looking for anything that might give them a clue. The Canning River Road was a dust road hardly used by anyone but sheep farmers.

They had been driving for about two hours when Tom said, 'Stop, mate.' They both got out the vehicle and walked up to what looked like a corpse, 'It's a roo, mate, the crocs have just had a roo.'

They stretched their legs and drank from their canteens. 'This is a dirt track road mate; they won't have been travelling at any great speed. I know they won't be at Denny's farm mate, Coppin would have had that checked out, so they didn't make it there, so they must be along this road somewhere.'

They both got back into the vehicle and drove on, suddenly Tom thought he saw something. They backed up and got out to see just part of a truck wheel inches below the water, very easy to miss. Heinz stood guard for crocs as Tom waded out to the truck and disappeared under the water.

Breaking the surface Tom shouted to Heinz, 'It looks like two trucks mate, a burn out and the other one crashed into it.'

'What do you reckon, mate,' asked Heinz.

'Dunno, mate,' said Tom, 'In one truck there's a bloke with half a head and in the second truck there's two dead blokes in the back.'

'Let's have the bodies out, mate,' said Heinz.

Both men dragged the bodies to the bank. 'Look at that face, mate; half his head has been blown away he's beyond recognition, looks like by a shotgun but look at his arm, no twat is gonna have Bingo tattooed on their arm if it's not their fucking name.'

'It's bingo alright,' said Tom. 'He's known for his tattoos and he's a fat bastard and that's definitely Ridgeway and Weeronga and it looks like holes through their necks, I had plenty of run ins with them bastards.'

'They've been killed with a crossbow mate, there's only a short list of men who kill or would risk killing like that,' said Heinz, 'And I already have an idea whose work this is, Tommy boy; obviously, nobody has found these bodies so let's get rid of 'em so no fucker ever does and let's drag them trucks down river into deeper water where there's more reeds.'

'We're still missing the girl and Denny mate, now I know Denny is not a solo act and I also know he's not clever enough or stupid enough to cross Coppin, so he must be round here somewhere.'

The men buried all three bodies in the soft bank mud under some reeds and laid big rocks on top of them. They took it in turns to wade the river in a crisscross fashion while the other walked the bank with a rifle watching for crocs. After a couple of miles Heinz found part of a leg of a pair of jeans in reeds.

It had part of a human leg inside the boot, Heinz brought the leg to the bank and said to Tom, 'Them three all had both legs mate, so this is part of number four.'

They concluded that with the teeth mark and rips on the thigh it was obviously a croc attack, that this leg had not been in the water for long, it was a man's boot, leg and foot, both men agreed that this leg was likely to be Denny's leg. They disposed of the leg and then dragged the trucks in the river to a deeper part of the Canning River where the trucks sank out of sight of the road.

Even though it was late they began a second search for the girl, but when it started to get too dark, they agreed it was time to call it a day and since there had been no reported missing persons or river searches in the last few days, they were also quite confident that no one was aware of these bodies.

Heinz and Tom went to a shearer's bar, it was dark and late, talking quietly in the corner over a couple of beers, 'We've got three definite ID's mate,' said Heinz.

'And we've got a probable ID on Denny,' said Tom, he went on, 'Ridgeway and Weeronga were executed by a crossbow and the tracks in the bush were made by their boots and a girls footprints mate, but no sign of a girl now.'

Tom continued, 'On the river bank where we found Ridgeway and Weeronga mate there was another man's boot prints and a girls bare footprint and then no girl footprints after the bodies, that means unless she can fly, she stepped into a vehicle, the boot prints belong to our cross-bow killer who stepped into the same vehicle, that's why we found no more foot prints going north or south from the river. I think the girl has been taken by some farmer or hunter or was rescued, by whoever used that fucking crossbow and he knows how to cover tyre track's.'

'Them killings haven't been reported or that river would be crawling with cops,' said Heinz, he went on, 'Nobody knows about them killings apart from us, some fucker with a crossbow and the girl. Coppin doesn't need to know about the crossbow, Tommy boy, that little secret could make us a few more Aussie dollars mate.'

Coppin

Coppin was in the office when Jonesy came back and told him they'd found Lol, Jonesy said, 'We found him, boss, he was pissed in some brothel, so there'll be no witnesses; they were glad to get rid of the cunt, they'll think we were just taking a drunken sailor back to the ship.'

'Is he on the ship now,' asked Coppin.

'Yes, boss,' said Jonesy, 'After we'd got him on board and pumped him full of morphine, we broke both his legs, it was quieter that way.'

'Jonesy,' said Coppin, 'Get it touch with Patrick, he's in the returning crew, tell him there's a big bonus for him when he returns to Fremantle in three months. First, he needs to see Peterson put Lol over the side in the Indian Ocean on the return voyage and then Peterson needs to disappear the day The Pharaoh docks in Liverpool.'

The phone rang and Jonesy picked it up, 'Its Heinz, boss,' said Jonesy handing the phone to Coppin.

'What you got, Heinz,' said Coppin.

'Do you want the good news or bad news first,' replied Heinz.

'Don't fuck me about Heinz, just tell me what you've got,' said Coppin, indicating to Jonesy to get a couple of beers.

'In the Canning River we've found three and a half bodies, Coppin and two wrecked vehicles, the three full bodies are definitely Bingo, Ridgeway and Weeronga, the half body is almost certainly Denny, we've dragged the trucks to deeper water and buried the bodies, but the girl has gone.'

'What do you fucking mean gone,' said Coppin.

'From the tracks it looks like she was taken or rescued by someone, there's no female body and her tracks just disappeared, so unless she can fly or has been taken by a croc, she's been lifted into some kind of vehicle, a boat or more likely an off roader.'

Coppin paused and then said, 'OK, Heinz,' then hung up and told Jonesy what they'd found.

Heinz Bergen

Heinz and Tommy both drank in the shearers bar, Heinz said, 'That must have been the easiest 1,500 Australian we've ever earned, Tommy boy. I'm warming to these fucking amateurs,' he said as they clanked their beer glasses together laughing.

Heinz said, 'Do you remember two years ago, Tommy boy, when we did that job in Darwin and two slave traders working for Ronnie had already been dealt with.'

'Yeah, I remember,' said Tommy.

'They were both killed with crossbow bolts, weren't they,' said Heinz.

'Oh, yes,' replied Tommy.

'That's why I told you Coppin don't need to know how his men were killed, we might get another pay day, Tom; let's pay Ronnie a visit.'

Skinner 1946

Theresa asked, 'I'm glad you're doing this for me Skinner, but why, you don't even know me.

'You'll pay me back, don't worry,' replied Skinner.

'How can I do that, I have no money.'

'We haven't got time to discuss this now, we have to move but there are some good men in this country who want this white slave trade finished, I am part of that. I am a mercenary, do you know what that is?' asked Skinner.

'No what is a mercenary?' Theresa asked.

'I kill people for money,' replied Skinner, 'Not anyone, only certain bad people and I get paid to do it by high officials in the government, in a few weeks when we're all safe I will inform my official friends where the bodies are in the Canning River and they will pay me.

The men I kill and the women are all known to the authorities and when they cease to be active, it's usually because they are dead. I have been killing these men and women for a long time. I am well known by the good and the bad and if I report someone dead, my official friends trust my word and pay me, they'll know it's true because that person will no longer be on the radar.

I am doing this for you and your sister but you are two of the first white slaves who can help me end this trade and that's how you'll pay me back; you are living witnesses and with some of my legal friends we can put an end to ships like The Pharaoh; they won't have safe docks and then the slave farms will just die a death, but first we need to rescue Bridget and go north where we cannot be found.

Now, let's not waste any more time, you must learn these hand signals and quickly, we cannot shout where we are going or they will hear us, we must work in absolute silence,' Skinner said.

He then went through a series of hand signals like the ones used by the marines and explained what they meant. 'Now, are you sure you understand,' he asked Theresa.

'Yes, I understand, Skinner,' she replied.

'Tell me now if there is anything you are not sure of, our lives and Bridget's life depend on what we do in the next few hours. What do you do if the sun is shining in your face,' he asked Theresa.

'I mustn't use the field glasses,' she replied.

'Why not,' he asked.

'Because they could reflect the sun like a mirror and give away our position,' she replied.

'Good girl, you are a very brave girl and today you must try to remember everything I've taught you, there will be a lot of bad men and there are only two of us, we have to leave, we'll be there in 30 minutes.'

They finished their coffee, covered their tracks and left.

Croc Lake

Marcus instructed Johnny and Dave to be at the back of the convent for six in the morning on their way to the farm, where they would meet up with Sister Brenda and collect the girls, Marcus knew very well what most of his men would do to any girl they were going to lose permanently, so he was quite specific in Sarah Jane's and Amanda's case.

'Don't even think of touching either girl,' said Marcus to Johnny and Dave. 'They both have syph,' he went on, 'Coppin said, any more syph cases at the farm and the finger points straight at you two, you understand.'

'Yeah, OK,' replied Johnny.

They drove to the convent, Sister Brenda was waiting there with Sarah Jane and Amanda they were both heavily sedated, they had no cases with them, their cases had been taken off them and they were too heavily drugged to realise, they wore only their nightdress's. The other children had not yet been awoken for breakfast so none of them had witnessed Sister Brenda take the girls out the back to wait to be picked up.

Johnny and Dave loaded the girls into the back of their truck and drove away from the convent, 'Well, mate if we can't shag'em, let's have a little bet which one gets taken first,' said Johnny laughing. 'I bet 10 Australian it's the blonde one.'

The girls were coming around from the drugs as they arrived at Croc Lake, Sarah Jane said in a slow drawling voice, 'Where are we, Amanda.'

Amanda tried to reply as she was lifted from the truck and taken to the lake. Both girls were carried out several yards into the lake to where the water was about three foot deep. Johnny and Dave stood the girls in the water and quickly went back to the bank where they stood and watched.

Sarah Jane put her arms around Amanda and said, 'My mum will come and get us both, Amanda and get us better again, you'll see.'

The two men heard the splash as the crocs entered the water and saw several crocs approach the two girls, 'Remember mate 10 Australian says the blonde goes first,' with that Amanda was ripped under the water as the first croc dragged her under by her legs. 'I win, ya bastard,' shouted Dave as he clapped his hands together, 'Yahoo.'

Sarah Jane heard the men cheering and turned to look at them on the bank in her drugged state she really didn't know what was happening, she was still talking to Amanda as the giant jaws of a second croc snapped around her small body blood filled the water as the huge croc took her under, both girls were gone.

'You lucky bastard,' said Johnny to Dave. 'I was fucking certain that little blonde would have gone first.' They both laughed, then got in their truck and drove on to the farm, still laughing.

Skinner 1946

Skinner drove very slowly as he approached the farm, for two reasons, to keep the noise down and keep dust clouds from the wheels to a minimum, they parked the truck and slowly crawled to a vantage point, as planned. Theresa went to the left and skinner to the right both were careful not make any noise they could see each other and through the field glasses both could see the farm entrance and as Skinner had anticipated there were at least ten men guarding the farm, most were armed with assault rifles.

Skinner hand signalled to Theresa to make her aware the guards had field glasses and not to move for any reason. He had also told her to stay where she was hiding and wait for him to return from the farm and to keep her weapon with the safety off and if he was not back within two hours she must drive off.

He had told her to shoot any man who approached her from the farm as soon as he got within twenty feet, take his weapons and then to drive away in the truck north as fast as she could, he would make his own way back.

It was not difficult to get into the farm, after all the guards were really only expecting to be raided by armed police or the military and in quite big numbers, they were not expecting one man. Skinner got to a staircase and looked through a window where he could see the auction without needing to get into the building. The children had all been separated by gender and age and placed in paddocks like a horse fair, each paddock had the age of the children on a big sign above them and each paddock had their own auctioneer.

Girls were wearing colour coded arm bands according to age because it was an international market, no need to speak English or even ask their age or talk, just bid and pay in cash. The girls wore lighter colours as their age increased, the area attracting the most interest were the young teenage girls 12 to 15, they were the only age group stripped naked and their wrists tied together above their heads and the rope pulled over a beam so each one of the girls was standing at their full height.

All had make up, nail and toe nail polish and lipstick applied by their female 'nurses' to make them more desirable and saleable and of course, to increase their value, any body hair was removed by the 'nurses' and if the girls had pubic hair it was trimmed or shaped to cater for the clients. The girls of Bridget's age wore yellow arm bands and the boys were colour coded in the same way. The nurses, nuns and morphine all played an important role in these auctions.

The nurses were a mix of oriental and middle-eastern origin, although there were some Aussie girls in charge of the nurses. It was in the interest of the nurses to make 'their' girls as attractive as possible there were big bonuses to be made.

Skinner counted approximately thirty guards inside and probably ten outside, he knew these types of auctions were over in a matter of hours to avoid the police or authorities getting onto them, the clients were varied and always there by invitation and a good proportion of these children would be out of the country in the next 24 hours. There was a lot of foreign buyers although most of the end clients were not there personally, why would they risk being caught when an agent could do all the risky jobs for them based on historical purchases and the end client's personal preferences.

Skinner looked towards the 11-year-old girl pen, but there were only six or seven girls there, none of whom matched Bridget's description, there were trucks and vans all over the place loading their cargos as soon as they were purchased, they always loaded their vehicles inside the building so that when the doors were opened there could be one very quick exit.

Suddenly, Skinner saw a 'nurse' putting foundation on the face of a girl who was wearing an 11-year-olds arm ribbon, she had plats and it looked as if the 'nurse' was trying to cover a beauty spot on her right cheek, not all nationalities saw beauty spots as a mark of beauty. That must be Bridget, he watched the 'nurse' bring her back and several bids were made before the final bid and she was loaded into yellow truck and Skinner noted the colour and the registration plate, he had seen what he needed to see.

He had watched this slave trade flourish in the past few years and the British and Australian authorities turned a blind eye, even the churches and convents didn't have clean hands. Their main objective was to rid Britain of war orphans and populate Australia, if a few thousand kids fell by the wayside so what. The Australian authorities didn't have anything close to the resources needed to police the whole of Australia so why publicly admit that the trade even existed and make a rod for your own back.

The buyers would soon leave, the whole essence of this type of operation is speed and the immigrant ships would arrive and discharge the illegal slave cargo. They would appear at auction farms within days and often be shipped to another country, the whole business relied on speed and usually it was conducted within 36 hours, the bidders always travelled separately from their new purchases, why would they take risks, after all they could enjoy their new acquisitions when they arrived back in their own country, now Skinner needed to get back to Theresa.

Marcus

Clients attended these farms by invitation only, they were allowed just forty minutes to view the goods before the auction and as normal there were only thirty to sixty 'items' available. Everyone knew it was time critical, after forty minutes viewing there was one hour and twenty minutes to bid, buy and disappear, as soon as two hours had passed the sale was finished and the farm completely dismantled.

Coppin employed Marcus to organise his farms, he was an expert at setting up the slave farms with his men, conducting the auctions and clearing the farms at speed. It also meant Coppin had clean hands, nothing connected Coppin to the convent or Marcus, all transactions where in cash.

The Holiday

In the ops room the team were assembled and Paul pointed at the clip board and started, 'From the witness statements of the hit and run, we've identified the car; it was stolen from a Birmingham railway car park, the real owner was out of the country and he is clean.' Paul went on, 'The car was then left in the corner of a market car park but blood samples from the car match the victim's blood type, there is no doubt it was the car.'

Colin continued, 'Further from witness statements we can confirm that it was a killing, witnesses saw the car accelerate into the victim and then reverse over him, the killer chose this particular car to steal because it has a small rear screen which makes it difficult to see the driver, part of the reason we have no clear description of the driver.'

Paul continued, 'However, eight of the ten witnesses did say the driver looked small and it so happens that the entry wound from the cross-bow bolt would suggest that the killer was smaller than the victim.'

One of the detectives said, 'Gov, if that's all we've got, that the killer is small, with respect sir were clutching at straw's.'

The Watching

Theresa had laid perfectly still for what seemed like hours as she watched the farm through the undergrowth and as instructed, if she needed to urinate, she would have do so into her pants where she lay, rather than move and give her position away.

Theresa was just a 14-year-old girl, she had only learned to fire a rifle today she was not an elite soldier trained in the art of warfare and just couldn't bring herself to wet her own pants as she lay in the undergrowth and after all she was hidden in bushes. She quietly moved to her left, sat up, pulled down her pants, careful not to move the bushes and squatted behind a bush to urinate.

At the farm Johnny said to Dave, 'Did you see that.'

'What,' said Dave.

'Look at that bush area across the road,' said Johnny, they both stared through their binoculars towards the spot Johnny had indicated.

Theresa got ready to move back into her lying position to watch the farm, as she pulled up her pants her binoculars around her neck swayed forward and backward acting like a reflecting mirror and sending out another flash.

'There,' said Johnny, 'did you see it that time.'

'Yes, I did, mate,' said Dave. They both concentrated their binoculars and focused on the area and as Theresa got back down in her position, Dave said, 'Did you see her.'

'Yeah, I fucking saw her,' replied Johnny. 'Go and get Ricky, tell him what's happening.'

Ricky came immediately with two more guards and said to Johnny and Dave, 'How many are there.'

'We can only see one teenage girl or in her early twenties by the look of it Rick,' said Johnny, 'She's not moving Rick and I'm certain I could take her out from here.'

'No, for fuck sake don't do that Johnny, a teenage girl won't be working alone and we don't want to frighten her mates away, do we,' said Rick, he indicated to Johnny and Dave saying, 'You two go and get her, don't kill her, bring her back to me as soon as possible, we need to know who she's working with.'

Rick turned to the other two guards and said, 'You two watch this gate.'

Oblivious to the fact that she had given away her position, Theresa lay very still and watched intently and saw a tiny movement 300 or 400 metres away moving towards her, she could only make out it was someone approaching and slowly raised her rifle ready to shoot.

The person still moved towards her but she couldn't make out who it was because the camouflage they were wearing was so good, but they moved so quickly toward her, she just wet her pants in fear. Then the figure disappeared from sight and as Theresa looked into the far distance another man appeared and through her binoculars, she could see this time it was Skinner.

She saw him raise his sniper's rifle and point it straight at her, Theresa began to panic and then suddenly heard a twig snap behind her and turned quickly to see a big man behind her with a rifle, he reached down to grab her as his chest exploded and liquid spattered across the back of her thighs, as the man fell heavily right next to her with a heavy thud. She looked to her left and saw a second man raise his gun, but before he could pull the trigger his face became a mass of blood and bone as it blasted out the back of his head, he also fell behind her.

She lay silent between the two dead men petrified, shocked and covered in their blood spatter, she buried her face into the ground from pure fear and to stop her screams from being heard. She summoned all of her courage to bring herself to look up and realised it was Skinner, she breathed a deep sigh of relief, he was hand signalling her to remain silent and keep still. If you were not looking for Skinner or aware of his previous position you would never have picked him out in his camouflage.

Skinner edged towards Theresa and signalled her to carefully and very slowly move backwards, they both quietly retreated not making a sound and moved back away from the two dead men back to their truck and drove safely out of sight of any more farm guards.

Theresa was still in shock and covered with blood as they drove away, she began to sob, 'I didn't see them creep up on me, Skinner. I'm sorry, I'm so sorry.'

'It doesn't matter, Theresa, they could have crept up on me just the same, these men are trained killers and do it all the time.'

Theresa calmed down for a moment and then suddenly remembering why they were here said, 'Did you see Bridget, Skinner, tell me did you see her,' she pleaded.

'Yes, she's there, she was loaded into a yellow Ute truck,' said Skinner, 'and we're gonna follow it and get her back,' he replied.

Skinner 1946

Theresa looked at Skinner in shock, saying, 'Really, really, thank you.'

Skinner had to pull her face into his chest, saying, 'Shuuush, be quiet, they'll hear us.'

As she began sobbing uncontrollably, she threw her arms around him saying, 'Thank you, thank you.' She kissed and hugged him in gratitude, he hugged her back recognising her relief that they'd found her sister. 'What's a Ute truck,' asked Theresa.

'It doesn't matter, just look through your binoculars for a yellow van with white wheels, it'll be leaving that farm very soon,' they stood and hugged for a few minutes.

'Now listen, Theresa, they knew we were here,' said Skinner. 'Those two guards did not find you by accident, they knew we were here and someone sent them to kill us, it will only be a matter of time before they send more guards and find those two bodies, they'll almost certainly be looking for us now, they know our position, so we need to be extremely careful.'

'How did they know we were here,' asked Theresa, 'And what do we do now.'

'We wait,' said Skinner. 'These markets need to be over quickly, especially if they think they have uninvited visitors, we wait and just hope this market disperses before they discover two guards are missing and come looking for them and us.'

Marcus

Marcus shouted with urgency, 'Move, move, move it,' he was telling Jack who was second in command to get the farm cleared as soon as possible as two of his men, Warragul and Ricky came running to him, 'Marcus, Johnny and Dave are dead,' said Warragul.

'What,' Marcus shouted in surprise, Warragul spoke up, 'Ricky here, sent them out to investigate what he thought was a teenage girl in khaki's lying in the undergrowth over the road from the farm.'

'And,' shouted Marcus questioningly.

'Well, they were gone for about fifteen minutes and then you shouted to wrap up and move out and Ricky went to find out where Johnny and Dave were, he found 'em both dead.'

'How were they killed,' asked Marcus.

'It looks like high powered rifle, both were blown apart.'

'Fuck me,' said Marcus, 'a teenage girl on her own did all that, I don't fucking believe it. Johnny and Dave weren't beginners, Coppin will go fucking berserk. Ricky check no one else is missing and make sure Johnny and Dave won't be found anytime soon and be fucking quick about it and be careful that girl won't be working alone I guarantee. I need to let Coppin know what's happening.'

'Warragul, you go and tell Jack I want this farm deserted in ten minutes, go.'

Skinner 1946

About twenty minutes later vehicles started to leave the farm and just as Skinner had predicted the new owners left in their own cars to go back to the city. Their new purchases left in a variety of other vehicles heading mainly to northern and eastern coast ports.

Skinner and Theresa watched carefully through their field glasses, scanning the occupants of each vehicle, suddenly Theresa hand signalled to Skinner both of them focusing on a yellow truck with white wheels. The vehicle approached the farm exit and the barrier was raised, skinner noted the registration plate, it was the vehicle Bridget had been loaded in. There were two men occupants in the front seats and a 'nurse' and at least two of the occupants wore yellow, the vehicle turned north.

'Is it Bridget,' asked Skinner as Theresa fixed her binoculars on the truck, she focused in on the van as it sped toward them, 'Is it Bridget,' repeated Skinner urgently.

Theresa was looking harder and harder and then she replied in an excited voice, 'Yes, it's Bridget.'

She collapsed on the ground with relief and started crying. Skinner knew there were not too many destinations north on that road, they were heading towards Alice Springs, but they wouldn't be stopping, they were almost certainly on their way to Darwin, these young white slaves could triple their price abroad. Theresa pulled herself together and asked, 'When those guards came looking for us, how did they know we were here.'

'It doesn't matter about that,' replied Skinner, 'What's more important is, are you absolutely certain that Bridget was in that yellow vehicle.'

'Yes,' said Theresa without hesitation, 'She was wearing her red hat that mum made for her,' she went on. 'Did I give our position away while you were at the farm,' asked Theresa.

'Theresa, it really doesn't matter, all these men are trained hunters and killers, you have only just learned how to fire a gun and you were a very brave girl today and we're going to get your sister back and we better leave now, they'll be looking for us as soon as the farm is empty and they've notice the missing guards.'

They both jumped in the Jeep and drove off, 'We're going over country to catch up with that truck,' said Skinner. 'There are too many vehicles on the road from the farm at the moment to follow them directly but there are no places to stop for over 80 miles and that is the only road north, they can only follow that route and by then most of the vehicles will have veered off to different destinations.'

Skinner stopped the Jeep and found two small bush clumps, he quickly tied them to the rear of the truck and put them on the rear seats, told Theresa, 'When I tell you throw those bushes out the back of the Jeep, they'll create a dust cloud, now get in, let's find Bridget.'

Sure enough after miles of cross country driving Skinner reached the road going north and ahead of them they could see tyre dust from a vehicle, they had driven for miles and miles and for what seemed like days but eventually they had caught up with the vehicle ahead, as they got closer Skinner told Theresa to use her binoculars and see what vehicle it was, she identified the yellow truck and confirmed the plate.

Skinner said to Theresa, 'We've got 'em, now listen carefully, when we get close, you must not be recognised by Bridget as we pass their vehicle so make sure your 'Akubra' covers your face completely.'

After about twenty minutes they were right behind the vehicle and close enough to see it was the truck. Theresa looked intently from under her hat and said, 'I can see Bridget.'

'Keep your Akubra covering your face as we pass them,' said Skinner. They passed the truck and raced on ahead Skinner was deliberately creating a great dust cloud with the bushes tied to his truck, it forced the truck to slow down until there was some distance between both vehicles.

When they'd put about four miles between themselves and the truck, Skinner said, 'Theresa, listen to me very carefully, next time we drive over a rough holed surface of road that'll force the truck to slow right down, that will be the perfect spot for you to wait to get a clear shot at the tyre. I'm gonna drop you off at the next convenient undergrowth or trees on your side of the road so you can hide,

OK. After the truck hits the holes in the road it will not have picked up much speed as it gets to you, do you understand,' asked Skinner.

'Yes, I know what to do,' she replied.

'I will drive a little further along that same road, I will not be far away do not be scared,' said Skinner, 'You will not be on your own but if you want to get Bridget back, you must do exactly as I say. Are you frightened,' enquired Skinner.

'Yes,' replied Theresa.

'You'll be OK.'

Jess

One of Jack's new boys went along to the tailor's shop, Jack knew Rose had never seen Keith. He walked into the shop and Rose came to the counter, 'Can I help you, sir,' she said.

'Yes,' said Keith, 'I'd like to be measured for a new suit, can I speak to the tailor.'

'I'm afraid he won't be back for an hour or so, sir; he's with a client but I can show you the materials catalogue and even measure you if you wish.'

'That sounds OK to me,' said Keith, 'and I've got another colleague who'd also like a suit.'

'Well, you know where we are,' replied Rose as she walked around the counter with her tape measure.

'No, he's here with me today just outside,' said the man.

'Well, call him in,' Rose answered.

The man went to the door and gestured for his friend to come in and then returned to the counter where Rose began to measure his chest, Rose heard a man walk in and stand behind her, she turned to say hello and froze on the spot, it was Billy with two other men, she nearly passed out.

Skinner 1946

A few miles further on Skinner said, 'I can see a place up ahead with some bushes on your side and a big dip in the road, can you see it.'

'Yes,' replied Theresa. I'm going to drop you there, stay hidden and out of site,' said Skinner. 'Just do as I say, stay low in the bush and then as the truck approaches and has to slow down, fire your shotgun at the tyres, just like we practised, after your shot do not stand up, stay lying down so they do not see you, be sure to keep the gun low, it's just the tyres your aiming at and do not fire high or at the windows, just the tyres, do you understand.'

'Yes,' replied Theresa.

'Make sure once you have shot out the tyres, you remain perfectly still and hidden, do you understand,' said Skinner.

'Yes,' said Theresa, 'You don't need to keep telling me the same thing, Skinner. I'm not eight, you know.'

'Repeat to me what I've just told you,' demanded Skinner.

'Shoot just the tyres, after the shot do not stand up, stay lying down so they can't see me, keep the gun low and do not shoot at the windows and when I've shot out the tyres remain perfectly still,' said Theresa.

'Good girl,' said Skinner, he went on, 'Leave the rest to me but make sure once you're on the roadside and settled that your safety catch is off, the truck will only take three or four minutes to get here, are you ready.'

'Yes,' replied Theresa.

'Here we are, jump out quickly,' Skinner said as he skidded to a stop. 'I'll be up ahead where you see those bushes on the right hand side of the road, remember as soon as you're in position make sure your safety catch is off.'

He stopped quickly and briefly and Theresa jumped out and hid in the roadside. Theresa did exactly as she was told and lay down under the cover of the bushes, she took off the safety catch and waited for the truck.

Skinner drove off into the bushes three or four hundred yards ahead of Theresa and out of site of the road. He picked up his sighted sniper's rifle and took up position, he could see Theresa through his field glasses and beyond her in the distance he could see the dust cloud of the truck. He quickly tied some rope around the trunk of a tree and passed the barrel of his rifle through it to keep the rifle perfectly still for an accurate distance shot, he cocked the rifle and took off the safety.

Through his rifle sights he could see the driver and passenger talking to each other as they approached the spot where Theresa was hiding. He saw the truck slow down and suddenly swerve and came to a stop, Theresa had done her part as instructed she remained perfectly still. The truck driver would simply think a rock had punctured his tyre and would not even hear the shotgun on the noisy bumpy road.

Marcus

This was a phone call Marcus did not want to make. 'Boss,' said Marcus, 'the farm's cleared but I've got some bad news.'

'Don't use names,' was the first thing Coppin said in reply, 'You're starting to give me bad news a bit too fucking often, mate, what is it this time,' said Coppin to Marcus.

'We've lost two men, boss.'

'Whaaat,' bellowed Coppin. 'Who was it this fucking time?' asked Coppin,

'It was Johnny and Dave, boss,' replied Marcus.

'How the fuck did that happen, you're supposed to be setting up and breaking down a fucking auction and these were your own hand-picked men, weren't they,' asked Coppin in an angry voice, 'Now I'm losing men every fucking week, is the farm secure.'

'Yes, boss,' replied Marcus.

Coppin went on, 'How did we lose these two.'

'All we know at the moment boss is that it looks like it was a girl,' replied Marcus.

'A fucking girl,' shrieked Coppin, 'What do you mean a girl, Johnny and Dave have done work for me in the past, they were too experienced to both be killed by one fucking girl and how did this girl kill 'em,' Coppin went on.

'They were both killed with a high powered rifle, boss,' replied Marcus.

'Well, it sounds to me like she's got some fucking mates with her then, what do you reckon.' Just then Coppin heard Jack say to Marcus, 'We're all done, Marcus, the farm's clean, we're ready to go back to Fremantle.'

Coppin said, 'Now you fucking listen to me, keep the men out of sight of that farm, but do not come back to Fremantle and don't fucking move from that phone till I phone you back,' he slammed the phone down.

Coppin

Coppin turned to Jonesy and told him what had happened at the farm, he didn't want to hear he had more dead men, he had been in this business too long not to know that something was seriously wrong, if someone was killing his men and taking his property other white slave traders would see him as a soft target if he took no action to recover them and avenge the killings. This was not the work of the Australian Authorities or any police department or it would have been all over the TV and radio channels, this was either another 'trader' or a mercenary.

Jonesy suddenly broke Coppin's thought pattern and brought him back to reality, 'Boss, I don't think Heinz is gonna find that girl at the Canning River, she just disappeared without so much as a footprint. I think the Canning River girl and the girl they saw at the farm are the same person and some fucker took her to the farm.'

'But why, Jonesy,' said Coppin.

'Well, boss, when you sent Ridgeway to find Denny, I had a quick look at the ship's Manifest in case that girl disappeared permanently, did you know she had a sister on-board with her boss and that the sister went to the auction, I think the older girl has been saved by some fucker and now whoever saved her has gone to try to save her sister; just think, boss, a blonde teenage girl disappears without a trace yesterday at the Canning River and suddenly, today we've got a blonde teenage girl mercenary across from the farm, it's just too much of a fucking coincidence for me, boss.'

Coppin sat and thought for a while and then said, 'If the girl is the same girl, she's free but how does she propose to rescue her sister, we've got about thirty armed guards at the farm.'

'I don't think they will attack the farm, boss, it's too well protected, if I was trying to rescue a girl from the farm I would watch the vehicles leaving and try and identify which one she was in, boss,' said Jonesy. 'Then you've only got a driver and perhaps two guards to deal with boss.'

'I think you might have a point Jonesy. Why would someone who was not the police or a government authority look for white slave girls or even worse try to save them.'

Coppin went on, 'Who would employ a mercenary to save a couple of sisters and what would be the gain, get me the names of the two sisters Jonesy and we'll find out who bought the one at the farm, then if you're right we'll know which truck they're following and which way they're heading.'

Jonesy replied, 'This could be another trader attempting to cut into your business boss, both girls are serious collateral, either way we better find out who's responsible and eliminate them and their business as an example to others.'

'Yes,' said Coppin, 'And we'll start with that one who killed Johnny and Dave and it will not have been that fucking girl I'll bet diamonds on it, get Marcus on the blower.'

Jonesy phoned Marcus and handed the phone to Coppin.

Coppin knew just how serious this all was, he had judges, police and government officials on his payroll and in his pocket but they will only bend so far, they all turned a blind eye to what they thought was just gun and whiskey smuggling and they did it for a price and the odd case of whiskey or something free from England.

Most of the officials knew nothing of his white slave trade empire let alone his gangster and IRA resettlement programme, Coppin knew he had thousands of living witnesses to his operation, but they were all children and most were in Arabian or African harems, foreign brothels or dead, but these two sisters could ruin him, one had already escaped and if she saved her sister there'd be two living witnesses free right here in Aussie.

If it was another trader muscling in, it could be dealt with, it would be effectively a gang war and although it would be expensive and bloody the press and authorities would still not be involved, but if this was a do-gooder or mercenary the media could be involved and the whole business exposed, his contacts in high office would disown him and run for their lives.

Coppin did not want Heinz involved to any extent, he didn't really want Heinz involved at all, but he had little choice, Coppin could not afford living witnesses to his empire running around in Aussie and he needed to take drastic action or his entire business would just crumble. He could leave Heinz to clear up the loose ends on the Canning River but at this moment any escapees were far more serious, they could blow the whistle on the whole operation, particularly if some fucker is helping them, he needed Marcus to eliminate this problem.

Marcus

The phone rang at the slave farm; a guard took the call and shouted to Marcus, 'It's Coppin, Marcus,' and handed him the phone.

'Boss,' said Marcus.

'Shut it, I won't use your name and don't use mine,' said Coppin. 'This is urgent but I'll keep it brief, I want you to get two teams of four together immediately, a mix of the men that we generally use, get it,' said Coppin.

'Yes, I get it, boss, what's the job,' asked Marcus.

'Never mind for now, do you know the 'Outback' north of where you are,' asked Coppin.

'Yes, I know it, boss,' replied Marcus, 'Get your men together and get there as soon as possible, leave as soon as we end this call and phone me at the 'Hunters Lodge', here is the number,' Coppin told Marcus the number and hung up.

IRA

Coppin arrived at the 'Lodge' with eight armed heavies and met with the group of Irishmen and some English criminals all in a discrete snug at the back of the pub, Jonesy closed the door as Coppin walked in and immediately addressed them all, in a quiet voice he said, 'You men arrived a few days ago on The Pharaoh and you're all on the resettlement programme, I'll give you all an envelope with new documents and ID's. However, in our type of business there's always something popping up and as a matter of fact something just has. I have a little bit of work for a few men, now are any of you boys looking for work.'

'What kind of work,' asked one of the Irishmen.

'Don't act fucking stupid, Paddy, you've just escaped a fucking firing squad in Ireland and been on a ship for six weeks, don't pretend you don't know what fucking business we're in, I'll ask again and only once. Does anyone want work.'

One of the Manchester murderers said, 'I'll work for you Coppin but I won't fucking work with paddies.'

One of the Irish men stood up and Mike and Scott stepped in and kept them apart to prevent a fight. 'You don't have to work with each other,' said Coppin, 'I need two groups of two, they can be two Irishmen and two others, who's in.'

'How much are you fucking paying,' asked one of the Irishmen.

'The job pays £600 for a few days' work,' answered Coppin and went on, 'If you're frightened of flying or have never used a Browning Hi-Power, fuck off, I haven't got time to piss about.'

Two Irish cousins said, 'We're in' and the two men from Manchester agreed to be the other team.

'Right, we've got our teams,' said Coppin. 'The rest of you pick up the envelopes in front of you and fuck off and if you want to enjoy a long and healthy life, this meeting and conversation never took place.'

As Coppin spoke, Barret and Jinxy stood up with their guns out and the room emptied very quickly except for the two Irishmen, the two Mancunian's, eight heavies and Coppin.

Jonesy closed the door and all the men sat down and Coppin began, he pointed at the two Irishmen saying, 'Tomorrow you two will fly with me and Jonesy to Darwin, I have some other business to take care of there anyway, he went on, have you used a Browning Hi-Power before.'

'Yes,' O'Hara replied.

'How many rounds does it hold,' asked Coppin.

'Thirteen,' came the reply.

He looked at the Mancunian's, 'You two will fly to Alice Springs with Barret and Jinxy; you'll be met there and all four of you will have 'clean' browning's. Bobby and Jim will stay in Fremantle by the phone 24/7 and keep you all informed of how things are progressing.'

Coppin explained the job to all four men, 'Tomorrow one of my men will identify a vehicle to all of you, this vehicle could be somewhere between Alice Springs and Darwin and your job is to kill all the men and boys in that vehicle, all the girls must be brought back safely, is that clear.'

They all said yes then O'Hara asks, 'Is there only one fucking truck.'

'Yes,' replied Coppin.

O'Hara went on, 'But if they're in fucking Alice Springs and we're in Darwin only one team will do the fucking killing, is that right.'

'Yes,' replied Coppin, 'I don't know at this moment in time how far north the targets are, so one pair will be paid for doing fuck all, is that clear.'

They all answered yes and then Coppin told all four men to be here tomorrow at six in the morning, then he told them to leave, the heavies stayed.

Jonesy asked, 'Boss, I thought Marcus was already on this job.'

'He is,' replied Coppin. 'This is just insurance, you've already said it yourself, Jonesy, that girl who disappeared from the Canning River without a trace is almost certainly the same girl who was at the farm and she won't have killed four men at the river and two men at the farm on her own, she's 14 and arrived with fuck all so where did she get the gun and how did she get to the fucking farm, I'll tell you how, she's got some fucker or a couple of 'em helping her and they've already killed six men, taken a girl and we don't even know who they fucking are, there could be several of them, but whoever they are they are good.'

'Well, so is Marcus, Boss,' said Jinxy.

Coppin replied, 'Judging by his or their performance so far he or they might outrun Marcus, he did have a good start on him and this job is so important I can't take that risk, he won't outrun a plane to Alice or Darwin.'

'But, boss, why employ outsiders for a job we could do ourselves,' asked Scott.

Coppin replied, 'If it goes wrong, these men don't even exist here and we can deny all knowledge of their actions, but you four are already known to the cops and authorities and you can probably be tied to me, this needs to be a clean job.' Coppin went on, 'Marcus is on the job right now he's tracking 'em from the farm.'

'Get some drinks, Barret,' the drinks arrived, Coppin leaned forward and spoke in a hushed voice, 'As soon as the planes arrive back in Fremantle, Bobby and Jim will meet you and four people who don't even exist in Australia need to be disposed of and I mean disposed, they will disappear permanently and there will be no trace left, do I make myself clear.'

'Yes, boss,' came the answer from all eight men, 'let's drink to a successful job,' said Coppin.

Barret was sent for a round of drinks when the phone rang, Jonesy took the call and handed the phone to Coppin. 'I'm at the 'Outback', Boss,' came Marcus's voice.

'Have you got your two teams, Marcus,' asked Coppin.

'Yes Boss, we're ready to go now,' replied Marcus.

'This job is so fucking urgent, I need it done as quickly as possible and as clean as a whistle, I don't want any loose ends this time, Marcus; there's some wild man or men, who killed Johnny and Dave and they've got a girl with 'em, I don't want to hear anything about the men ever again, they'll disappear, but the girl comes back without a scratch; got it, Marcus. I'll meet you in Alice Springs where you will tell me the job is fucking done; it's simple, Marcus, track, catch, kill and dispose of all the evidence, only return the girl; here's Jonesy to fill you in on their last known position,' Coppin handed the phone to Jonesy and went back to the table.

Race across Aussie

Skinner had carried out killings such as this on many occasions and knew the first target always had to be the passenger as they were more than likely to be holding a gun. Theresa had done her part and stopped the truck, now he had the first target in the passenger seat in his sight, they could not see him in the bush, he squeezed the trigger and the passengers head exploded in a ball of bone and tissue, his blood covered the driver.

The rest of the occupants screamed and lay on the floor of the vehicle but before the driver realised what had happened or could grab his gun a second bullet had found its way through the windscreen through his left eye and into his brain, both men were perfectly still in their seats, they were both dead. After a short pause Skinner walked slowly towards the truck, with his rifle in his hand and cocked, as he approached the vehicle, he could hear the children screaming in terror as they saw him approaching.

Theresa remained out of site and motionless as instructed, skinner reached the truck and slammed open all the doors, making as much noise as possible, he threw open both back doors pointing his rifle at the occupants, he had to be certain there were no more armed persons in the truck. He told them all to be quiet and step out of the vehicle, slowly one by one, they did as they were told and there were five children and a nurse.

Skinner checked there were no others in the truck and searched the nurse for weapons, he then called Theresa to show herself. Bridget could not believe her eyes and screamed with happiness and excitement when she realised it was Theresa and ran toward her, they hugged and cried and kissed, the other children relaxed a little as they watched the sisters enjoying their reunion and they all realised this man was not going to kill them, he was gonna save them.

Meanwhile Skinner, unnoticed by the children took the nurse to the back of the truck and asked who she was and for some ID. She produced an Australian Passport and said she was from Brisbane, she was petrified. He asked her where she lived in Brisbane, skinner knew Brisbane very well and he knew from her answers that she was lying and with that accent he also knew she was no Aussie. She looked Egyptian, exactly the type the slavers use to transport children across Australia.

The slavers kill single Australian girls, normally back packers and often feed their bodies to crocs or sharks so there is no trace, then they use their passports and ID for their slave nurses. Skinner took her out of site of the children, who did not notice him take her to the opposite side of the road and she did not notice because he walked behind her that he had screwed a silencer to his hand gun, it was silent and efficient, no-one would find her body in the road ditch until it was convenient for Skinner for the body to be found.

Skinner returned with the nurse's bag, purse, passport and documents he put them in the truck with her medical supplies and told Theresa to take the children quickly to the bushes up ahead where his truck was parked. He drove the yellow truck to his truck and stopped he took the fuel can from it and put it in his own truck.

He syphoned the fuel from the truck, retrieved the guns and ammunition from the two dead men and then drove the truck as far into the undergrowth as possible, so it could not be seen from the road, he marked exactly where the truck was located on his pocket map, he then returned to his truck hurrying the children to get in, he tied a large branch over each rear wheel.

'Listen to me and listen good, soon some very bad men will try to follow us and if they find us they will kill us all, you must do as Theresa and I tell you, don't ask any questions, just do as you're told.'

With that Skinner sped off as fast as the truck would go with the five children in the back seat and Theresa in the passenger seat. Skinner drove for about 5 miles before turning off road. He drove about 2 miles into the outback and then removed the branches from the rear wheels and continued slowly until out of site of the road in order not to create any visible dust clouds.

Now Skinner was several miles into outback he needed to pick up the pace he knew Coppin was behind 'The Pharaoh' operation. Coppin would need to cover a lot of tracks to keep the authorities from catching him this time. All these killings one way or another led to him and he would be anxious to find who was responsible. Skinner had already left too many clues, four men dead in the Canning River two guards at the farm and two men and a woman dead near the truck, all nine deaths related to that ship and Coppin.

The bodies may not have been totally destroyed but sooner or later they would be discovered and the two guards killed at the farm would definitely have told other guards they were going to investigate movement in the undergrowth and they may well have seen Theresa through their field glasses and mentioned her, then the bodies in the missing truck and the nurse.

Coppin would not be pleased that six of his 'cargo' were missing, he had some powerful and ruthless friends and it wouldn't take long for his ex-police friends to come up with a short list of possible suspects. Skinner knew how ruthless Coppin was and put his foot down he needed to get as far north as possible, he would only be safe in Darwin. Going back to his own cabin would be suicide. Coppin and his associates would have already put together all the pieces of information they had and his name would almost certainly come up and unwanted guests would arrive, they may even be at his cabin now.

Heinz Bergen

Heinz saw a brilliant opportunity to double his money and get paid by Coppin for killing the Canning River crossbow killer and get paid by Ronnie for delivering the body to him. Heinz and Tom went to a late-night bar, he was known by many there and he was not alone. The bar was loud and rough and he sidled up to a big rough looking sheep farmer.

'You don't smell no better than the last time I ran into you Ronnie, remember?'

'That won't happen again, Bergy,' replied Ronnie.

'I hear you're renting out your farm these days, Ronnie,' said Heinz

'A little birds told me you're having a bit of a do in six weeks, it's all arranged and the invites are already out, the Carrington farm is such a nice big place Ronnie, ideal for the business you're in.'

'Don't know what you're fucking talking about, Bergy,' said Ronnie.

'I'm glad you said that Ronnie, 'cos I was thinking of advising the police about a bit of a do going on at that very farm in a few weeks,' said Heinz.

'This ain't one of your fucking country clubs, Bergy, I've got muscle in here that can wave good bye to you forever, right here, right now,' said Ronnie in a threatening voice.

'Let's not get nasty, Ronnie,' said Heinz, 'Like that nasty bastard in the corner, oh and him over there look, Ronnie, or perhaps you hadn't noticed I didn't arrive alone, there are a few more outside Ron and even though you are a thick bastard you know what the fuck this is.' Ronnie looked down to see a sawn-off shotgun pressing into his groin.

'What do you fucking want, Bergy,' said Ronnie.

'Well, even though I know what a ruthless piece of shite you are, I might be able to settle a score even for you, Ronnie.'

'And why would you do that fucking favour for me, Bergy,' Ronnie asked.

'I heard you had a couple of your boys about the beginning of last year died of crossbow bolt syndrome, it could happen again, Ronnie, who knows.'

'Is that a fucking threat,' said Ronnie.

'No, it's a warning, Ronnie; you never got anybody for them killings, he's still on the loose and there are other interested parties who'd like to see the back of the bastard,' Heinz had a drink of beer and continued, 'For a small financial consideration and a little bit of information, I could forget about Carrington Farm business and bring you a crossbow man's corpse Ronnie, you could sleep better at night.'

Race Against Time

As Skinner's truck raced across miles of outback the children were huddled in the back of the truck not knowing what was happening. They drove for what seemed like hours and then stopped in a deserted place, right beside a waterhole. The children were tired and ached from the race across the rough stony and rocky desert but were glad to see water.

'Theresa, get your sister to get the kids fed and watered,' said Skinner, 'And do it quickly, we haven't got long, then I need to talk to you, be quick.'

Theresa did as she was told giving Bridget two steel mugs and telling her to give the kids a drink but stay clear of the water's edge and then she came back to talk with Skinner. Skinner sat her down and began, 'You've been a real brave girl today, Theresa, braver than a lot of blokes I know, but because of what we've done there'll be a lot of men after us and they will be coming to recapture all you kids and to kill me, men have been killed at the river, at the auction and now on the road.'

Theresa interrupted, 'Did you kill that nurse, Skinner.'

'Yes,' replied Skinner.

'But she wasn't armed, was she,' enquired Theresa.

'No, she wasn't,' said Skinner in an enraged voice, he went on, 'But all those men I've killed were and all of them would have sold you and your sister as slaves to whoever paid the most money and that nurse was paid to make all the girls look more attractive so that she could earn more money from selling them.'

Skinner went on, 'She was no angel, believe me and if I'd let her live she would have given the man hunters all the information they need to find us and they would pay her for that information, like how many men, vehicles and guns we have, which direction we are travelling in and how much water, food and fuel we have, she would have been very happy to sell that information even though she knows they would kill us, we're in enough trouble believe me without giving them more information.'

Skinner calmed his voice and spoke to Theresa, 'You must listen to me very carefully, Theresa, the men who are after us are killers and highly dangerous, they use professional man hunters and they use trackers to find people and kill them. I imagine there will be several interested parties, firstly they will have almost certainly discovered the bodies in the river or what's left of 'em, they will already have found the two guards at the farm and there will be a halfway house where your sister and the other kids should have stopped to eat and change drivers and of course, they'll never arrive, so they'll have a good idea what's happened, where it happened, where the bodies are likely to be and where we're likely to be.'

Skinner stopped for a drink of water and then continued, 'Those two guards at the auction will have responded because someone had seen you, so they'll know you and the five kids are alive and with someone, they will want their property back, we must all disappear and quickly.'

'But where can we go so they won't find us,' asked Theresa in a desperate voice.

'One thing at a time,' said Skinner.

'First, tie branches to the back of the truck to cover which direction we leave this watering hole.'

'But we've left tracks behind us for three or four hours,' said Theresa.

'Yes, we did,' replied Skinner, 'Do you also remember when we left the truck we covered our tracks when we left the road with branches for over an hour, even professional trackers will take a long time to find our exit tracks, but don't forget water is a very rare commodity in the outback, the aborigines and man hunters will know this water hole exists and they will definitely visit it for their own water and also to see if we've been here. My guess is we're being hunted as we speak, get the kids back in the truck we've got a long journey ahead.'

When the children were loaded in the truck, skinner filled all the water cans and then tipped diesel into the watering hole and attached two large branches over the rear wheels before driving northwards.

'Won't that poisoned water kill the animals, Skinner,' asked Theresa.

'No, they won't touch it and it'll be clear in a couple of days, but any man hunters won't be able to use that water and they can't afford to wait two days for it to clear.'

He drove at just ten miles per hour so as not make too big a dust cloud, after two hours he quickly stopped jumped out with Theresa and removed the branches.

As Theresa helped him, he said, 'If they find we were at the waterhole, they'll have to scout for around twenty miles or so to pick up our tracks and that'll take them a fair while and should give us about two or three hours.'

Skinner drove for what seemed like an eternity and as darkness fell he told Theresa and Bridget to keep talking to him and not allow him to go to sleep, he also told Theresa to make sure her shotgun was loaded, by her side, pointing out of the truck and had the safety catch on, she did that and Skinner continued to drive into the night.

In the morning Skinner was shattered and Theresa had fallen asleep, she suddenly awoke and saw Skinner with what looked like fruit, she walked across to him and said, 'Skinner, I am so sorry, I didn't mean to fall asleep,' she went on, 'What are they, Skinner.'

He replied, 'These red things are a kind of peach called quandong, these smaller ones are riberries and them over there are wild oranges, the kids will need some breakfast and they wouldn't eat wild grubs or frogs and I can't light a fire to cook anyway.'

'I'll wake the kids,' said Theresa.

'No wait till we've talked,' said Skinner, 'Because today is really important.' He explained, 'We're gonna drive about three hundred miles north,' he drew a map in the dirt as he spoke, 'Then about sixty miles to our east there is a farm, we will need to attach branches to the rear wheels and drive to that farm and then return to the same spot leaving no tracks and then drive north again.'

'Why do we need to go to the farm,' asked Theresa.

Skinner replied, 'The farm is safe, it's a sheep farm and that's where we're leaving the kid's.'

'No,' screamed Theresa, Skinner immediately gagging her. He slowly released his grip.

'I'm not leaving Bridget,' said Theresa.

'We can't take her with us,' replied Skinner, 'She's only 11.'

'Listen, mister,' said Theresa, standing up, 'We have both been dragged to this country, she is only 11 as you say and I'm only 14 and I have had to learn how to please men with sex, so they don't kill us, kill men with guns, so they don't kill us and now run away from men so they don't kill us, you have taught me a lot and I will never forget how you saved my life and Bridget's but I will not leave her at a farm now.'

'It will not be forever,' said Skinner. 'She can't do what we can do.'

'No, no, no, she's coming with us, she can learn what I know, I learned all I needed in one day and she can learn too.'

'I will teach her, I'm not fucking leaving her, Skinner.'

They drove for miles and the heat never let up, Skinner spoke after an hour or so, 'Theresa, we are going to a place called Docker River about four hundred miles to the north.'

Theresa snapped, 'I don't fucking care where we're going, I'm not leaving her.'

Skinner continued, 'No we're not leaving her, she's coming with us but yo—'

Theresa immediately interrupted him as she flung her arms around his neck and kissed him, he nearly lost control of the truck. 'Thank you, thank you,' she screamed.

'Calm down,' said Skinner, 'Now listen to me good, Theresa, we could be ten hours or just two hours in front of the man hunters, we just don't know so everything we do today in vitally important are you ready to help.'

'Yes,' replied Theresa with a big grin on her face.

'Right, get a drink of water now,' said Skinner as he stopped, 'Let the kids stretch their legs, give them all water and make sure they go to the toilet this could be our last stop for a long time and don't let the kids wonder off too far, keep them all together tell them nothing at all and send Bridget to me.'

Theresa did as she was told. Bridget came over to Skinner. 'Listen, Bridget, I know you and Theresa and the kids have been through some tough times but it will soon be over and we'll all be safe, from now on you must do everything I tell you to do, do you understand.'

'Do you mean like the sailors on the boat,' Bridget replied.

'No not like——' he paused and then went on, 'Just do as you're told, go and find two broken branches, do not break any new branches, find branches that are already on the floor about as long as your leg and bring them back here, do it quickly.'

Bridget did as she was told and then Skinner called Theresa and the other children back to the truck. 'Theresa come here,' said Skinner. 'The rest of you get back into the truck,' turning to Theresa he said, 'Show Bridget how to cover any footprints near the track left by the kids then get in the truck but keep the branches.'

The sisters cleared any footprints and then climbed aboard.

Scott the Sheep Farmer

Scott rode his camel, it's common practice in Australia, camels are perfect for this climate, sitting high on the camel's back he looked to his left and noticed an unusually large flock of Black Kites and there was a smell in the air, he went off the track to investigate, among the kites there was a woman in the undergrowth wearing Arabian clothes.

Scott got off his camel and walked closer, he frightened the remaining birds away from the woman, she had not been dead long, he felt her body still warm as he turned her face from on its side to look at her full face. He jumped back in horror, vomiting as he scrambled away backwards, her teeth were visible through the holes in her cheeks and nose from the pecking and her eyes had been completely pecked out by the birds.

Scott climbed back on his camel, threw up again, he saw the truck in the bushes but did not investigate, he'd seen enough horror for one day. He rode back to his farm and phoned the police, it would take the police some hours to reach the crime scene, but it did not take that long for Coppin to find out what had happened from his police informers, the police had found the three bodies and Coppin got all the details he needed to know; as a matter of fact, Coppin knew everything before the police detectives even arrived at the murder scene.

Race Against Time

Skinner got into the driving seat and told Theresa to look at the compass, which she did, 'In which direction are we driving,' said Skinner.

'North,' replied Theresa.

'Correct,' said Skinner as he turned the wheel to the left. 'Now which direction are we driving,' asked Skinner.

Theresa looked at the compass and said, 'West.'

'Good girl, correct again,' replied Skinner, 'Now why do you think I'm doing this.'

'To lead the man hunters to the west,' Theresa replied questioningly.

'Correct again.' Skinner drove for about two hours before stopping again, almost racing the Jeep, it didn't matter about any dust cloud, he knew at this point the hunters were too far away, but they wouldn't be for much longer.

'You and Bridget tie those branches over the wheels,' said Skinner, they did as they were told, then Skinner said, 'Theresa, you said you would do anything to keep Bridget with us, even teach her what you know, is that correct.'

'Yes, I said that Skinner,' Theresa replied.

'Well, now's the time to keep that promise. There will be men hunting us who are trained killers and trackers, few of them will be expert at both, but I am and I probably know this country better than anyone of the men who will be hunting us but there will be more of them than us. They will have at least two drivers and their trucks will never stop, they will drive night and day and even eat and drink on the move to try and catch us and to stay ahead of them we must do the same, so you're gonna drive for four hours, I need to rest.'

Skinner climbed in the back and said to Theresa. 'Drive west for two hours then north for a further two and then wake me, you said you could teach Bridget so get her in the front with you, she will have to talk to you to keep you awake and you can talk to her explaining to her what you are doing so that she can learn how to drive. Drive as fast as the road will allow, Theresa, don't wake me up unless you see another vehicle and Bridget, keep your eye on the track behind us for dust clouds, Theresa, keep your eye on that compass, west for two hours and north for two hours, now let's go.'

Theresa drove as fast as she dares and after driving for four hour's she woke Skinner.

Skinner could see both sisters were shattered and told them to stop telling them both to get in the back and sleep, he quickly tied branches to the rear wheels and turned east and looked at Theresa and asked, 'Now what do you think we're doing.'

'Covering our tracks to the east, so that the hunters will get here and our tracks just stop.'

'Correct,' said Skinner, 'So what do you think the man hunters will think.'

Bridget interrupted from the back, 'Can I tell you.'

Skinner was surprised to hear Bridget but said, 'Yes, what do you think the man hunters will think, Bridget.'

'They'll think we deliberately turned west and left tracks for a few miles and then turned north covering our tracks but continuing north and will go north looking to pick up our tracks.'

Skinner clapped his hands in approval and then said, 'Exactly right Bridget we're heading east but want them to think we have continued north to deceive them. Now what do you think we should do, Theresa.'

She thought for a moment and replied, 'With the branches still over the back wheels covering our tracks, I think we should now keep going east for as long as we can and then turn north, because you said we needed to go four hundred miles north anyway.'

'You are both exactly correct,' said Skinner.

'I hope we've deceived the hunters as Bridget said and when the tracks stop they assume we have continued north.'

Skinner said to Theresa, 'I will keep driving east with the branches over the wheels but remember at this moment in time we are just driving back to where we were two hours ago and all the time the man-hunters are coming north gaining on us, we're just hoping that the trackers will be fooled and take at least five or six hours to pick up our tracks.'

Skinner said to Theresa, 'When I've gone as far east as I dare, I'll turn north until I can't drive anymore, you will take over in four hours, now get some sleep.' Skinner told Bridget, 'You also get some sleep Bridget, when Theresa takes over the driving she'll need you to help her stay awake by talking to her, do not let your sister fall to sleep at the wheel.'

Skinner drove as fast as he dared without creating too much dust and conscious that if the man-hunters saw a dust cloud all this trickery would be just a waste of precious time, the girls slept in the back with the kids but he was getting very tired, he eventually woke the girls to change places with Theresa.

As the girls woke Bridget said, 'Look Skinner a smoke cloud to the south.'

Skinner sprung into life slowing the Jeep to a crawl, he drove into some thick bushes and stopped, turning off the engine and telling the children not to make a sound, he knew that he was about half a mile north of where he first turned west off the track, *will these man-hunters fall for the trick,* he thought.

He watched through his field glasses as they just kept coming towards them, you could almost hear hearts beating as one of the children began to cry saying, 'They're going to catch us, aren't they,' Theresa cuddled the little girl and said, 'Shuuush.

Suddenly the dust cloud stopped, obviously the vehicle had stopped. Skinner could just make out the front of a truck sticking out of the thick bush and could clearly see two men walking around looking for tracks. He saw a man kneeling checking tracks, his heart was in his mouth, then the vehicles engine fired up again throwing up a great dust cloud as it turned west, 'Do not cheer or make a noise,' he said to the girls, 'But I think they've gone for it, they're heading west, we could have bought 6 hours of time let's go.'

Theresa got into the driver's seat, 'Do not start the engine yet,' said Skinner. They waited until the sound of the hunters had disappeared. Then Theresa started her engine and drove very slowly for about 20 minutes to make as little dust as possible and then she picked up speed, Theresa headed north as the man-hunters drove west. I just need to sleep now said Skinner. With that Skinner pulled down his Akubra over his eyes, leaned back in his seat, crossed his arms and said, 'Do not wake me up unless you see another vehicle,' then he collapsed into deep sleep.

Skinner did sleep, it had been some days since he had the opportunity to rest at all. When he awoke some hours later it was dusk and Theresa's head was nodding backwards and forwards as she desperately tried to stay awake, Bridget was also a whisper away from slipping into a deep sleep. Skinner gently put his hand on Theresa's shoulder and told her to stop the truck, she was exhausted and glad to do exactly as she was told.

'You have both done very well,' he said to the sisters, 'You are both good and brave girls, now get in the back with the kids and sleep.'

They did not need to be told twice, Skinner had to lift both of them into the back, one after the other they were both completely exhausted and asleep within seconds.

Kaltukatjara

To many people Western Australia is featureless, just endless outback, with nothing to give you an indication where you are, but not to the Anangu people, this is their land and has been for thousands of years. In this area there were many Pitjantjatjara aborigines and the Anangu are part of this aboriginal mix, made up of many tribes of aborigine's and they can live in what many westerners would see as a barren landscape. Skinner's father knew Western Australia almost like the Pitjantjatjara he lived here and this was Skinner's playground as a boy, he looked around and knew exactly where they were.

Theresa and Bridget had done fantastically well and now Skinner drove through the night to an area westerners called Docker River but to the Anangu and Skinner it was known as Kaltukatjara its aboriginal name and that's where they were heading. As dawn broke it was only thirty or so miles to Kaltukatjara and the children began waking, however Theresa and Bridget slept on until they reached the kids final destination.

The Pitjantjatjara are aboriginal people of the Central Australian desert. They are closely related to the Yankunytjatjara and Ngaanyatjarra their languages are, to a large extent the same and they are all Anangu. The Pitjantjatjara live mostly in the northwest of South Australia, extending across the border into the Northern Territory to just south of Lake Amadeus and west a short distance into Western Australia. The land is an inseparable and important part of their identity and every part of it is rich with stories and meaning to Anangu.

Track and Kill

Marcus and his trackers and man-hunters were on their way at speed, he had a crew of eight experienced men including himself who were totally ruthless, they already knew they were heading north and how many they were tracking thanks to the police on Coppin's payroll, so they didn't have too many routes to choose from, it did not take them long to pick up the trail, but it was their job to track experienced men and they were expert at it.

Warragul, the head aboriginal tracker knew their quarry were experts by the way they left no fire trace or obvious tracks, Warragul was such an experienced tracker he could practically track sitting in a slow-moving vehicle, he was in the lead truck driven by Jack. All eight men could track and man-hunt but some were specialists.

Marcus's men had the edge, they had their information from police informants, a starting point to begin the hunt and they knew approximately how much of a lead their quarry had. They had at least two drivers in each truck so they could drive continuously twenty-four hours a day, seven days a week and of course, they also had eight men with guns. Skinner would have to be at his very best to outrun them.

Caroline

Andy and Caroline were expecting Skinner, but as always none of them could be sure what day or time he would arrive, in this part of the world they measure time by season or by night and day. They had been warned by a bullroarer (an ancient aboriginal tool for sending sound warnings, simply a piece of wood on a length of rope swung around the head in large circles).

Andy went back to the kitchen to speak with Caroline. "Let's talk about Skinner,' said Caroline, she continued, 'You know I know exactly how he makes his money darling, he collects the bounty, but he only needs one bent cop and he'll be dead.'

Andy said, 'Come and sit here.' Caroline sat down; Andy held her hands, looked into her eyes and spoke in a very quiet and serious voice. 'You know how much I love you, my darling woman and you are my best friend, so what I'm about to tell you must never ever be repeated, do you understand.'

'Of course, darling,' replied Caroline, recognising that Andy was deadly serious. 'This promise of silence must never ever be broken.'

'I promise, I promise,' repeated Caroline.'

Andy went on, 'Skinner does not hunt and kill men, he frees child slaves who cannot defend themselves.' Andy paused, 'His business often results in men dying, these men are nearly always wanted in one state or another and Skinner collects the reward, he never delivers a man alive, that would compromise his identity, he kills all of them.'

Caroline sat back in her chair shocked covering her mouth with both hands. Andy said, 'Don't be shocked, darling; every last one of 'em are murderers or deal in this filthy white child traffic business, they are not worthy of your sympathy or compassion, in the dangerous business he's in, he cannot afford a living eye witness.'

Caroline composed herself leaning across the table and once again holding hands with Andy. 'But when he delivers the body, the officer who gives him the money will see him, won't he.'

'No, darling,' Andy replied, 'No, since his father died, no one apart from you and me have ever seen him, they don't know his name, how big he is or how tall he is, he even darkens his skin with berry juice so that people who think they've seen him give conflicting descriptions, he just disappears like a ghost, he learned all these skills from his very famous dad.'

Andy went on, 'Skinner is known in all the states under a different alias, he never ever shows his face and he's known by a different name in Northern Territory, Queensland, New South Wales, South Australia, Victoria and Western Australia.'

'Well, how does he exchange his prisoners for the reward money then,' asked Caroline.

Andy replied, 'There's only New South Wales with enough resources to hunt men across Aussie, the other five states just have to rely on and pay bounty hunters to catch criminals, dead or alive no questions asked, Skinner has a senior police officer contact in every state, he phones a day ahead of delivery using his alias so they know it's him and they have time to get the reward money.

Skinner's rules are simple, on the day of delivery Skinner nominates a place; only hours before the exchange the police must arrive at the designated time and place and identify the body that Skinner lays on the floor, then they open the case with the reward money and slowly turn it through 180 degrees so that Skinner can verify it's money in the case through his field glasses then, leaving the case and body the officers drive back in the same direction as they came for two hundred yards, stop and turn off the engine, get out of the car. The driver on the driver's side and the passenger on the passenger's side, kneel on the floor and face the direction the police car is facing, they must not turn around.

Skinner watches the police arrive from a safe distance, open the case and then retreat to a safe spot. He then drives to the money, checks it picks it up and leaves, the cops must wait five minutes before retrieving the body. He always picks a remote spot where he could see for miles and all of his senior officer contacts know the procedure.'

'The problem is darling,' said Andy, 'Skinner has been doing this for years ever since his dad was caught and killed at a white slave child auction. Senior police officers in all the different states know he's a bounty hunter and they know his method of operation, they also know each other and must talk about work at the national police conferences, they will know that they're dealing with the same man.'

Caroline had listened intently and said, 'But why is that a problem, darling, they're all police just using a bounty hunter to get rid of criminals.'

'But Australia is changing, darling,' replied Andy, 'It's not like in 1880 Aussie and the days of Ned Kelly, the ships will stop coming at some point and Aussie wants to move forward with the rest of the world and loose this wild outback image and then Skinner will just become another outlaw, only he'll be hunted by both the gangs and the police, he needs a retirement plan and needs to disappear soon.'

Andy then went to bed but as he slept, Caroline had driven north to round up the various Anangu tribes from the Docker River. They trusted Caroline, she was Anangu and she spoke aborigine and her own tribe knew this part of Australia like the back of their hands, they owed Skinner's father a debt of honour he had prevented this land from being sold to westerners and he'd also played a major political role in ensuring this land remained the property of Anangu

Track and Kill

Warragul knew every water hole for every season in this part of Australia, he was Aboriginal, he walked around the water hole as the others took a well-earned rest, it was the first time the trucks had stopped for over three hours of fast pace over rough terrain.

Warragul squatted by the water hole and lifted two blonde hairs from the water's edge, 'They were here and not long ago,' he said as he scooped up a handful of sand near the water and carefully sniffed it, 'Human urine,' he said. 'It's not dry, we're less than fifteen minutes behind them, let's go, Jack.'

All the men jumped into the trucks and sped off. Jack driving the lead truck said to Warragul, 'If you're right mate, they'll only be six or seven miles ahead of us in this terrain.'

'I am right, Jack, they must be racing to be this far ahead and they'll be giving themselves away, everyone keep your eyes open for a dust track.'

The hunters raced on not caring if they gave away their position with dust, they were not the hunted and they were closing in on their quarry.

Race Against Time

Skinner was driving again, he knew he was close to where he would turn west.

'Skinner,' shouted Theresa, 'I can see dust clouds behind us, they've caught us, Skinner.'

Bridget began to become hysterical and cry, 'Don't let them catch us, please Skinner, don't let them catch us.'

'OK,' said Skinner from the driving seat, 'Now, we all have to be braver than we've ever been, listen very carefully, if you can see their dust cloud they're probably racing to catch us, right.'

'Yes,' said Theresa.

'So when I tell you hang over the back of the truck with Bridget and drag the branches on the road to hide our wheel tracks.'

'But we'll create our own dust cloud for them to easily follow Skinner,' said Theresa.

'Just do as you're fucking told and shut up,' bellowed Skinner to both girls.

'It'll take them around fifteen minutes to get where we are now, so I'm now turning east, get ready girls.'

Theresa and Bridget hung over the back of the Jeep as instructed, 'Not yet, not yet,' said Skinner, he slowed to a crawling pace and said, 'Now.'

Both girls wiped away the tyre tracks one on the left and one on the right as the Jeep crawled along. Skinner turned around 180 degrees back towards the road he'd just left as the pursuers dust cloud got closer and closer. Skinner continued at a snail's pace, crossing the north road and disappearing into quite thick bush heading west, a few seconds more and the man-hunters would have seen them, their dust cloud was already within sight.

Track and Kill

Jack turned off the north road following the tracks going west and Marcus followed, then Jack's truck came to an abrupt halt.

'Where now, Warragul,' said Jack, as all the men jumped out of the trucks with their guns at the ready. Marcus spoke, 'They can't be that far ahead of us, we're using two drivers non-stop, he can't drive all day and night on his fucking own, so we're missing something; could there be two blokes, could we have missed 'em.'.

Warragul replied, 'I've been tracking you stupid whitey bastards who get lost in the outback for 30 years, I'm telling you there is only one male, the other foot tracks we've found right up to the last water hole were not big enough or heavy enough for a man, they were a Sheila's or kid's tracks.'

'So what are you thinking, Warra,' asked Marcus.

Warragul knelt to study the tyre tracks, he shouted, 'Everyone quiet, look for a dust cloud they're only minutes in front of us, they are very close.'

'Where, which way,' bellowed Jack looking at Warragul for a reply.

'Shhhhhhhhsh,' said Warragul putting his finger to his lips. Everyone was deathly quiet for a couple of minutes listening for any give away noises.

'They have covered their tracks very well,' said Warragul, 'But they will not be going east, I think they've turned west.'

'West,' shouted Jack, 'There's nothing west, just outback, he's trying to escape for fuck sake, he'll have turned north,' said Jack to Marcus, 'This bollocks is just to slow us down.'

'They are ahead of us and definitely nowhere we've already been, said Warragul one of the older kids could be sharing the driving, there's Lake Amadeus west of here and that's Anangu country, they could be resting there.'

Marcus said, 'I agree with Warragul, they are not going east, there's nothing but a couple of thousand miles of outback and ocean and they have covered their tracks well, but they are close and they can't cover their tyre tracks indefinitely or go so slow as to make no engine noise or leave no dust cloud, so they have either stopped and hiding or moving north or west.'

'Jack, take your crew west and search for tracks, we'll go north, we're a few hours from Alice, meet me there, if you catch them, kill them all except any girls and burn the evidence, if I catch 'em, I'll do the same.'

Race Against Time

Skinner maintained his crawling pace east to keep the engine noise to an absolute minimum and to create no dust and just disappeared into the bush heading towards Anangu Territory, the girls still hanging over the back of the Jeep covering their tyre tracks. After twenty minutes, Skinner told the girls to stop and increased his speed.

Caroline

Caroline and Andy saw the dust cloud as the truck approached and then heard the truck as it got closer, they came out of the farmhouse with their shotguns as usual to see who was approaching. As soon as they saw it was Skinner they lowered their weapons to greet their old friend, the Jeep stopped, Skinner was exhausted.

He had driven the best part of 400 miles without a rest Andy shook Skinner's hand and embraced him, 'Gudday, mate, glad to see you,' he said.

Caroline put her arms around him and kissed him, 'Good to see you Skinner mate,' she said, 'Let's get you and these poor little tykes inside.'

Andy was the son of a sheep farmer and had grown up in this area and Caroline was Anangu. Her Anangu name was Coolaliah meaning south wind but all the sheep shearers and farmers called her Caroline and it stuck. The children all went into the house and immediately fell asleep, driving in the outback for days was just physically exhausting for adults let alone kids. As the children slept Skinner spoke to Andy and Caroline over a very welcome cup of coffee.

'I've got to leave four kids with you,' said Skinner as he enjoyed his first hot drink for days. 'We're taking Bridget with us, these kids just want a home mate and a bit of kindness; they've already been through too much.'

'Don't you worry, Skin,' replied Andy, 'They can have all they can eat and they can swim in the lake, I've fenced the pool off from crocs.'

And then Skinner said, 'We're being hunted mate, I've killed the tracks to here but some of those trackers are real good, mate.'

'No worries,' replied Andy, 'It's the same old story mate, the best trackers are abo's, Oh sorry Caroline I didn't mean anything.'

'I know you didn't, ya whitey bastard,' replied Caroline laughing.

Andy went on, 'There's no aborigine who will track on Anangu land, it's sacred, you know that, that's why you brought the kids here.'

'I've gotta get some sleep, mate,' said Skinner, yawning. 'I'm absolutely shattered but I've gotta leave early in the morning with the sisters.'

'You sure you don't wanna leave them here,' said Caroline, 'You know they'll be safe and you would have a better chance on your own against the man-hunters.'

'You'd never understand, Caroline,' Skinner replied, 'You are just too beautiful for this wicked world and the kids couldn't be in safer hands I know but the sisters are coming with me,' with that he kissed Caroline and said, 'I have to be gone by noon, so please don't let me over sleep, wake me.'

Andy walked Skinner to his room and said, 'How long are you gonna carry this on mate, everybody loved your old man and I know you felt you had to avenge his death but you're shortening the odds every time you kill, if you don't stop, they'll catch you; how many have you killed already and how many more mate.'

Skinner replied, 'When those fucking ships stop bringing little white slave kids to Aussie, I'll stop killing these bastards.'

'Don't forget most of the bastards I kill are scum, they deal in kids as currency and most are wanted for violent crimes, many of them are murderer's.' With that Skinner embraced Andy and said, 'Don't worry about me, mate, just wake me around noon,' he lay on the bed and went to sleep immediately .

Caroline was sitting on Skinner's bed waking him with a hot cup of coffee, it was five minutes to noon, 'Wake up, Skin, it's nearly noon,' said Caroline as Skinner awoke and rubbed his eyes.

'Oh thanks, Caroline,' he said as he took the coffee, 'Would you wake the sisters please, Caroline, we've got a long drive ahead of us, it's about 400 miles to Alice and about 1500 to Darwin.'

The Anangu were native here and knew this land, they could do much to delay the man hunters. Andy came in and said to Skinner, 'I've put new tyres all around and put you two spare wheels with tyres on in the truck, I've topped up your fuel and put six full jerrycans of fuel on board, I've changed your oil and you're good for about 5000 miles, mate.'

'Thanks, mate, how much do I owe ya.'

'Fuck all Skin, with what your dad did for me and Caroline and her whole Anangu tribe, I think the Anangu, Caroline and me still owe you a million Australian debt, Caroline has put fifty gallons of water on board and enough food for about four days, mate.'

The girls were crying and saying their good byes to the other children and Caroline when Andy took Skinner to one side, 'Listen, mate, we've had a bullroarer message, there ain't one fucking truck following you, there's two and there are eight men, you'll need me to come with you mate.'

'No,' said Skinner. 'You and Caroline have done more than enough for me.' Skinner asked, 'Where are they now, mate.'

'They must think they're making ground on you, mate, 'cos they've stopped, they did make good time but they must be shattered and they're about 30 miles east, an hour and a half away,' said Andy.

'Stopped,' said Skinner in surprise.

'Yes,' said Andy, 'They must think they're catching you so convincingly that they can afford to stop, they must think you've only got one fucking driver. You need all the help you can get, mate, so I've put two machine pistols in the glove compartment, two sawn-off shotguns and a rifle on the back seat, they're all loaded and there are eight boxes of ammo and if you leave now and go north for an hour then east to Alice, I think you'll have a couple of hours on 'em. Caroline's brought some of her mates to help us and we'll do our best to delay them for another couple of hours, mate, good luck, go go go.'

As Skinner drove away from Andy and Caroline's he headed for Alice Springs about 400 miles away, over outback roads this could take as long as 15 hours. Then the most dangerous part, 1500 miles on to Darwin, on the one and only available road and in a Jeep with two kids, they would stand out like a sore thumb.

Track and Kill

Warragul and Jack, turned north as Marcus had said, they drove slowly in order to hear any movement or any other vehicles, they searched intensely trying to pick up the tracks again, Jack said after a while, 'They haven't come this way Warra, the must have gone east.'

Warragul said, 'Jack, we are dealing with a professional here, he knows how to cover his tracks better than most, anyway why are you so pissed off that we've not found them yet, whoever finds them first will have a fight on their hands and we could die.'

Warragul had no idea that Jack was on a big bonus that he thought was easy money. Marcus had promised him £500 for every right hand of every male kid he killed, as proof of the kill and £250 for every Anangu, he had not mentioned this in the company of Warra, 'cos just like the Anangu he was aborigine.

Suddenly Warragul said, 'Stop,' he jumped from the truck and knelt to check the tracks, he had found Skinners renewed fresh tracks going east. Jack jumped up and down with excitement and hey followed the tracks for a very long distance probably seventy miles but now they were losing light fast, Warragul hand signalled Jack to stop and he did, they listened in the bush.

They could hear voices up ahead and Warragul crept quietly ahead peering from his bush hide, he could see a cabin, fire and hear voices, he crept back and told Jack. Jack said, it's been a good days work, but it's getting late and they still don't know we're here let's keep it that way we can pick our time to take 'em anytime now so let's have some food.

Warragul was well aware that they were in Anangu Territory and knew very well that Jack and the other two man-hunters hugely underrated the skill, hunting and tracking ability of Anangu, as they did with all Aboriginal tribes. Just yards away a face lowered himself slowly into the bush and signalled to others to do the same, the Anangu had been there some time and were already only yards from the man-hunters Warragul and Jack had no idea of their presence.

The Anangu had gathered spotted gum and bloodwood tree sap, the favourite food of the grey headed flying fox bat and while the man hunters made food around a fire the Anangu smothered these substances all over both vehicles, this would attract the bats and make night driving almost impossible as they swarmed over the vehicles for their food. They had also brought the orange beans from the strychnos nux-vomica tree (strychnine) and they had put them into all their water jerrycans.

Jack said, 'we've just about lost the light today but, in an hour or so when it's completely dark, Warra and you Billy will go to that Anangu settlement and if those kids are there, kill them all except the girls and all the fucking Anangu you can find who must have helped them.'

Just as Jack finished speaking thousands of bats engulfed both vehicles making an enormous row with their flapping wings and leaving their putrid scent over everything, the gang scattered firing guns and swearing but to no avail. Jack had four problems now, he was only aware of two, the bats and they'd lost the element of surprise, but the other two were far more serious, poisoned water and the Anangu who were just yards away in the bushes and had heard every single word that Marcus had spoken.

By the time the bats had cleared the Anangu had disappeared as silently as they had arrived into the bush and Andy and Caroline were well aware how many men were coming their way thanks to bullroarer. Jack approached the Anangu territory cautiously and as quietly as possible, he saw a cabin and stopped. In a whispered voice he told Warra and the other two to approach on foot, they did as he had told them.

Jack used hand signals to advance the men towards the cabin, he knew that recovering the children was not going to be easy, they were a long way from help and he knew that he was up against an aborigine tribe. Jack indicated to one of his men to take up a position behind the cabin and for the other man to move forward in the bush, Jack and Warra approached the cabin slowly watching for any movement from inside.

They hand signalled each other to wait, they both took aim at the cabin door and were totally unaware that they had passed within feet of Caroline and Anangu concealed in the undergrowth they were also totally unaware that they were now completely surrounded by Anangu tribesmen.

The Holiday

In the ops room Paul called the detectives to order and pointed at the clip board and started. 'We have a thumb and index finger print from the bolt used at the Liverpool killing and we also have smudged finger prints from the poison dart and door handles of the car.'

A detective interrupted, 'Sir, with respect smudged fingerprints are hardly going to reduce the suspect list are they, sir.'

A ripple of subdued laughter went around the room. 'If you'd just let me finish, detective Thompson,' said Paul. 'I think I can reduce the list significantly, the fingerprints have been checked against our records but not matched yet, but more importantly the fingerprint department informs me that the prints are very small, almost certainly too small for a man and the car that was stolen from a Birmingham car park, just happened to be parked next to a nurse's car. This nurse, Helen was finishing her shift at the hospital with two other nurses, all three of them saw the driver and all three said it was a woman, gentlemen and ladies, we think our serial killer is a woman.'

Caroline

Jack would never know that his one of his best men was dead within seconds without even a whisper as he took up his prone position on the ground behind the cabin, he would not have heard the four or five poison darts that hit him simultaneously.

Meanwhile at the front of the cabin, Caroline's shot was precise and clean, Jack's head exploded, the same time as a single shot from the cabin took out Warra, the other man was overwhelmed with arrows, spears and poison darts. Caroline was first from the undergrowth not knowing if all the man-hunters were dead, but after checking the bodies she signalled to all to come forward. Andy approached Caroline and hugged her, 'Are you OK baby,' he asked.

'No probs,' only one man was alive but the poison from the darts would kill him soon.

'Kulu pushed his spear into the dying man and said where were you going to take the kids, the man groaned in pain and tried to speak, 'We were—' he paused, again Kulu pushed the spear into him, he blurted out, 'We're going Alice,' before vomiting and falling into complete silence.'

Caroline and Andy looked at Kulu. 'So they were gonna meet up in Alice,' said Caroline. Caroline spoke in aborigine to the tribesmen, Andy could speak some aborigine but she spoke very quickly, it was her native tongue.

Andy asked Caroline what she had said, she told him, 'The vehicle and these men must disappear in Lake Amadeus very soon, before they were missed because the other man-hunters would definitely be coming back when they didn't show up at Alice, they'd come looking for them and the children,' she knew this was not the end of this matter.

Darwin Kill

Barret and Jinxy arrived in Alice Springs with the two Mancunians they were met at the airport by two men each driving a car, one of the men handed the keys of one of the cars to Barret, who said to him, 'Take us to a filling station on the main road north to Darwin,' he turned to the Mancunians and said, 'You two get in that other car and follow us.'

It was a short drive, when they arrived Barret said, 'Jinxy, fill the car up, I wanna talk to the owner.'

Barret pulled the man at the filling station to one side to pay for the petrol and said has a guy with about five kids been through here recently.'

'A guy with five kids,' said the garage man, 'You must be fucking joking, nobody brings kids to Alice, this is no tourist town mate,' he went on. 'I've only seen one kid through here today, she was in the back of a jeep, there was a bloke and a Sheila in the front, the Sheila was a pom, mate.'

'How did you know she was a pom,' asked Barret.

'She spoke pom, mate, she was asking how much further to Darwin and she was wearing a loose top, ya could see her pomey white skin, like the kid in the back.'

'How long ago did they pass through, mate.'

'Bout an hour.'

Coppin, Jones and the two Irishmen arrived in Darwin, they were also met by his men who brought a car for them. It was not a comfortable flight but then again this was no pleasure trip.

Coppin said to one of the men, 'Are both cars filled up and water on board as instructed.'

'Yes, boss,' Came the reply.

'Good,' said Coppin, while all the men gulped down water, he went on, 'We need to be at Joe's bar about sixty miles south of here out in the sticks, do you know it.'

'Yes, I know it,' came the reply, 'We need to go now straight to Joe's place he's got a phone and food, we'll follow you.'

The two Irishmen got into the lead car and Coppin and Jones got in the following car the journey was about three hours.

Escape North

Skinner was in the back seat looking backwards into the distance through his binoculars and Bridget was driving, he told her to pull over which she did.

'Somethings not right, girls,' said Skinner.

'What do you mean,' asked Theresa.

'They should be right behind us by now,' he replied, 'And they are not.'

'How do you know they're not,' said Bridget.

'We're on an open flat dusty road, we'd see a truck behind us at least three miles away and do you see a dust cloud following us,' replied Skinner.

Both girls looked intently into the distance and then they sat for a while in the jeep on the side of the road, Skinner was thinking as they all briefly got out the truck, stretched their legs and drank some water.

'They've given up 'cos they can't catch us,' said Bridget.

'The one thing those men will not do is give up, Bridget, they were following us to catch all the kids and take them back and to kill at least me and they still want to do that, believe me.'

'So what do you think they're up to,' asked Theresa.

'I think they were told to stop the chase after they'd discovered we'd passed through Alice,' said Skinner.

'But how would they know that,' asked Bridget.

'How many white girls do you think come north through Alice Springs with a white man travelling from Anangu territory, if that happens twice a year I would be amazed Bridget, believe me they know because we stand out like a sore thumb and someone has been watching us.'

'So what do you think is going to happen now,' asked Theresa.

'You have both been brave girls, but now you have to listen to me carefully, I think someone has called off the chase because we were too far ahead, but they know it's a day and a half drive from Alice Springs to Darwin, so they have plenty of time to come from the north, that means someone has seen us and knows there is only three people on board, that means they also know that the rest of the kids are in Anangu territory somewhere and if I was a guessing man, I would guess the four men who were chasing us have been sent back to join the other four to find the kids.'

Theresa started crying, 'They'll kill Andy and Caroline and all the children, won't they; we should go back to help them, remember they helped us, please please, Skinner, we have to go back.'

'You're forgetting, Theresa, Caroline and Andy know this country and the Anangu territory better than almost anyone on earth, even better than many aborigines, Andy grew up there and Caroline is Anangu, they will not be easy to find or kill and don't forget their cabin is amongst the Anangu warriors, absolutely no one will be sneaking up on them; they want the children back, I don't think they'll kill them, they are worth a lot of money, but if the worst has happened and we went back, we would be no match for eight armed men, there are just us three; we must carry on north but we need to be less obvious to the men who want to kill us, we need a plan.'

'But we can't change what we look like,' said Bridget.

'There is a way Bridget, but it will be very dangerous, especially for Theresa, are you up for it,' said Skinner.

'Do we have any choice,' asked Theresa.

'No' said Skinner.

'OK then, what's the plan.'

Skinner pulled out two black fly veils from his rucksack and said, 'From now on Theresa you will be the only person driving into a filling station,' he turned to her and said, 'You will wear both of these fly veils, it will darken your face and you'll also wear my Akubra with the corks fitted, it will be very difficult for anyone to see your face.'

'What will I have to do, Skinner,' asked Theresa.

'When we approach a filling station, you will drop me and Bridget off out of sight of anyone, you'll drive up to the bar, but not too close, you will first make sure there are lots of people in the bar, they would not attempt to kill you with witnesses. You'll walk in alone at the chosen place, buy a cold drink and quickly but very carefully check out the people in the place without staring at anyone and then you'll leave.'

He continued, 'You won't speak to anyone apart from saying 'Gudday,' which we will practice till you get it right and you sound like an Aussie and then we'll try out our plan at the first place we come too.'

'When you've dropped me and Bridget off, while you're driving slowly up to the bar, I'll take up a position on the opposite side of the road and will have you in my sights through my sniper's rifle, every step of the way. If anyone tries to grab you, Theresa, I will shoot the person or fire a shot into glass bottles to make as much noise as possible as a distraction.

The crowd in the bar will panic and almost certainly drop to the floor and you'll have about 40 seconds to escape before the crowd in the bar recovers, you'll run back to the Jeep immediately and return here as quickly as possible, do you understand,' said Skinner.

Now Bridget started crying, 'It's too dangerous, Skinner,' she said as she hugged her sister.

'Look,' said Skinner, 'We're gonna try it out to see if it works, the first place up ahead is a sheep shearing stop off, I guarantee the killers would not pick this as a place for a killing, there will be too many witnesses and most of the farmers are armed with rifles and shotguns and they would shoot the killers, we are too far south for them to be here this soon, we're still over a thousand miles south of Darwin. This is just a practice run, Bridget and if it doesn't work, we'll scrap the plan. I would not put you, Theresa, at any more risk than necessary and those men won't be looking for a girl on her own, they'll be looking for three people in a truck, one man with two girls.'

After an hour or so the first shearing stop-off came into view in the distance and they all followed the plan, Theresa dropped off Skinner and Bridget and drove in alone, bought a drink and left. She sat with Skinner when she returned and told him it all went perfectly, just as they had hoped. Skinner said to pull over and have a rest, they were not being chased anymore they could take a break. Bridget yawned and stretched her arms and lay down on the back seat and went straight to sleep. Theresa placed her finger on her lips, indicating to be quiet and looked at Skinner she took him by the hand and led him away from the Jeep.

When they were twenty yards or so away out of ear shot of Bridget, Theresa spoke, 'It went wrong, Skinner, they knew I was English, I didn't want Bridget to hear.'

'What do you mean,' enquired Skinner, 'I stopped as we planned not too close to the bar, it was crowded and as I walked in all the men whistled, I only said Gudday and bought my drink and left and as I left one farmer shouted what's a pom Sheila doing in the middle of nowhere and they all laughed, whistled and cheered, they knew I was English Skinner.'

'OK,' said Skinner, 'Calm down and just try and remember every little detail of what you said or did in there.'

'I've just told you,' said Theresa, raising her voice.

'When I walked in they all whistled.'

'Shuuush,' said Skinner, 'Bridget will hear us.'

Theresa lowered her voice and continued, 'I walked to the bar because the machine was out of order, I sad Gudday and pointed at the can, he handed it to me, I paid and said thanks and left.'

'You've just told me how they knew, Theresa,' said Skinner.

'How,' asked Theresa.

'You said thanks.'

Theresa paused for a moment, 'Oh, fucking hell,' said Theresa.

'Don't worry,' said Skinner.

'You've had your first rehearsal and most of it went well, you'll get better at it, remember only 'Gudday,' nothing else, no thank you, no goodbye, nothing. In a few hours we'll be at another sheep station and we'll try again, now get some sleep while I drive, you did very well, Theresa.'

Darwin Kill

Coppin finally arrived at Joe's bar, they were all glad for a rest, as they got out of the vehicles stretching their legs, Coppin said, 'Jones'y, check around the back, how many vehicles are here and then organise some food and a room.'

He walked into Joe's and Joe was there to greet him, 'Gudday boss.'

'Any news from Fremantle, Joe,' said Coppin.

'No boss, but Barret's been trying to get in touch with you from Alice for the last couple of hours.'

'Give me the number,' said Coppin, Joe gave him the number and Coppin phoned Barret.

The manager answered and turning to Barret said, 'It's for you Barret.' Barret took the phone.

'What you got, Barret,' asked Coppin. 'Bad news boss, I've been trying to —'

'Never mind about the bollocks,' interrupted Coppin, 'What's the fucking bad news.'

'He went through Alice about half hour before we arrived boss, about three hours ago.'

'Fuck, fuck, fuck,' screamed Coppin as he stamped his foot, 'Had he got all the kids with him.'

'No that's another thing boss, there was just him and two kids.'

'WHAT,' shouted Coppin,' is Marcus there.'

'Yes, boss.'

'Right, put him on.'

Marcus took the phone, 'You couldn't catch the bastards and now you've lost half the fucking kids where the fuck are they,' Coppin screamed down the phone to Marcus.

'They're in Anangu territory, boss. I was delayed 'cos I sent Jack and Warra to find them and bring them to Alice where we'd meet up.'

'Well you better fuck off back south and find Jack and the kids, 'cos they're not in fucking Alice, are they, but the rules have changed, I want the boys, men and any fucker who has helped 'em gone permanently without a trace. I only want the girls back, do I make myself crystal clear.'

'Yes boss, I understand.'

'Barret and Jinxy will be coming with you, got it.'

'Yes, boss.'

'Now put Barret on and fuck off south as soon as I've finished talking to him, this job is urgent, put him on,' with that Marcus handed the phone to Barret.

'Barret, you and Jinxy get this fucking mess cleaned up, I want all the males and any fucker who has helped them gone forever without a trace, I only want the girls back, now tank up and finish this job.' Coppin slammed the phone down.

'What's the problem, boss,' said Jonesy, as they sat down with a beer to discuss what happened next.

'What's the fucking problem,' Coppin shouted in reply, 'That fucker's killed about eight of my men, taken my property and Marcus and his fucking crew still couldn't catch the bastard, he went through Alice driving north probably three hours ago and with only two of the kids.'

'Well, where are the rest of 'em,' asked Jonesy.

'Don't worry it's sorted,' said Coppin.

'Boss, we're only about sixty miles south of Darwin and if he passed through Alice about three hours ago, he won't have travelled 150 miles north yet, he'll still be the best part of a 1000-miles south of us, he'll be lucky to cover that distance in 30 hours boss, we've got plenty of time to sort out a plan, so no sweat.'

Caroline

Caroline spoke to Andy, 'these four are dead but without Kulu and his tribe, it could easily have been us and the children and we are no longer secret, baby, at least four man-hunters know approximately where we are and that we have their property, you know they'll be back and they could bring a lot more men, we need to make a plan now and prepare.'

Andy spoke, 'If they were going to meet up in Alice, let's assume they are waiting in Alice for them and if they are there now, it won't take long for them to work out something has gone wrong.'

Caroline said, 'If they're coming south from Alice, the quickest route is past Lake Amadeus and that will take them around four to six hours, that gives us about 12 to 36 hours and if they come past Amadeus, I have a plan.'

Marcus

Marcus, Barret and Jinxy headed south to Anangu territory, they were taking the shortest route past Lake Amadeus which stretches for nearly 200 miles, it is a Salt Lake and although it's shallow there are only a few places to cross because of quick sand, it will take about four hours to reach from Alice. Marcus's best man for this territory was Walla who was with Jack, he knew all the short cuts and places to cross Lake Amadeus. It had taken quite a few hours to get to Amadeus and now they either have to cross a shallow section or do a 200 miles detour taking another six hours.

Both vehicles drove along the shore line, suddenly Marcus saw multiple tyre tracks exiting the lake and indicated to Barret and Jinxy to follow him. Marcus tentatively entered the water but as the front wheels followed the tracks, the Jeep began to sink past the axles and the floor pan began to fill with water.

Marcus yelled to his driver to reverse and has he attempted to reverse a bullet shattered the windscreen and blew his head apart, Marcus tried to return fire but all four occupants of the leading truck were being attacked and they were all dead within seconds. Barret and Jinxy opened fire on an invisible enemy whilst under a hail of arrows, spears and poison darts. A single rifle shot killed the driver Jinxy, Barret kicked him out of the Jeep and jumped into the driving seat in a vain attempt to reverse into the bush.

A bullet hit him in the arm and he lost control of the Jeep, a second bullet ripped open his chest and he slammed into a rock in reverse and came to a shuddering stop, a hail of darts and spears hit him and everything was still. After a short time, cautiously Caroline and Kulu were the first to break cover, both went toward Alura who had been hit in the shoulder but was the only Anangu casualty, he was not hurt badly.

Andy joined them from his cover, they all looked at the four dead men in the slowly sinking Jeep and then look towards the wheels from Jack's truck in the undergrowth, the wheels that had created the exit tracks from the lake. 'It was a great plan, baby and it worked, only Alura was injured and all eight of the man hunters are dead,' said Andy.

'It wasn't that greater plan, darling, now we need to lose 12 bodies and 3 vehicles,' said Caroline.

Warra knew Lake Amadeus, he was aborigine and if he had been alive, he would have told them that the soft mud and sand bed of Lake Amadeus could not even support a Kangaroo's weight, let alone a Jeep.

Escape North

After a couple of hours, the second shearing stop could be seen in the distance and again they all followed the plan, Theresa dropped off Skinner and Bridget and drove in alone, she walked in bought a drink and left, Skinner watched her every move through the telescopic sights.

When she returned she told Skinner, this time it had gone perfectly, exactly as they'd planned, but unfortunately, the place was full of mainly Italians and they can't tell Aussies from English, there was whistling of course, she's a young attractive girl on her own in a bar full of men.

'Don't worry,' said Skinner, 'You've had your second rehearsal, it went well and you're getting better, Theresa, you remembered to only say 'Gudday' and nothing else. In a few hours we'll be at the last sheep station and it'll be your last chance to practice, every stop after that will be for real. You're both very brave girls and, Theresa, you've done very well, now get some sleep while I drive.'

Darwin Kill

Coppin was getting impatient at Joe's bar and called a meeting with Jonesy and the two Irishmen. They ate some food as they talked, Coppin said, 'No more fuck up's, the target is on his way north, it's gonna take the best part of a day to get here and after this, there are no more chances for a discrete kill, do you all understand.

'Yes, boss,' the Irishmen replied.

'I've got two rooms, one for me and one for you three,' said Coppin, 'You'll work a rota, Jonesy will organise it, one of you will cover that bar looking south 24/ 7, if anything suspicious comes north I want to know, at the moment there are only two people staying here apart from us and that's perfect for our work. Jonesy, sort out the shift pattern. I'm going for a lie down.'

With that Coppin went to his room. Jonesy said to O'Hara, 'You take first watch and you McGuiness, get some sleep you're on next, come and get me if anything happens, I'll be in the other bar at the back.'

Escape North

The drive to Darwin seemed endless, broken only by the occasional kangaroo or bush on the right or left, Bridget took over the driving and Theresa took a well-earned sleep after about two hours another bar up ahead came into view and Skinner said, 'Bridget, pull over into that bush ahead and we'll have a rest for ten minutes.'

Bridget stopped the truck and yawned she was shattered. 'After this one,' said Skinner, 'We will pull off the road and all sleep for a couple of hours, we need to be on our toes from now on, I'm almost certain they will not have come this far south, they wouldn't have had the time it's nearly a 1000 miles from the nearest airport, but still treat it seriously, Theresa. We'll only get one chance and this might be your very last chance for a rehearsal, but I promise both of you when we get to Darwin you can sleep as long as you like.'

Bridget spoke, 'Skinner, if it's getting dangerous, why can't Theresa take a gun with her.'

'Yeah, why can't I take a gun,' said Theresa.

'Both of you pick up a shotgun and come with me,' shouted Skinner, the girls did as they were told, they followed him into the bush for a few minutes and they saw two Koala's in a tree, 'Shoot the Koala,' Skinner said to Theresa.

'Why,' said Theresa.

'Don't fucking ask,' shouted Skinner, 'Just kill it.'

'No, I can't,' said Theresa, throwing down the gun.

'You kill it, Bridget, do it now,' ordered Skinner.

'I can't, I won't do it, I'm not gonna do it,' screamed Bridget. She threw down her gun and both girls went into hysterics.

'Calm down, calm down,' said Skinner as he put his arms around both girls. 'That's why I can't give you a gun, Theresa, if you can't shoot a koala bear, how will you stack up against an armed man who kills for a living. Apart from which, Theresa, if you walked into any of these bars with a side arm, shotgun or rifle you would immediately become a target for men who kill every day, they would see a side arm and out draw you, a rifle would be out of the question in such a confined space and if you tried to use a sawn-off shotgun against a professional killer, you could accidentally and easily kill innocent travellers, farmers or hunters or even yourself.

Even if you managed to kill one of these men with a shotgun, everyone in that bar with a weapon would shoot back at you to protect themselves, you are much safer without any weapon.'

The next few stop offs were the same, Theresa went through her well-rehearsed routine as Skinner watched her every move through his sniper sights, she bought her drink and left, it went exactly as planned. When Theresa got back to the truck she said to Bridget, 'I'll drive,' and pushed her over into the passenger seat and drove off.

Skinner said, 'Drive past the place for about 20 miles and then pick a spot in the bush, we're gonna sleep in a parked truck for the first time in a long-time, girls,' both girls cheered. They slept for three hours and when Skinner woke up it was still light so it was safe to make a fire so he made some coffee and woke the girls. 'We slept a bit longer than planned,' said Skinner.

'Yes, but I feel much better,' said Bridget, 'if Theresa checks the next stop and no one is there, can we stop for some proper food, Skinner,' asked Bridget.

'That's not possible now, Bridget, until we get to Darwin, we're getting closer to the places that they would choose to kill us and I don't know how many or who Coppin has got in his pocket. We are about 200 miles north of Alice and they would travel at least 400 miles south of Darwin to be in the outback and avoid witnesses, so we'll just carry on doing what we're doing all the way north.'

'And how long is that for,' asked Theresa.

'I estimate about 700 miles,' replied Skinner.

'Oh no,' said Theresa, 'I don't know how many more times I can do this, Skinner.'

'Listen,' said Skinner. 'Everything before has been a rehearsal and you've become very good at playing this part, but you've only had to cope with wolf whistles, soon it will be the real thing and we'll have to cope with men who have guns and have come to kill us all.'

After a couple of hours another sheep shearing stop could be seen in the distance and again they all followed the plan, Theresa dropped off Skinner and Bridget and drove in alone, she walked in bought a drink and left, Skinner watched her every move through the telescopic sights. When she returned she told Skinner, this time it had gone perfectly, exactly as they'd planned, but unfortunately the place was full of mainly Italians and they can't tell Aussies from English, there was whistling of course, she's a young attractive girl on her own in a bar full of men.

'Don't worry,' said Skinner, 'You've had another rehearsal, it went well and you're getting better, Theresa, you remembered to only say 'Gudday' and nothing else. In a few hours we'll be at the last sheep station and it'll be your last chance to practice, every stop after that will be for real. You're both very brave girls and Theresa, you've done very well, now get some sleep while I drive a few more stops.'

It was just more of the same and Theresa didn't want to drive, she thought she was making her contribution with her acting role and didn't mind voicing her opinion. As she got out at the next stop she dropped them both off and turned and said, 'You two can fucking drive the rest of the way north, it's me doing the dangerous bit,' she said as she drove off.

The Holiday

In the ops room Paul opened with an apology for calling an earlier meeting. He called the detectives to order and began with, 'New information has come to light, I have discovered that 'The Pharaoh' has been investigated before, in 1947, the suspicion was, that wanted criminals and even IRA members were being given a safe passage to Australia, that the ships manifest was not accurate and that guns and drugs were being brought into Liverpool on The Pharaoh and other ships returning to England. However, resources were so limited after the war ended that there were insufficient police or harbour personnel to conduct a thorough search of a ship the size of 'The Pharaoh'.'

Paul went on, 'There was also a political imperative to maximise the speed of these ships to get as many immigrants to Australia as soon as humanly possible and very little support from either the English or Australian governments to be too particular about small quantities of illegal cargo or passengers. Australia wanted a population and we were only too willing to oblige. We need to concentrate our investigation around 1945 to 1948.'

A voice from the back of the room screamed, 'Sir, that's a lot of people for our small team to investigate, it will take months or even years.'

Paul replied, 'We have no other option people, so let's just get on with it, thank you,' with that Paul closed the meeting.

Escape North

Theresa was thinking this could all be a waste of time, what if Skinner was wrong and all of this was for nothing. It was getting monotonous and Theresa was getting fed up of the repetition but reluctantly went through the routine, parking not too close, walking to the machine or bar, getting a drink and looking for anyone suspicious.

She walked into the bar and was about to order as an Italian looking man came up on her left-hand side standing uncomfortably close and offering to buy her a drink, she turned to look at him, he was quite handsome but she'd seen it all before, it was all so repetitive, like doing a school play and Skinner was becoming annoying like a school teacher.

Theresa was thinking, 'I'm gonna tell Skinner I'm not doing any more bars, fuck him.'

A second man walked up and stood to Theresa's right side, again this was nothing new, they would probably both try to buy her a drink, it happened in nearly all the bars, both men were 1000 miles from the nearest women, she knew exactly what they were up too and what they wanted.

The man too her right slammed his glass on the bar and shouted for a cold beer, he had the thickest Irish accent she'd ever heard, he towered above her, she looked down under her Akubra and froze in fear as she saw a scorpion tattoo on his hand, she peeped under the rim of her Akubra as the barman served him beer and she saw his scarred face, it was the man at the pub in Liverpool with Jack, she was petrified and tried to think what to do, her mind went blank.

Theresa deliberately turned her back to the Irishman turning her face to the Italian man, she accepted the Italians offer of a drink and trying to say as little as possible she pointed and just said one word, 'Coke.' It was one word too much for the very astute Irishman.

'Well, we have an English gal here,' said O'Hara standing behind her, he grabbed her shoulders and quickly turned her around snatching her Akubra and fly veils away from her face, he pulled, grabbed her tightly by the arm and said, 'Well, hello Theresa, have you come to see your daddy.'

Skinner saw the man grab Theresa's arm through his sniper sights he thought he was just a horny punter as his finger tightened on the trigger, but even if it was the hit, the Italian guy was in the line of fire and he didn't have a clear shot. O'Hara attempted to pull Theresa away from the bar, he did not want to kidnap her in such a public place, many of the drinkers were hunters and farmers who were armed, the Italian man buying her drink said, 'Who the fuck are you, paddy.'

'I'll tell you who the fuck I am,' said O'Hara, pushing Theresa to one side, drawing his gun and pushing it into the Italians right eye. 'I'm here to do a fucking job and I might do you for fucking free,' shouted O'Hara, he'd attracted a lot of attention and Skinner had watched Theresa's every step and O'Hara's actions confirmed Skinners worst fears, this was the hit. Both men had moved from the bar and now O'Hara was in Skinner's sights.

Before O'Hara could pull the trigger of his Browning his face exploded across the mirrors at the back of the bar as Skinner's finger squeezed the trigger and an explosive bullet from his high powered rifle found its mark, O'Hara immediately released Theresa as his blood and bone were spread across the walls of the bar, a farmer in the bar had also fired his rifle at O'Hara at the same time after watching his threatening behaviour and the bullet passed straight through O'Hara's shoulder as he fell to the ground.

Theresa, just as planned and rehearsed ran to the Jeep faster than she'd ever run before, as she cleared the bar, Bridget kept firing randomly into the bar to create panic and confusion, just as rehearsed. Everyone panicked and dropped to the floor for cover, glass flew everywhere as the optics, glass and mirrors in the bar were blown apart, no one in the bar knew where all the shots were coming from as noise and gunfire filled the place.

McGuiness had heard the gun shots in the bar from his room and ran out towards the veranda following Theresa. He saw her run toward the Jeep and started firing at the truck to disable it and prevent her escape as he ran after her.

Two shots ricocheted off the Jeep and only missed Theresa by inches, she dived headfirst into the front foot well of the Jeep and McGuiness managed to get off a further shot from his Browning aiming at the tyres, before his throat was ripped open by a high-powered rifle shot, he was blown back into the bar by the impact. Theresa jumped into the driving seat and sped away. Skinner and Bridget continued firing into the bar at glass windows, bottles or mirrors, anything that would create noise, panic and confusion which bought Theresa additional and valuable seconds to assist her escape.

Skinner looked through his sights for anymore 'guns' and saw a figure run from the back rooms with a gun in his hand and dive for cover behind the bar, he recognised the man as Coppin who kept his head down as Skinner kept firing into the bar to keep everyone on the floor and Bridget emptied another magazine into the bar.

Skinner saw Jonesy run from the back of the bar with a shotgun but two shots from Skinner made him jump for cover. Theresa drove back to Skinner and Bridget at break neck speed, the tears poured down her face as she cried with fear and relief at her close escape, she skidded to a halt raising a great dust cloud, she was in shock, 'Get in Bridget,' shouted Skinner, as he fired more shots at the bar, 'Get in the back,' he shouted to Theresa, both girls jumped in the back seat as Skinner took the wheel and sped off back south, Bridget continued from the back of the Jeep to shoot at the bar as they sped away.

Theresa was screaming to Skinner, 'It was the Irishman from Liverpool, the one with the tattoo on his hand who tried to kill me, Skinner. I remember him from the pub with Jack and he must have been on The Pharaoh with us.'

'Bridget, cuddle your sister, keep her warm, she is in shock,' shouted Skinner, 'Put that blanket around you both and stay warm.'

A mile or so down the dirt road Skinner slowed right down to prevent creating a dust cloud and turned into the outback and turned back north, making a big two-mile arc around the bar.

'Coppin's men will follow us soon and the state police will be following our tracks and they may use a plane,' said Skinner, as he drove the Jeep as slow as he could to keep down noise and dust. It was now completely dark and driving was difficult enough using lights and Skinner drove with no lights to avoid detection from the air.

Back at the bar the dust settled and gradually people stood up, Coppin waited until quite a few men were standing before slowly and carefully standing up. Jonesy joined him, 'They're both dead, boss,' said Jonesy.

'Get the envelopes off 'em, Jonesy,' said Coppin, 'Let's not leave any money or fake ID's and then let's fuck off discretely before the cops arrive.'

'Aren't we gonna try and catch her, boss,' asked Jonesy.

'We're up against a professional, Jonesy, that sniper might still be out there expecting us to follow her, it's still over 500 miles to Darwin, phone Blackie and have him watch for them.' Jonesy collected the envelopes from the dead Irishmen.

Coppin looked around the bar, he did not want to be there when the police arrived, his two Irish killers were already dead but they had no connection to him, in fact they had no identity at all, they would never be traced. Coppin's quarry was still free and still unknown and had escaped again and he had still not got his girl back, he needed another plan, but more urgently him and Jonesy needed to slip away into the night and disappear.

Skinner drove until first light and he was absolutely shattered when he woke the girls, 'Where are we, Skinner,' asked Theresa.

'I don't know exactly,' he replied, 'But we don't seem to have anyone following us at the moment, but we need to be into Darwin's suburbs before we're safe.'

Skinner did not know how many men Coppin had with him, if they were being followed or even if there'd be another hit, he just knew he had to disappear in Darwin. He stopped, he was shattered and told the girls to get out just for a stretch. We're almost there girls but we can't stop now, Bridget you drive, the girls jumped back in the Jeep.

Skinner climbed into the back seat and said, 'Don't stop until you see the next garage or shearers stop, wake me up then,' he lay down and slept as they set off.

About 2 hours later, Theresa was shaking Skinners leg, 'Wake up, wake up, Skinner,' she said. Skinner awoke and took a drink of water, he poured some on his hand and flushed his face before he collected his thoughts and spoke.

'OK, we've done brilliantly so far girls we're not too far from Darwin and I don't think Coppin would have set up two kill sights so close to each other, especially so close to Darwin, that's why he was at the last place, he wanted to witness the killings. I was surprised to see him, did you see him, Theresa,' he asked.

'No Skinner, if you remember I was just running for my life, I didn't see the second Irishman, Coppin or any of his men, I haven't got a clue what Coppin looks like, I only saw the Irishman from Liverpool and the Italian at the bar.'

'What shall we do now,' asked Bridget, as they approached yet another shearers stop. 'Well, I think that we should treat this the same as the last place but I'm sure this will be the last time we'll need to go through our routine, but you girls have been so brave and taken even more risks than me, so what do you think,' asked Skinner.

'I agree with you, Skinner,' said Theresa, 'And by the way Skinner, we've taken no more risks than you, without you I wouldn't have my beautiful sister, thank you,' both the girls wrapped their arms around Skinner and each other, finally they were beginning to believe this nightmare was coming to an end.

Skinner was right, they went through their routine and everything was fine, now they passed a road sign 'Darwin 40 Miles,' they knew they'd won. Everything was more relaxed it was time for Skinner to tell Theresa and Bridget about the complete plan to shut Coppin's slave trade down forever.

Skinner pulled over and all three of them got out, he reached under the passenger seat and felt around until he found a sheet of paper. 'What's that,' asked Theresa.

'This is a list of twenty men who all served on The Pharaoh over the past ten years and who were all recently seen in Darwin.'

'So what's your plan, Skinner,' asked Bridget.

'When we get to Darwin, we'll go to a very safe house both of you girls can have the bath time of your life, we'll all eat a wonderful meal and have a long and wonderful sleep in a comfortable bed, then tomorrow morning when we're all completely rested you will meet some of my legal friends over a big breakfast and we'll all talk about how we intend to stop this slave trade so no other girl will ever have to suffer what you two beautifully brave girls have just come through.'

Legal Darwin

The girls awoke in a beautiful bedroom and got out of their soft warm beds and there were khaki shirts and shorts on their beds, for once it was a beautiful morning, no one was chasing and trying to kill them. Skinner heard them talking in their bedroom and said, 'Hurry up and get dressed we're going for some breakfast.' The girls were both hungry and gladly did exactly as they were told.

As the three of them walked to a café, Theresa asked, 'Skinner, what happened here?'

'That's the rubble left after the Japanese bombed Darwin in the war, but it's finished now, but ya can't rebuild as quick as you can bomb,' replied Skinner.

Both girls were surprised they thought only Liverpool had been bombed. They walked past the bombed-out buildings and down to the water's edge, the ocean was beautiful and everything seemed so calm, quiet and peaceful compared with the last few frantic, hectic and dangerous days.

They sat outside around a big round table and Skinner asked them what they wanted for their breakfast. Theresa and Bridget had spent the last few days eating wild fruit and strange food, they were pleased to enjoy bacon and egg with all the trimmings, it was like heaven. When they had finished eating, they had a brief moment of happiness telling Skinner how wonderful it was to be safe again and how much they'd both loved that beautiful bath time last night, for a moment they all laughed in safety.

'In a moment some people will be joining us,' said Skinner. 'Don't be afraid, they are some of my best friends and they are all here to help.'

Theresa put her hand on Skinner's strong arm and said, 'Skinner, before your friends arrive Bridget and myself would like to say something, We were just too exhausted last night to say thank you properly, Skinner,' Theresa went on. 'Me and Bridget spoke last night before we went to sleep and we thought where would we be now if you hadn't saved us both.

Thank you just doesn't seem enough when you risked your own life over and over again to save ours and here we are sitting in this quiet beautiful place and listening to the sea softly washing up the beach and we are alive and safe, only because you were so brave, wherever Bridget and myself go in the future and whatever happens in our lives, we will never forget you, Skinner, not ever.'

A car pulled up across the street and two men got out, both the men were massive. Skinner felt Theresa's fingers dig into his arm, he put his other hand on her hand saying, 'Relax both of you, these are my friends.'

The two men waited at the kerb side looking up and down the street and then another car pulled up and parked behind them and a woman got out. All three of them walked to the table. 'Gooday, Skinner,' said one of the men as Skinner shook hands with the two men and kissed the woman.

The woman spoke first saying, 'My name is Angie Bacon, I'm a lawyer and I've heard a lot about you two brave beauties from Skinner and very pleased to finally meet you.' Angie pointed at Theresa and said, 'Now if I'm right, you're Theresa,' and then Angie looked at Bridget and said, 'And you're Bridget, the Gun.'

All at the table laughed. 'I'm not Bridget, the Gun,' said Bridget shyly as she blushed, 'And how did you know our names,' she enquired.

Angie said, 'Before I tell you, would anyone like something to eat or drink.' Food was ordered for the two men and drinks were ordered for everyone. As they waited for the food to arrive Angie went on, 'I knew your names because after your exhausting few days racing across Australia, you arrived here in Darwin yesterday completely shattered and when you had gone to bed Skinner and myself spoke on a long phone call about your experiences and bravery, Bridget the Gun,' Angie looked and smiled at Bridget.

She continued, 'You two beauties have faced more danger in the past few days than most people face in their lives, well that's going to stop and so we arranged this meeting today. I want you to remember the faces of these two men opposite you, they are Laurie Tandy and Mick Tandy,' both the men smiled across the table and said Gudday to the girls, 'They are brothers and whilst you are here in Darwin, they will shadow you everywhere you go and protect you.'

'What does shadow mean, Mrs Bacon,' asked Theresa.

'Call me Angie please, both of you,' she went on. 'Shadowing means guarding you all the time without being seen and that's what Laurie and Mick will do while you're here in Darwin.'

'If we ever need protection, we have Skinner,' said Bridget. Angie smiled at the girls and went to speak.

Skinner interrupted, ''Scuse me, Angie,' he said, 'I think we're moving a little too quickly after what the girls have been through in the past few days, can we slow it down, how about some ice cream girls on this lovely sunny morning,' both the girls said, 'Yes please.'

When the girls were eating their ice cream Theresa said, 'I thought you said we were safe now here in Darwin.'

Skinner said, 'Bridget, you are safe now you're in Darwin but Coppin is still around and sometimes I will need to go to places with Angie and on those occasions, Laurie and Mick will guard you with their lives.'

'You're right Skinner,' said Angie. 'You two brave girls have been through a lot, so today no more business, instead Skinner will take you both shopping or to the beach or anywhere you want to go,' with that Angie put 50 Australian dollars on the table and said, 'Have a fabulous day, I have to go now, Laurie and Mick will shadow all three of you and then Theresa and Bridget can get used to them being around, but tomorrow the work starts and I may have to disappear with Skinner for some time, have a lovely day girls you have earned it,' and Angie was gone.

Skinner took the girls around Darwin and they had a wonderful day, it was so hot they swam in the sea under the careful gaze of three of the best man hunters in Australia. It was the best seaside holiday they'd ever had in their lives, they had suffered a war-torn country on desperate food rations, a terrible trip half way around the world and a life-threatening race across Australia chased by killers and now just for a while they could be safe and happy, eating ice cream and become kids again briefly.

It had been a fantastic day for the girls and they were shattered and they went to bed and slept, as Skinner, Laurie and Mick talked tactics, for tomorrow

Angie arrived at the safe house and was let in by Laurie, 'Gudday, Angie,' said Laurie as he led her through to the back yard where the girls, Skinner and Mick were having breakfast.

'Gudday, girls,' said Angie, 'Hope you had a great time yesterday.'

'Yes, thank you, Angie,' came the reply.

'Do you want some breakfast,' asked Skinner.

'No thanks, mate,' said Angie, 'We've got a lot of work to do today, mainly around the harbour, we're going to the sailor's mission first to speak to Dixie Bacon, I know he's there I checked the register yesterday, Skinner.'

'I don't really like to ask,' said Bridget, 'But isn't your name Bacon Angie.'

'Don't ask those questions,' said Skinner.

'It's not a problem,' interrupted Angie, 'Yes Bridget, he is my uncle and he will either testify against Andrew Coppin or just like all the other men on our list, he'll go to prison for a very long time.'

Angie took over the conversation, 'I know it's confusing for both of you,' she said as she looked directly at the girls, 'Let me try and explain. Skinner saved you because no girls should be slaves, but we would also like you both to help all those other girls by being witnesses in court, that's where I come in as a lawyer, we are trying to convict a man called Andrew Coppin and stop this slave trade forever.'

The Holiday

Colin opened with, 'This team has uncovered evidence to support the allegations that 'The Pharaoh,' was used for serious criminal activity, we have discovered that two crew members on the 1946 May sailing, did not return to Liverpool.'

'Scuse me sir,' came a voice from the back, 'It's not unusual for sailors to jump ship.'

'I agree with you, detective constable Macki,' replied Paul, 'But these two sailors were happily married with children and even more suspiciously, the two men who claimed to be them and settled in Australia, had thick Irish accents and yet the two crewmen, Peter Swan and Philip Buxton were scousers with thick Liverpool accents.'

Again, DS Macki asked, 'How do you know that, Sir.'

'Witnesses, DS Macki,' Paul replied, 'Witnesses,' he went on, 'Family, friends, workmates and neighbours in both Liverpool and Aussie have given us reason to believe that two Irish men who were not on the ship's manifest arrived in Australia and took on the identities of the two crewmen, who were on the ships manifest when it left Liverpool.'

He continued, 'Then either on route or in Australia, both crewmen simply disappeared and according to the Australian authorities, later on so did the two Irish men who I believe were using their identities. In itself this information does not help our investigation but it does implicate the ship 'The Pharaoh'.'

Colin continued, 'We have had a stroke of luck, one of the three crew members killed in our investigation was only part of the crew with the other two victims on two sailings, in May 1945 and 1946 and we think that something happened on one of these two sailings to cause either a crew member or passenger to take revenge on as many of the crew as possible.'

Paul continued, 'There are just too many inconsistences on the 1946 sailings to ignore, the new findings around Peter Swan and Philip Buxton and not least of all the disappearance of the captain two days after returning to Liverpool and

226

now because of these new developments, I want you all to concentrate your investigations on the May 1946 sailing of 'The Pharaoh'.'

Legal Darwin

Skinner went on, 'Yesterday, I showed you both a list of men who have served on the ship 'The Pharaoh' and many of them live in Darwin, we only need a few of those men to speak up about the slave trade and that combined with your statements as living victims should be enough to end the slave trade and put Coppin in prison for many years.'

'But why are Bridget and myself in any danger,' asked Theresa.

'For the same reason the men on that list are in danger,' replied Skinner. 'All of you can put Coppin away in prison for the rest of his life.'

'But Skinner, you said that some of these men who worked on The Pharaoh have lived in Darwin for years, so why haven't you done this before now,' asked Bridget.

'OK,' interrupted Angie, 'Please let me explain to the girls, Skinner,' she went on.

'Theresa and Bridget, we have a team, Skinner, myself and many others are part of it and we have been trying to end this white slave trade for years, often we have no information about the ships or the farms, we could always find ex-crew members who were willing to talk for the right price, but unless those men thought it was a rock-solid case and Coppin would go to prison, they wouldn't talk because they knew they would be killed.'

Angie continued, 'This time we have two living victims, you two girls and enough evidence to prove that you were chased half way across Australia to re-capture you or to kill Skinner.'

Skinner continued, 'That's why Coppin spent so much time and effort to catch us, no one can find any living witnesses and Coppin knows this, he is a very cruel man but he is far from stupid, so I will bet diamonds that he's here in Darwin to eliminate all ex-crew and he still hasn't completely given up on finding you two either and that's why you have Laurie and Mick.'

This was the plan, Angie and Skinner, would use two of her Darwin men, Piper and Wilson and the four of them would approach all the men on the list of ex-crew members on The Pharaoh and offer them the deal. The deal was, for a written statement from them, they would receive a financial reward and protection from Coppin, they would also be offered immunity from prosecution for their part in the slave trade on The Pharaoh, Angie and her legal team wanted the big fish like Coppin, the tiddlers like the ex-crew men were just thrown back.

At this point Skinner and Angie were unaware that Coppin was also looking for an ex-crew member, Dixie Bacon. Coppin wanted Dixie Bacon dead for speaking to Denny Harris and causing him all this trouble and enormous expense but he also wanted to send out the perfect message to all ex-crew members by making the killing particularly gruesome, he had the perfect man for the job who was an expert at killing with meat hooks, but first he needed to find Dixie.

Angie, Skinner, Piper and Wilson drove to the harbour and parked outside the Ocean Hotel just across the street from the sailor's mission, Wilson stayed with the car and Piper walked along the street a small way. As Angie and Skinner walked across the street a car pulled up just past the sailor's mission, Skinner put his arms around Angie pushing her into a shop doorway as he kissed her, she was taken aback with his sudden embrace, 'Look over my shoulder,' he said.

'It's fucking Coppin in the back of that car.' Angie looked and confirmed it was Coppin in the car.

A heavy got out of the car looking around, 'He's here for Dixie, Angie, do you know what room he's in,' asked Skinner urgently.

'Yes, 24 on the second floor.'

'Quickly pull your hat over our faces,' Skinner said, as he took her hand and walked into the sailor's mission.

The heavy looked up and down the street, ignoring the kissing couple across the street, as he opened the back door for Coppin. 'Quick, quick,' whispered Skinner as they both went into the mission and flew up the stairs, Dixie's door was partially open and as usual he was lying pissed on the floor. They quickly scooped him up as they heard Coppin downstairs looking for Dixie's room key.

'Fuck it,' they heard Coppin say as they dragged Dixie onto his feet. Skinner quickly stuffed pillows under the sheets, as they heard footsteps coming up the stairs and voices saying, 'He's in 24, it says on the register, boss, we'll break the door open.'

Skinner quietly pulled the door closed and together Skinner and Angie dragged Dixie along the landing to the fire escape, they'd just made it out of the fire door to the top of the fire escape when they heard a door being kicked in along the corridor and two noises like bullet from a silenced gun, this had been Dixie's luckiest day that he knew nothing about.

On the fire escape Skinner pushed Dixie to Angie and said, 'Hold him, I'm gonna kill Coppin,' as he pulled his gun out.

Angie said, 'No Skinner,' as she pressed her hand on his gun hand, 'If you kill him here, like this, my whole legal credibility goes out of the window and this case that we've worked so hard all these years for goes up in smoke and Coppin will just carry on.'

They heard one of the heavies walking along the corridor towards the fire escape door and Skinner cocked his gun, but another pissed up merchant sailor came to his room door fell onto the heavy, grabbing him and asked for help 'cos he'd pissed his bed. The heavy shrugged him away slid his gun back in his shoulder holster, turned around and went back along the corridor. From the top of the fire escape, they watched Coppin and his men drive off.

Next day back at the safe house Skinner, Angie, Piper, Wilson, Laurie, Mick, Dixie, Theresa and Bridget all sat around the table.

'The reason I've called this meeting,' began Angie, 'Is because my uncle Dixie has finally agreed to be a witness against Coppin, he has finally realised after his near murder yesterday that he will never be safe until Coppin is dead or in prison for a long time; he also tells me that he knows other ex-crew members who will testify, so yesterday was a complete success thanks once again to the bravery of Skinner.'

Everyone around the table applauded. Skinner said, 'Angie was just as brave, she faced the same threat and the same killers as me and she was not armed,' again the table applauded.

The Holiday

Paul opened with, 'Ladies and Gentlemen, thank you for your hard work,' and pointed at the clip board. 'With the evidence so far gathered, we are convinced that our killer is female.'

There was a huge sigh in the room. 'What makes you think this, sir,' came the first question.

'There are a number of things,' replied Paul, 'firstly, the small hand print sizes, the trajectory of the entry wounds on two of the victims from the cross-bow bolt and the three nurses who were eye-witnesses.'

Paul took over, 'Because none of the crew were female, we have to assume that our killer was one of the girls being transported to Australia on The Pharaoh in 1946, we need a list of everyone aboard that sailing, especially the female passengers, this number should not exceed five hundred.'

Paul pointed to two male detectives and said, 'DC Scott and Mason, I want you two to get this list, particularly the female passengers as soon as possible.' Paul then turned to two women detectives and said, 'DC Bennet and Taylor, I want you two to work with the passport office and compile a list of all females arrivals who have entered the country in the last 3 months, on either British or Australian passports.'

He went on, 'Then all four of you cross reference the lists and see if you come up with a single or multiple names that appear on both lists.'

Colin again took over, 'As a matter of urgency we also need a list of all ex-crew members, as these men are potentially the next targets, any crew members still alive who were on that sailing, needs to be contacted and informed of the potential threat, this should not exceed 150 men. We need to provide as much protection to these men as possible.'

Legal Darwin

Angie went on, 'Because of Theresa and Bridget's age I hate to include them in these graphic discussions of a total monster and killing machine like Andrew Coppin, but because they are the final nail in his coffin that will destroy this man they need to be in the team,' the whole table applauded Theresa and Bridget as Angie walked around the table and cuddled both the girls, saying, 'These two beautiful young girls are the bravest of the brave and my uncle Dixie sitting there should be crying an ocean for what you did.'

Again, the whole table applauded the two girls. Theresa put her arm around Bridget and spoke, 'You keep telling us we're brave but everyone around this table is brave and please don't think we're just little girls, the last few days and the voyage on The Pharaoh forced us both to grow up and we'd love to put Coppin in prison and then none of you, especially Skinner will have to keep risking your lives.'

Skinner spoke first, 'I think both girls know what I think of them, they were stronger than many men I know but to put Coppin away for life, our case has to be watertight, we have to know exactly what we have got on him, over to you, Angie.'

Angie began, 'Well, to start with we have a lot of suspicion within the Fremantle community because of some very unusual financial transactions, but let's talk about the hard evidence we have. We have Coppin's finger prints on illegal guns and the guns serial numbers, we can prove they were imported from England, we have bodies of dead IRA members identified by fingerprints, dental records, body scars and tattoo's and evidence of how they got to Australia with links directly to Coppin, we have trace elements of morphine from the convent in at least five girls blood samples and now we have statements from ex-crew members and more importantly living child slave victims.

'The population of Darwin is a little under 6000, in many countries that would just be a village and so it is easy to find and track people who we think may be of help.' Angie continued, 'Because Skinner's and Andy's fathers were key in political change in the Northern Territory their statements will certainly carry some weight.'

Theresa looked at Bridget as they both jumped up hugging each other as they danced and screamed with delight at hearing Andy was alive. 'Is Caroline OK as well,' Bridget asked excitedly.

Skinner said, 'They are both fine, I was gonna tell you at the end of this meeting, but Angie spoilt the surprise.'

'Sorry Skin,' said Angie and they all laughed, but at least sometimes there are still some happy endings.

Angie again continued, 'I was going to give a complete list of casualties, but it is not all good news, the main losers as always are the children, they didn't all have a Skinner. No key players in this operation were killed, but because of how certain individuals needed to be dealt with a lot of evidence cannot be submitted in court, chasing and catching Skinner, Theresa and Bridget was so key to Coppin protecting his operation, for once he worked very sloppily and made quite a few mistakes that can be traced directly back to him.

Coppin was photographed for the first-time passing money to nuns, gun runners and convicted criminals, in his efforts to cover up his operation I have been able to produce clear photographic evidence that he cannot deny, there are 40 photographs on the table please examine them all so that you are quite familiar with them should you be called as a witness and quizzed in court by some highly paid illegal barrister on Coppin's payroll.'

The photographs were passed around, Skinner asked, 'Anyone want a drink,' and went on.

'I've seen enough of Coppin to last me ten lifetimes so I don't need to look at them, but the girls need to see what Coppin looks like,' said Angie, 'In court Andrew Coppin and any of his men will try to frighten and intimidate Theresa and Bridget by staring at them, so do not look at him, but you do need to know what he looks like as you have never seen him before.'

Bridget picked up a photo and dropped it immediately as she let out a scream nearly falling off her chair covering her mouth with both hands. Angie, ran around the table to comfort her, 'Are you alright, Bridget,' she said.

Bridget said, 'I have seen him before.'

'When did you see him?' asked Skinner.

'In Liverpool,' she replied, 'It's my dad Jack.'

'You must be mistaken,' said Angie.

Theresa picked up the photograph from the floor, looked at it and, with a gasp, said, 'No she's not, Angie. That's a picture of Jack Grantham.'